THE WATERS OF CRYSTAL LAKE

MELISSA DAVIS BAIZE

First Edition

PAGE PUBLISHING, INC.
New York, NY

First originally published by Page Publishing, Inc. 2019

ISBN 978-1-68456-274-9 (Paperback)
ISBN 978-1-68456-275-6 (Digital)

Printed in the United States of America

PROLOGUE—1979

The hurt from mindless deeds done long ago,
By others may be hidden in the subconscious.
But memories of such pain, not forgotten or forgiven,
Could be simmering, simmering, waiting to explode.

IT WAS A picturesque town, a Norman Rockwell type that covered a broad plateau and was surrounded by steep mountains. From the interstate five miles away, a traveler could see it shimmering in the sunlight and might think it would be a good place to live. The beauty of the region was breathtaking, and it was far from the strife and turmoil of a large city. The town's name was Greenwood, not a very original name, but chosen by the first European settlers for the heavy foliage that grew there. A group of twenty pioneers from North Carolina had struggled for weeks through the wilderness, exhausted and hungry before they arrived at a spring. Deep in the woods, they set up camp and, after resting several days, decided to break ground for a permanent site they were so impressed with the terrain.

After that austere beginning, only a small settlement existed for the next hundred years, made up of a few families who scratched out a living from what they could grow or shoot. Then the area slowly grew into a larger village, which served as a marketplace for farmers in the area. By the twentieth century, light industry moved to the region, and more families came, drawn by better-paying jobs and the growing reputation of the town. The population doubled and then doubled again. The richness of the area's natural resources actually fueled much of its expansion and the stately trees themselves were cut by the thousands for a hungry lumber industry.

Also visible from the interstate was a large lake that lay to the left of the town. The water on the surface of Crystal Lake, as it was called, glistened in the sunlight, which offered the traveler a cool mental reprise from the waves of heat that radiated from the earth in the hot September sun. It was the last Saturday in September. Labor Day was long past and had been celebrated with the town's usual parade and street fair. The children had returned reluctantly to school, but warmth still engulfed the area like a shroud and belied the cool air, which would descend later at dusk. The leaves of the trees hung limply on their branches and exhibited that peculiar yellow-green color that would give way to the vibrant reds and oranges of October in the Tennessee Mountains.

The willows at the southern end of the lake cast a welcomed blanket of shade, and the shore was lined with bursts of color from purple ironweed and goldenrod. Birds splashed in the warm water along its shallow edges, while the iridescent blue of dragonflies flashed by in the brilliant sunlight as they darted over the water's surface. A few turtles could be seen sunning on large rocks surrounding the lake. The wildlife in the area depended on the lake for their water, and even though the forest animals couldn't be seen hiding in the deep shadows of the forest, when night fell, they, like apparitions, would cautiously creep to the shore to drink.

Since the lake was also the source of water for the people in nearby Greenwood, large industrial pipes ran from its northern end to the water purification plant a few miles away. The area around the lake was beautiful and had been transformed into a park for Greenwood residents by the thoughtful board at the water company. A gravel path ran around the shore for joggers, and at the opposite end of the lake, several picnic tables had been set up under two majestic oaks. A boat dock close to the tables extended out into the water, where a few weathered fishing boats were tied. It was rumored that in the forties, a man had rowed out to the center of the lake with his girlfriend and drowned her in the deep water then allowed her body to sink to the muddy bottom, but that is a story for another time.

Abruptly that Saturday morning, the usual tranquil setting around Crystal Lake was broken. At the edge of the water, a man's figure suddenly appeared. He had made his way silently down the steep path to the water, carefully, like a cat stalking its prey. His motorcycle had been parked off the small road that circled the water company's property and was hidden from the view of others.

The man paused briefly, looking to see if anyone else was in the area. Satisfied that he was alone, he sat carefully down on a large flat rock at the water's edge. For some time, he seemed buried in thought, his head in his hands. Finally, he pulled from a backpack a brown bag with a small lunch inside. He quickly ate a simple meal of cheese and fruit, which he washed down with water from an old aluminum thermos. When he had finished, he carefully cleaned up all traces of his meal, even picking up any bits of paper and putting them in his jeans' pocket. Standing up, he slowly walked toward the lake, crouched down by the water, and started at the town.

Hate began to swell in him like dark violent clouds gathering wrath before an approaching storm. Thoughts of the wrongs he had suffered as a youth in the town washed over him. Memories of the teasing, the ostracisms, even blows he had suffered there poured out from emotions that were buried in the deepest part of his mind. Many times, as a boy, had he not sat on the same rock, lonely and rejected.

Finally, he returned to his backpack and, with great resolve, pulled out a large glass bottle. He held it up to the sunlight and studied the fluid as if to memorize its appearance. He then walked swiftly to the water's edge and unscrewed the bottle's cap. He slowly stooped down and carefully poured the liquid contents into the reservoir. He watched with fascination as ripples spread from the spot where the milky contents of the bottle mingled with the clear lake water. Swiftly, like the release of electricity in the air after a storm passes, the tension and anger drained from his body. He smiled slightly, even though he rarely smiled, and stood up. Slowly he turned and began to make his way back up the path to his motorcycle to return to the cabin five miles away.

CHAPTER ONE

IN THE CENTRAL part of the state, Nashville to be exact, a lab employee contemplated her surroundings with little enthusiasm for the pristine laboratory. Debra Chandler sat on a lab stool in the University's Medical Center and studied the list of reagents she had to prepare for her boss, Dr. Joe Steiner. His domain covered part of one wing of the medical center's fourth floor. The sheer size of the layout was the envy of other researchers. The suite consisted of two labs, an office, two walk-in incubators, a coatroom, and a storeroom for chemicals and medical equipment.

From the windows in the back of the main lab, a beautiful view of midtown Nashville could be seen, not that Debra ever had time to appreciate the view. She had arrived before eight o'clock, anticipating a large number of reagents to prepare for the week's experiments, but the list was even longer than she had imagined and involved careful measurements of the various radioisotopes protected by lead shields in the storeroom.

Debra twisted on the lab stool and realized it would be hard to finish the preparations before her lunch, which was scheduled for twelve thirty. Regardless, she wished she could take a break now even though she couldn't finish everything. Not only was the work tedious, but her back hurt from sitting on the hard metal. Today she felt chilled because the air in the lab was too cool even for her tastes. Summerlike temperatures were still hanging around Nashville, and she had made the mistake of wearing under her lab coat a thin summer skirt and sleeveless blouse.

Debra's long brown hair was tied back in a ponytail, but one strand hung over her white lab coat as she tried to decipher Dr.

Steiner's strange hand writing. Hearing a sound, she turned and saw Dr. Steiner himself standing behind her, looking over her shoulder. She shrank slightly inwardly. Any other man would be suspected of trying to peer down her V-necked blouse, standing at that angle, but not him. As far as she could tell, he was more interested in the periodic table than any interaction with a fellow human being, be it male or female.

"Ms. Chandler, here are the names of four more reagents that I also need by this afternoon. Please add them to the list you already have. Remember to label all the flasks carefully, and don't forget to add today's date." He spoke curtly as he handed her a sheet of paper. Then he turned and left the lab for who knew where.

"Yes, Dr. Steiner," Deborah demurely replied as she glanced over the list and turned back to her work, thinking as usual he was acting like a jerk. *Does he think I'm an idiot and incapable of doing anything correctly?* And she bit her lip.

When she first interviewed for the job, she was struck by the inconsistencies in his manner and dress. He was not an unattractive middle-aged man. At a distance, he appeared to be well dressed, though by 1979, few researchers bothered to wear a dress shirt and tie to work. Upon closer inspection, she later noticed the shabbiness in his attire. The cuffs of his white shirt were permanently stained a dull gray. His ties, which were always either dark gray or blue, had small grease spots splattered on their surface. He was of medium height with a slender build. His hair was coal black and straight, which he wore slightly long and parted on one side. His eyes were piercing blue, but he seldom looked one in the eye, so most at the hospital would say that they weren't sure what color they were.

She was surprised when he called her a few days later to say she was hired. He held his emotions in such check on the day she was interviewed she couldn't tell what he thought of her application then.

After working there a few weeks, she began to notice that he never shook hands or touched another person if he could avoid the contact. In order to open a door at times, she saw him twisting the knob with a paper towel. His hands were washed well and often using a strong disinfectant, as if he were a surgeon preparing for the operating room. Debra wondered how his skin could stand such abuse, and at times his hands did look red and irritated. She washed her hands too but followed nothing like his procedure. She reasoned many of the reagents, which included the radioactive chemicals and cell cultures in his lab, could be considered dangerous, which would explain the strange behavior.

Debra had been working for Dr. Steiner for over a year after she received her master's degree in microbiology. In 1979, the work done at his research lab for recombinant DNA was at the cutting edge of science. Dr. Steiner had received a grant for the unheard amount of a million dollars from the federal government. The research for which the federal grant had been awarded and the one for which she had been hired concerned the insertion of bacteria viruses, or phage, as they were called, into defective mice cells growing in tissue culture. The viruses had been artificially tricked into being carriers of DNA from human pituitary cells. It was hoped the viruses would infect the cells growing in tissue culture so that the new genetic material would code for the production of various hormones and proteins. The human DNA was inserted into each virus using techniques developed exclusively by Dr. Steiner.

If all went well and with her help, Debra liked to think, the hundreds of tissues culture flasks in the walk-in incubators would soon be churning out gallons of hormones. These future genetic drugs could prevent the terrible pain and suffering associated with diseases, which had plagued mankind since the beginning of time. It was already rumored that California scientists were attempting to insert genes carrying the production code for insulin into host bacteria. If that proved to be the case, huge amounts of the hormone could be produced at a low cost compared to current methods.

The bottom line was that Debra felt she was fortunate to have found a well-paying and interesting job so soon after grad school. So she shut her eyes to Dr. Steiner's peculiarities and worked hard to please him. He left her alone for the most part as long as she met his demanding standards. Her professional manner in the lab at least seemed to be okay with him as far as she could tell.

She looked back over the last few years of her life and tried to understand how she had gotten into such a mess, divorced and living alone in a large city. Like many other girls in the seventies, she went to college and then had married soon after graduation. In fact, other girls in her sorority had only attended school for a couple of years before quitting for marriage. They joked about getting a Mrs. Degree instead of a BS or BA. At least she had told herself that she finished when she walked across the stage and received the diploma.

Debra had married her high school sweetheart after college, three weeks after she received the degree to be precise. To those curious and ill-mannered enough to ask what had gone wrong with the marriage, she would simply answer it had not worked out. After the divorce, she moved back into her parents' home, and several months passed before she decided to go back to school, not knowing what else to do. Her grades had always been good in college; in fact, her grade point average helped pull up her sorority from their previous low level to a respectful place in the Greek academic rankings.

She was lucky to ace the graduate record exam, which she took a few months before applying to graduate school. Several schools, all well-known in the South, sent her acceptance letters, but she had chosen to go back to the University in Nashville where she had received her undergraduate degree. The school was close to her parents' home in Clarksville, and its graduate school had an excellent reputation. After getting the advanced degree, she had a vague plan to land a job in research or perhaps a teaching position at a community college. With a master's degree in biology, she should have several options, as her campus adviser suggested.

It took two long years and more midnight hours than she would have thought to finish the degree. Now a large loan for the education was still outstanding. Of course, her well-to-do parents offered to pay the loan off, but she declined their help. Debra had felt so foolish with the problems in her personal life that taking care of the tuition was something she felt she should do, wanting to make it on her own without help from her parents. Perhaps it was her pride or stubborn personality, she told herself when she wrote a check to the loan company each month. She was still mad for making the mistake of getting married in the first place, because she knew it wasn't going to work. Deep down when she had attended bridal showers given by girlhood friends or was fitted for the elaborate wedding dress, she knew that she and her fiancé had become too different to have much success at a marriage.

When she made plans to move to Nashville, she had visited several apartment buildings to find a place to live close to the school, but after many discussions with her parents, she agreed to let them buy a town house in the Green Hills area of Nashville, which she could rent back from them. The value of Nashville real estate continued to skyrocket, so all three were happy with the present arrangement. Her father felt that the investment would pay off someday with handsome dividends. Since he was the president of a large bank in Clarksville, he was very conscious of getting a good value for his investments, as he told her and her mother more often than not.

Regardless, the place was perfect for her needs. Debra definitely loved living there, much more than the large one she had shared with her ex. The two-storied brick town house had two bedrooms and one and a half baths. The extra bedroom was used as her study, but she bought a sofa bed for the room so her parents would have a place to stay when they came to visit. Between the house and the garage was a small brick patio complete with two trees and several shrubs whose names escaped her.

The patio was of great importance because of the dog, Annie. Annie was a four-year-old Springer Spaniel whom she had bought while still living in Clarksville. Her husband was upset with her for getting a dog, but Debra didn't care and ignored his complaints. When she left him, she naturally took the dog along. She had been able to handle having her live in the city in spite of long school hours. Luckily, her schedule worked out so she could come home at noon between classes to eat lunch, take her on a short walk, and refill the bowl of dry food and water in the kitchen. If she felt the dog was feeling cooped up in the house, Debra would let her out in the backyard so she could run around in the tiny fenced space or doze on the patio.

When she first moved to Nashville, her favorite cousin, Elizabeth Chandler, would come over to visit. Elizabeth was several years older than Debra and had been living in Nashville for some time when Debra arrived for graduate school. Every few weeks the two had gotten together for dinner and drinks when Debra didn't have to study. Sometimes in the summer, they cooked steaks on the small grill the previous owners had left behind while they sat on the patio in the Nashville heat, sipping red wine with ice floating on top, and rehashing old stories about long-forgotten relatives.

Two years ago, much to Debra's sorrow, Elizabeth had to return to her hometown of Greenwood. As she told Debra, she felt there was no other choice because the great aunt who had raised her was now in failing health and could no longer live alone. Debra admired Elizabeth's unselfish decision, and even though she missed Elizabeth and their cookouts on the patio, she still found it pleasant in the summertime to sit there alone after work. She would pour a generous glass of wine and try to recover from a day of Dr. Steiner's moodiness and ill temper.

Debra shook herself out of the daydreams and said to herself, *Enough of this.* Thank heavens Dr. Steiner paid well. Her salary was generous, and that was important because she could pay off her student loan and still have a fairly comfortable lifestyle. Considering the mess she had been in few years ago, she was reasonably happy in Nashville even though loneliness crept through the house after dark when the shadows grew.

If she was honest enough with herself, she had to admit that Dr. Steiner was a creep. But certainly, she could stand working for him. There were worse things to consider doing with her life. She squared her shoulders, turning her attention back to preparing the solutions. At twenty-eight, she had energy to burn and didn't mind the long hours in the lab. Certainly, she had nothing exciting to do at home.

Suddenly there was a knock on the lab door. This was a shock. No one ever came by to see her. "Come in," she said in a low voice.

A resident from internal medicine, whom she had seen around the medical center, stepped through the doorway. "Miss, I'm Dr. Jim Tarkington, and was told I might borrow a jar of this compound from you. I placed an order for this stuff several weeks ago, and it apparently has been lost." And he smiled as he handed her a slip of paper with the name of the chemical written on it.

"Yes, sir, I believe I have this in the storeroom and could loan you some." And she smiled too.

Then just like that, the earth moved, though neither knew it at that time.

CHAPTER TWO

HARRY MORGAN, THE manager of the Greenwood Water Company, checked to see if the gun was still in the desk drawer. In recent memory, he had only one unfortunate incident with an employee, but it was a bad one, and that was the reason for the gun. It happened six months ago when he had to fire a troublesome and quarrelsome worker. The man had a bad chip on his shoulder and was continually stirring up problems with the others in the filtration plant. After a fight in the locker room at lunch with another employee ending up with a broken nose, Harry had had enough. He called him in later that Friday afternoon to tell him to pack up his stuff and not to plan to come back Monday. The guy, who was over six feet tall with a heavy black beard, cursed Harry out and shook his fist. He promised to get even as he went out, slamming the door.

The incident left a bad taste in Harry's mouth and spoiled the weekend for him. That night, he and his wife, Joyce, had gone to dinner at a friends' home whom they knew from church. He couldn't enjoy their company and was unusually quiet. Finally, Joyce asked him, what was the matter, but he wouldn't tell her, just sipped his beer in silence. On Saturday, he put a small revolver under the seat of his car, and Monday he added the gun to the desk drawer in his office. Already stored in the front coat closet of his house were several hunting rifles, loaded. There was no sense in taking chances when dealing with someone who seemed dangerous and filled with rage.

Later, Harry felt vindicated when he heard that the man had trouble getting along with other workers and had been fired from his previous job in Knoxville. Unfortunately, that information did not show up on a checklist Harry had run, or he never would have hired him in the first place. He was now wondering if he had a criminal record that didn't show up either. Anyway, Harry was thankful he was gone, and no more of his time would be wasted thinking about him or that unpleasant afternoon when he confronted the bully.

Harry walked briskly into the quality control lab of the water company. It was the last Monday in September at exactly seven o'clock, the usual time of his arrival, always before any of his employees clocked in. Harry's slim athletic build belied his forty-six years of age. A devotion to daily workouts kept him in superior shape. In spite of the heat, he had run five miles that morning before arriving at work. Once there, he had showered in the men's locker room and then slipped on clean clothes and a crisp white lab coat. Now looking around the lab, he ran fingers through his short brown hair. Unlike the popular long styles of the day, which he disliked, his hair was cut with military precision, and his face was clean-shaven with no side burns or mustache.

Pulling his belt a notch tighter, he opened a window and leaned out to check the temperature. The gage attached to the window frame was already registering eighty-three degrees. Down the street a two-storied red-brick building could be seen simmering in the heat. It was owned by a local lodge to which Harry belonged. As Harry looked at the building, he snorted with disgust, thinking about his former high school classmates who spent most Saturdays at the lodge in front of the TV, half drunk.

In the fall, they were addicted to watching football, particularly Tennessee football while drinking can after can of beer. With the season in full swing, he had stopped by a few times to visit some high school friends. As usual, bowls of chips and French onion dip had been conveniently stationed around the room, and the floor, not swept too often, was crunchy from peanut shells pitched on the linoleum.

Harry had played football at the local high school with some of the guys and tried to stay in touch. He always inquired about their families and how their jobs were going, but after so much small talk, he found he could think of nothing else to say and escaped outside to fresh air. He couldn't take the smoke-filled room for very long, because in the past, he had broken down in coughing fits before leaving. Harry worked hard to keep his good health and didn't have kind thoughts about the former teammates who were out of shape. He had told his wife, in jest, they were in such pitiful conditions they might have a hard time walking two blocks to the 7-Eleven if they ever ran out of beer.

He shut the window with a slam to lock in the cool air and glanced around the laboratory, admiring its gleaming perfection. Reagent bottles were lined against the back wall shelves like soldiers at attention. Lines of petri dishes filled with colored media were stacked on the black granite countertop, waiting to be used later in the day by his microbiology technicians. At that time, samples of the town's water supply collected during the weekend would be streaked over the media's surface, and the dishes would be placed in a warm dark incubator for twenty-four hours. Overnight groups of bacteria cells would grow and form colonies that would resemble round raised beads on the media's surface. The next day, the bacteria colonies on the surface of the media would be examined for atypical dangerous forms. If any were found, a more detailed search would begin for any problem lurking in the reservoir, which might threaten the town's water. Of course, nothing had ever been found, at least in Harry's memory.

The Greenwood Water Company where Harry worked was located at the very edge of town about a mile from the hospital. A devastating drought had occurred in 1920, and when the wells and springs couldn't provide enough water for the fast-growing population, the city fathers came to their senses and realized Crystal Lake would have to become a reservoir in order to furnish enough water for the town. Naturally, that water would have to be purified, and that was when a new state-of-the-art plant was built. After the grand opening of the new water company, everything went well, until the 1960s when an addition was added to keep up with the demand for more water.

Harry had been at the water company twenty years. He started as a technician, then was promoted to supervisor and finally named manager eight years ago. He wanted Greenville's water to be the purest and safest in the state. He kept accurate reports of everything coming out of the lab and made sure the facilities were spotless. His workweek usually lasted fifty hours because he was a perfectionist for detail.

The current board of directors of the water company was pleased how their company was run. There were very few problems for the board to discuss at their monthly meetings, which never lasted much more than an hour. Usually after the meeting ended, they retired to the Greenwood Country Club for drinks and dinner. They had complete confidence in their well-informed manager. Harry kept the board up-to-date on any items that might be needed for them to consider at the next board meeting. He had hired a competent staff, and was relieved there was little turnover among the employees. Harry himself was knowledgeable about all important research done in water purification and quality control. He kept everyone informed about any new developments that might help the company or save money.

Harry was confident the coming week would go well and knew of no major problems on the horizon. He walked toward the front of the building and glanced in the employee lounge.

As usual, it was neat and spotlessly clean. During lunch, some of his employees might have a card game at a table set up in the middle of the room, or others would play volleyball behind the building, weather permitting. Most of the employees got along well together, and he had observed they seemed to be friendly after work with some playing golf or hunting during deer season with each other.

As noted before, his reputation was excellent, and he was careful to see that no mistakes were made by anyone under his watch. He had survived handling a difficult board member a few years ago, but that was a thing of the past. The company had a board now whose members were pleasant and easy to get along with. The members seemed so pleased with the operations and budget report last year they hosted a Christmas party at Greenwood Country Club. The chairman put on a red suit complete with a fake beard to play Santa Claus and passed out gifts to the employees' kids.

Harry and his wife had been a fixture in the community for many years. He had come back to Greenwood after college and a two-year tour with an Army's medical unit. He could have gone to graduate school or settled in a large city. He chose instead to return home because he loved the mountains surrounding the town. The hunting and fishing available in the area was world class, as he told his wife, Joyce. They had met in college, and she liked his hometown though she was from another part of Tennessee. When they moved, she easily found a job teaching at a local elementary school. They had never had any children, but she always said that the third graders were like her own. When they first arrived, they joined the Methodist Church and made friends there in addition to socializing with Harry's classmates and wives from high school days.

All in all, it had not been a bad life, he thought. Some might say it was a little boring, but Harry didn't feel that way.

His biggest excitement these days, excluding hunting during deer season, was to attend the annual meeting on quality control for water purification systems. In fact, that meeting was coming up in mid-November and was being held in Atlanta this year, an easy drive for him. He would plan to attend all three days of the meeting and listen diligently to the latest research on water purification presented by some University types. Then he and a few of his friends would go to a fancy steak house at the company's expense, naturally. After the meal, they might drop by a bar and sip a little Jack Daniels. If the waitress was very attentive and attractive, and they usually were, he might give her a few extra dollars in a tip, but that was as far as it went. He was not like some of the others who saw the meeting as a chance to have some fun.

He and his wife had a good, solid marriage, and nothing would happen in Atlanta that would jeopardize their relationship. Yes, thought Harry as he walked toward his office in the front of the building with a satisfied smile on his face, it had been a good decision when he and Joyce moved back to Greenwood years ago.

CHAPTER THREE

THREE MORE WEEKS flew by, and by the end of October, the heat in Greenwood and for that matter the rest of Tennessee had not let up. The whole state suffered from a serious lack of rain. In Greenwood, the flower and vegetable gardens were dried up ghosts of their former selves. The water company and the local newspaper begged people to conserve water, and most residents did just that. They had resigned themselves to the weather and were waiting patiently for the first frost, but a few green yards remained. Those stubborn owners were using sprinklers and hoses almost around the clock because of the drought. They seemed to be oblivious of the water shortage or maybe just didn't care in spite of daily notices to conserve water.

Farmers in the area understandably were panicked about having enough water for their livestock and late summer vegetables. It would seem the situation was getting more desperate with each passing day for lack of rain. Their small farms usually produced an abundance of vegetables for the town with extra produce being trucked to Nashville and other cities, but not this year. Evidence of the drought could be seen just by looking around the town and countryside. Anyone walking on the gravel path around Crystal Lake could not help but notice that the water level of the reservoir had dropped several feet, and large cracks could be seen in the ground. But as usual, the surface of Crystal Lake was smooth and serene with its color a clear, beautiful blue. Though beneath the surface, an unknown invader was growing silently, multiplying faster than any organisms known to man, gathering its forces, and turmoil, yet unseen, was brewing for the town of Greenwood.

A mile away at Greenwood Memorial Hospital, Taylor Whitney walked briskly down one of the hospital's corridors, checking on his patients. He was one of seven family practitioners in the town, and his practice was the largest. Today he felt fortunate since only six patients were ill enough to require hospitalization. When Taylor first arrived, he originally hoped the rounds would only take a short time, and he could be out of there in one hour flat. But the rooms of the six patients were spread out at opposite directions of the five-story building, and of course, some patients' medication required changes, and new notes for the nurses had to be written. All this took extra time, and his rounds were taking much longer than he had planned.

It was a slow day at the hospital, which had only an eighty percent occupancy rate and was definitely not the answer to Ben Montgomery's prayer. Ben was his friend and the hospital administrator. He was constantly trying to get more beds filled so Medicare and insurance payments would flow faster into the hospital's bank account. While the hospital did well enough in their financial department, there was always a need for extra cash, as Ben reported. More patients equated to more charges, which equated to more money to pump up their balance at the Greenwood Bank. That increase could be put to good use. At the last staff meeting, Ben told them that the AC system would have to be replaced and soon—it was fifteen years old and in need of constant repairs. There was always something else to pay for, Taylor thought moodily.

Today, it was obvious that many beds were empty. With a lower enrollment and summerlike temperatures outside, a slight air of relaxation existed throughout the building. Some of the nurses and other staff members were on vacations, and two of the nurses' stations were even staffed by on-call nurses rather than the regulars. Taylor noticed the clinical lab seemed to have fewer techs working that day when he stopped by to check on some lab results. Fortunately, none of his patients were critically ill. Taylor glanced at an empty ICU area as he walked past. It was gratifying that nobody in the city was ill enough to be in there. Ben would surely comment about that in their next staff meeting. Then immediately he would turn around and point out just how much more money patients in the ICU generated than those in other parts of the hospital.

Suddenly, his concentration was broken by the hospital operator's voice blaring out in an urgent tone, "Dr. Taylor Whitney, Dr. Taylor Whitney, you're wanted on line five."

Ducking in an empty patient room, he quickly dialed the extension to answer the call, hoping it was not an emergency. His stomach churned in revulsion when he recognized the voice he knew all too well at the other end of the line. It was his estranged wife, Claudia. He pulled off his glasses and sat down on the empty bed as he prepared himself for a long and one-sided conversation.

"Taylor, we must talk about the temporary alimony check which arrived in the morning mail. It was much too small for my October expenses. In spite of what your lawyer thinks, I need five hundred more dollars each month to pay all of the bills. Also, maybe I didn't mention this to you, but I'm planning to go to Nashville for the last weekend in October and need you to keep the kids. Several friends and I are going to leave for a little shopping and to check out a new restaurant one of the girls has heard about."

According to the rambling story, a few more things were needed to fill in her wardrobe for fall social events and upcoming holidays. They would leave early Saturday morning, had reservations to stay overnight at the Hermitage Hotel, and would return Sunday afternoon.

She went on to say since she needed him to babysit over a weekend, he could stay in the first-floor guest bedroom at their home since she didn't want the children to sleep in his small apartment, and he could take the children out for all the meals so he wouldn't have to cook.

Taylor felt steam coming out of his ears at this inconsiderate behavior. The fact that she tracked him down while he was at the hospital seeing patients to talk about money and babysitting was inexcusable. She could have at least waited and called him at his apartment that evening. Claudia always wanted her way immediately—instant gratification, he called it. As he calmed himself down, he was reminded that such behavior was one of the reasons they were getting a divorce.

"Listen, Claudia, I'll be glad to stay with our children over the weekend. In fact, I'll look forward to it, but I'll be damned if you get one more cent from me! Do you have any idea what my expenses are? The office staff's salaries, the insurance premiums, my rent in that crummy apartment where I am staying, I have been more than generous with you. Hell no, not one more cent. Call my lawyer if you want more money." And he slammed the phone down. Taylor slumped over and put his head in his hands as he sat on the empty patient's bed and wondered if they had ever been happy.

It was hard to remember now, but perhaps the first few years had been good. He met Claudia on a blind date the end of his second year of medical school in Memphis. Her blond good looks and long shapely legs dazzled him, and he was smitten. A brief and passionate romance led to a society wedding at the end of his third year in medical school. It was covered by Memphis's *Commercial Appeal* in great detail.

Claudia belonged to a wealthy Memphis family whose money came from cotton and banking. Her family was at first pleased that their only daughter was marrying a future doctor whose profession would be approved by their prominent friends. Later it was to their horror they discovered the bridegroom had no intention of setting up a practice in Memphis and specializing in some lucrative field. Rather, he chose to go into family practice and move back to the area where he was raised. Claudia reluctantly followed. Thinking back, he supposed it was to her credit that she tried hard at first. Claudia dutifully joined the medical auxiliary, and the whole family belonged to the Baptist Church. She played tennis and bridge at the Greenwood Country Club every week unless of course she was in Memphis or Nashville.

After Taylor moved the family to Greenwood, Claudia's parents swallowed their pride, came to visit periodically, and sent a generous check each month. Perhaps the money made up for not being as close to their daughter and the grandchildren, a boy and girl, as they would have liked. During the summer or over the Christmas vacation, Claudia and the children would drive to Memphis for extended visits to pacify her parents while Taylor continued to work his normal fifty-hour workweek.

She certainly could not complain she had to work too hard as a wife and mother or even work at all, he sarcastically thought. Their household maid, Lilly, was the one who should complain. She faithfully came every day to take care of their house, and of course, she also helped with the children. Her cooking wasn't too bad either, maybe a little heavy on the salt, but better than Claudia's, so Taylor never said anything, at least not when he still lived there. They also had a gardener and general handyman, Archie. Taylor was too busy with his practice to take care of anything inside or outside of their home. Archie, who could fix anything, was a gem, and they were lucky to have found him.

His thoughts turned to their home. Claudia and he had built a large and impressive house on the outskirts of town eight years ago after much bickering among themselves and their Memphis architect. For the down payment, Claudia used money left to her by a wealthy grandmother. The house itself was a stately two-storied colonial with towering white columns. The interior had been furnished by the town's best-known decorator and reeked of old Memphis money with leather couches in its library and pricey art work on the walls.

Some would say the house looked too expensive for a doctor in family practice to build. Taylor once overheard two doctors talking about his home. They described it as a mansion more fitting for the president of the Greenwood Bank or the town's only plastic surgeon to own. If the truth were known, Taylor at times himself felt embarrassed to live in the house built and furnished by his wife's inheritance.

When Claudia was home, her weekends often started early on Friday clustered around at the club's bar with a group of friends. Taylor usually joined them later after he finished seeing patients. The group, made up of a few doctors and their wives or some of Taylor's fellow golfers, would then go to a popular restaurant in town or simply stay at the club for dinner. They both enjoyed their friends immensely but perhaps not each other so much and depended on the group for weekend activities.

But none of the luxury Claudia was surrounded by or the group of devoted friends she ran around with seemed to bring her any happiness. Six months ago, she announced that she was no longer sure she loved him and wanted a trial separation to think about their relationship. At times Taylor had wondered if there was another man in her life, but regardless, the announcement had been the final straw. He told her the separation was a good idea, but it would not be a trial. All these thoughts flashed through his mind as he got off the bed and carefully smoothed out the sheets.

Leaving the room, he finished his rounds as quickly as possible. He stopped by the nurses' station to see if the new orders for medication were being filled correctly and then stepped outside into the blazing heat. Taylor walked slowly to the parking lot, feeling a lot older than his thirty-nine years. He glanced at the sky but could see no suggestion of rain. The sky was a clear and brilliant blue. As badly as it was needed, no rain was forthcoming today. At noon the temperature already felt as though it was close to ninety. Waves of heat rolled up from the asphalt in the doctors' parking lot. The flowers in a bed by the entrance were wilted and flopped over toward the ground. He supposed Claudia's and his lawn still looked good since she was the type to ignore pleas from the water company to conserve water. He was reasonably sure she would have had Archie turn on the underground sprinklers every evening.

Taylor pulled off his tie and opened the doors of his black Cherokee to let some heat escape. He eased his lanky frame onto the hot leather seats and started down the hill toward Hopkins Pharmacy on East Main Street. There he would probably order his usual sandwich made with homemade pimento cheese and a Coke. If he was lucky, he would get to eat with some of his golf buddies from Greenwood's Country Club. Hopkins Drug Store was a local gathering place for friendship and good food with many men in the town. Taylor welcomed the relaxed atmosphere around its lunch counter. No medical problems were discussed, for which Taylor was grateful, and no serious world problems were brought up either. The conversations always were comfortable in a small-town kind of way. After lunch, he would drive to his office in a renovated Victorian house on Forest Avenue. There he would undoubtedly find an office crammed full of patients anxiously waiting his arrival.

CHAPTER FOUR

At noon in another part of town, the busy streets of the shopping district overflowed with people. Some were hurrying to favorite restaurants, while others ran errands during their lunch breaks. Greenwood's downtown looked ready for fall in spite of the unseasonable temperatures. Along the busy streets, Greenwood's Parks and Recreation Department had placed scarecrows sitting on bales of hay with pumpkins scattered around their feet. Gigantic baskets filled with arrangements of mums hung from lampposts at each street corner. Broadway's trendy shops had autumn goods in their windows, and flower boxes, attached to many buildings, were overflowing with more fall plants.

People from the surrounding counties swelled Greenwood's population since they often came to shop or visit their doctors or lawyers. Plus, with good weather, there were many tourists who came to hike, fish, or simply to camp and enjoy the beauty of the mountains. As the Chamber of Commerce liked to say, there was something for everyone to do in Greenwood. The residential areas were filled with stately trees, and a small stream had been conserved and flowed through the center of the town, guaranteeing that Greenwood's charm was unsurpassed in the region.

On a side street off the main area and away from its hustle and bustle, an elegant boutique sat rather proudly forty feet back from the street on a small rise of land. It had the well-deserved reputation as being the most exclusive shop in the Greenwood area. Heralding the fact were several expensive cars parked in front of the building waiting for their owners who were shopping inside. The Robin's Nest, as it was called, was owned by two middle-aged sisters who prided themselves on dressing the most fashionable women in that part of Tennessee.

The building itself was handsome, suggesting a refined atmosphere would be found inside. Its brick was painted a pale yellow, and there were pots of burgundy mums lining the stone steps leading to the dark oak door. Inside, a heavy brass chandelier hung from the ceiling, and ruby-colored Persian rugs covered the polished wood floors. Scattered throughout the rooms were comfortable chairs upholstered in pale-blue velvet. Customers could wander from room to room, looking at racks of beautiful dresses or inspect displays of costume jewelry tastefully arranged on antique tables. When entering the shop for the first time, the beauty of the interior could take one's breath away and, many said, also could its prices.

In one of the Nest's fitting rooms, Debra's cousin, Elizabeth Chandler, turned her blond head to catch a glimpse of the way the gray silk dress clung to her slender figure. The fabric draped around her neckline, nipped in at the waist, and flared below her knees, accenting the tan on her legs gotten at a friend's pool over the summer. A perfect dress to wear at the hospital's dinner dance in two weeks, she thought. The event was held each year at the end of October to celebrate the founding of the hospital eighty years ago. Everyone in the medical community, including the attending staff and their employees, received invitations. Since Elizabeth was in that latter group, her invitation had arrived in the mail last week.

Perhaps her boss, Dr. Taylor Whitney, would even ask her to dance, mused Elizabeth to herself as she fingered the silk, judging how her mother's pearls would set off the low neckline. She smiled in the mirror, pleased she did not look her thirty-five years but wishing again her chipped lower tooth had been fixed when she was a child. Perhaps she should make an appointment with that new dentist, in the office building next to Taylor's, to see about getting it fixed. Then she remembered her patients, some of whom were very ill, and realized a chipped tooth wasn't something with which to be concerned.

Thinking about the dinner dance again, one thing was sure. She would be going there by herself. In no way was she going to invite Doug Reynolds, whom she had met through a friend at church. She had been dating Doug for about two months, and after living in Nashville all those years, she was getting increasingly bored with his conservative attitudes and him in general. The men she had known in Nashville were interesting, and some, she might even say, were sexy.

Doug's idea of a fun date was to see a movie and then go to the local Shoney's for coffee and pie. He was the manager of Greenwood's K-Mart and loved to monopolize the conversation by describing the numerous problems he had dealing with his employees. Then he would go on about his relationship with the people at corporate headquarters at such length she almost felt she worked with them too. While he was a very nice person, as many would say, she had decided that she should tell him in a careful way that they should begin to see other people before he might suggest a serious romance and a worrisome topic, sex.

Elizabeth had left a great job in Nashville two years ago to come back home to take care of her maiden aunt, Susan. It was Susan who had raised her after her parents were killed in a plane crash when she was thirteen. Her aunt was now living in a retirement home outside of town, a victim of the complications of old age. Elizabeth continued to live in Susan's home while visiting her aunt several times a week. She tried to help Susan cope with the difficulties of living there, provide some company, and give her news about her friends.

Though at first, she missed Nashville and life in a big city, Elizabeth eventually found herself enjoying her childhood home and its small-town atmosphere. In spite of her better judgment, she also found herself more and more attracted to her boss, Dr. Whitney. Poor Taylor, she thought. He had too many patients and not enough time in the day to see them all. In addition, he was recently separated from his wife, Claudia. It was Elizabeth's impression that Claudia was fascinated with her own beauty and seemed cold and demanding with Taylor. She had tried to turn their two children against him and in general made his life miserable as the pending divorce proceedings rolled on.

Elizabeth knew she had used up most of her lunch hour and must make a decision. She turned to the sales clerk and said, "Margaret, I'm going to take the gray silk, please put it in a box. It's a wonderful dress, and I particularity like the way it fits."

She pulled on her green hospital scrubs and met the clerk at the front desk. Elizabeth had spoken to Margaret cheerfully but frowned as she wrote the check after entering the amount in her checkbook. The purchase was going to make a dent in her savings, and while she made a good salary as an office nurse compared to most women in town, she told herself that a splurge like this couldn't be repeated any time soon. Putting the dress box under her arm, she ran down the store's steps and decided to stop by a local sandwich shop and grab something to go before continuing on to the office.

Dodging small groups of people on the sidewalk, Elizabeth turned off Broadway and hurried down a shaded street lined with a canopy of mature oak trees. Many of the Victorian-era houses in this part of town had been converted into offices or shops after the regional medical center had been built at the end of World War ll. In spite of the beauty of the street, the dry leaves of the trees and wilted gardens detracted from its usual gracious appearance.

Elizabeth quickly ran up the steps of Taylor's office and flipped the Close sign to Open on the door of the gleaming white frame house, which served as both office and clinic. The business manager, Peggy, was already at her desk, which was separated from the waiting area by a glass partition. She was arranging the file charts for the afternoon appointments. Elizabeth gave her a friendly hello but also an appraising glance. An empty sack from Catfish Heaven lay on the floor next to her desk.

Taylor had tried with no luck to get Peggy to go on a diet since both her weight and blood pressure were sky high and off the charts. Many more fish dinners like the one she just consumed would put her in danger of not fitting in the desk chair, thought Elizabeth. But her constant good humor in dealing with the many elderly patients and her knowledge of government forms for Medicare payments were a godsend in a small doctor's office. Elizabeth for one was grateful she was there.

Elizabeth walked down the hall, checking on the setups in each examining room, adding supplies when needed. After rounds at the hospital and lunch, Taylor should arrive at approximately one thirty. Everything must be ready to go like clockwork so he could see all the patients in a reasonable amount of time. He prided himself in not having patients wait too long in the office.

She shook her head over the fate that brought her back to this small town after the excitement of living in a big city like Nashville. She worked in the medical center's emergency room where there was never a dull moment. Often one crisis after another came through its doors, and it was hard for a nurse to catch her breath. But because of Aunt Susan's failing health, she finally realized her aunt could no longer live alone and felt compelled to give up her job and a rather plush apartment shared with two fun-loving roommates and move back to Greenwood.

Elizabeth thought fondly of her life in Nashville when the days were filled with fast-paced events in the emergency room and many weekend nights were spent visiting the city's hot spots or country music bars. She and her roommates would meet others from the medical center for drinks and dancing. While Printer's Alley was a favorite for many, around Third and Broadway, some of the best new music was played by young musicians trying to break into the Nashville scene. That area was another favorite with her and her roommates. Though she was never bored, she also never met a man to fall in love with, so when she realized she needed to move back to Greenwood, there was no one holding her in Nashville.

Then for some reason, her thoughts turned to her cousin, Debra Chandler, who had gone with them to a popular club in Printer's Alley one night. Debra had moved to Nashville earlier to get her master's at the University. Though Elizabeth did not know any of the details, Debra had just gotten a divorce from her high school sweetheart. She had dated him for six years before finally marrying him after graduating from college. Everyone in the family was curious to know why the split had happened after such a long courtship, but Debra wasn't talking. She had even taken back her maiden name, so she must have been really bitter over the marriage, Elizabeth decided.

That night, uncharacteristically, Debra had a little too much to drink but still looked her fabulous self in a tight pair of jeans and black sweater. She was talking to a tall guy in a cowboy hat and boots, standing at the bar. The man was flirting seriously with her. He also was bragging to everyone around that he was a rising country music star and his name would be in lights soon. Her cousin was not her usual reserved self and seemed to hang on every word the guy said. She was about to leave with him to go to another bar when Elizabeth intervened. Elizabeth pulled Debra out to their car and drove her home while giving a lecture on making bad choices of men in bars.

The next morning, while she held her head from a booze-induced hangover, Debra called, very embarrassed. She thanked Elizabeth for coming to her rescue and preventing her from making an even bigger fool of herself than she already had. Elizabeth first replied that she had not needed to call but was glad she had been able to save her cousin from someone who was probably a jerk and liar.

Elizabeth recalled she had said, "Debra, just remember, half of the men you meet in a Nashville bar may say they're going to make it big in country music and never do. They just use that line to impress any woman they're talking to. That guy was sexy, but I could tell he was lying the minute he opened his mouth. Probably half of the stuff he was telling you wasn't true, and you were too naive to realize it."

Debra had replied, "I know, I know, Elizabeth. I admit I had too much to drink last night and wanted to believe every word he said. I could have almost made a stupid mistake if it wasn't for you," confessed Debra. "Now I don't even remember today what he looked like. Believe me, no more nights out like that. I'm just going to concentrate on getting my degree, finding a job, and staying out of bars or any other kind of trouble," and as far as Elizabeth knew Debra did just that.

Elizabeth smiled again, picturing the scene at the bar and a tipsy Debra who rarely lost her self control. She then put down the papers she had been reviewing and finished placing the charts on a table where they would be easy for Taylor to pick up. He always liked to review the patient's history before he entered the examining room. She walked down the hall and continued to prepare for the large number of patients they were expecting that afternoon. So far, no flu or other infectious diseases had hit the community, or the numbers of appointments would even be higher.

CHAPTER FIVE

ANOTHER HOT AND sticky week passed in Tennessee. At 5:45 and one hundred miles to the west of Greenwood, Molly's Folly was in full swing. The restaurant had the reputation as the most popular place in Nashville, and the number of people crowded inside certainly testified to that statement. The heat still hovered above ninety outside, but inside the air was cool and heavy with the aroma of steaks cooking on kitchen grills.

Through a smoky haze, a potpourri of flea market finds could be seen nailed on walls for just the right touch of Nashville nostalgia. Here and there pots of sickly ferns were hanging from the ceiling on brass chains. The plants were a pale-green color due no doubt to the unhealthy atmosphere of smoke. The walls were covered with oak paneling, and the chairs were done in black leather with excessive numbers of brass nails pounded into the leather. On one prominent wall, there were pictures of well-known patrons, businessmen, politicians, and the like. All had inscribed on their photographs some type of well wishes to the owner of the restaurant.

Groups of rising young business executives were clustered around the antique bar while eying equally well-dressed women over the rims of their drinks. Like flocks of Magpies, friends huddled together discussing a recent promotion or perhaps a scandalous divorce. An overweight waitress dressed like an English milkmaid wove her way through the crowd, taking orders for drinks and food.

Debra Chandler sat uncomfortably in the corner of the bar area and waited for her date. The sound of voices and laughter bounced off the walls and engulfed her. From time to time, she nervously sipped on a glass of Chablis while searching for a glimpse of Jim Tarkington. She smoothed the maroon fabric of her skirt and brushed a strand of long brown hair back from her face. She wore no ponytail tonight, with her hair falling around her shoulders in soft waves. Her golden-brown eyes roamed the restaurant for any familiar faces, but there were none. Her eyes had been described by friends as her best feature. They were a color similar to that of a golden topaz but the shade seemed to deepen when she was concentrating or angry. She crossed her long legs under the table in a restless fashion as she continued to wait. One of the things she hated most was to sit alone in a restaurant and feel the inquiring glances of strangers.

After a long day in the lab, she had returned to her town house to shower and change. She glanced at her watch. Perhaps she had arrived a few minutes too early, or Jim was running late. This would be her second date with Jim and, in fact, one of the few dates she had had period since the divorce. Even though Jim was the chief resident in internal medicine and infectious diseases at the medical center, he was also doing independent research in a small lab in her wing of the building. A month ago, when he stopped by her lab to return a reagent that he had borrowed from her, he asked her to go to the cafeteria for a cup of coffee. Last week she had met him in Hillsborough Village for a movie because, as he suggested, they should both like the foreign film. Then yesterday at the last minute, he phoned to ask her to meet him for dinner tonight, on a weeknight, no less, she thought. In a hurry, he had explained he was on call that evening, and if an emergency came in, his plans could be cut short in a moment's notice.

Debra took a sip of wine and could not decide whether she felt excited or apprehensive about the developing relationship. After living in a painful marriage for three years, she was not sure if she was ready to get involved with another man. Emotions were like a crystal vase, she thought, strong but fragile when put under undue pressure. She had to admit, in all honesty to herself, if she saw Jim walking down the hall with a group of fellow residents or standing in the line in the cafeteria, she was more than just interested in a casual friendship.

Debra raised her eyes from the surface of the table and realized he was standing in front of her. His dark-blond hair was combed back from the left side of his face and his eyes glistened with warmth when he spoke to her.

"Were you about to give up on me? Actually, rounds took longer than usual. We have a bigger patient load than I realized when I called you yesterday. I should have told you to meet me an hour later than I did. But at least I thought ahead and called to reserve a table in the back. Let's grab our table and get away from this noise and smoke."

Jim pulled her up from the chair and guided her to a back table, with Debra balancing a half-full wine glass in one hand while holding a large leather purse under her arm. After sitting down, Debra sipped more wine while watching him as he ordered a Coke. He jokingly explained to the waitress that he was on call and couldn't drink anything stronger.

Earlier in the week, she had seen him in rumpled hospital whites, but he too must have gone home to shower and change. He was wearing a dark-blue jacket with gray slacks and could have passed for a young lawyer or banker rather than the hard-working and sometimes exhausted resident that he was. A complete metamorphous, she thought. At thirty, Jim was definitely a striking-looking man. She had not been attracted to him initially because of his appearance, like most women would be. Rather quite the contrary. Debra held some subconscious suspicion about very handsome men and their vanity, which led her to be somewhat reserved around him.

It was only later when she got to know him better that she grew to appreciate his warm personality and the depth of his intellect. His concern and empathy he showed for his patients particularly impressed her. But in spite of his easy manner and sense of humor, there was something in his gray eyes that suggested there was a part of himself that he would only share reluctantly with others.

Strangely, he seemed oblivious to the effect his appearance had on the women, especially those who worked at the medical center, but Debra wasn't. Before she had even met him and he borrowed the first batch of reagents, she overheard two nursing students in a hospital restroom discussing his good looks and single status with much giggling. So when he walked into her lab that first time, she could understand the attraction many members of the female staff felt. Later she found out he had done most of his undergraduate and professional training in Nashville, but their paths had never crossed. On that first visit, he was strictly business and only asked about the reagent he was about to borrow.

Her thoughts were interrupted when the waitress appeared and asked to take their dinner order. After she left, they began a conversation by talking about the unusual hot weather and a few other innocuous subjects concerning the hospital, but he suddenly switched the topic by saying, "I can't help but ask this, tell me how such a nice girl like you, as the saying goes, end up working for a screwball case like Steiner?"

Now that was the last thing she was expecting him to say, and at first, Debra was not only surprised but almost offended that Jim would refer to her boss as a screwball. After all, she had chosen to go to work for him. But trying to maintain a professional manner, she carefully explained that she was fascinated by Dr. Steiner's work with DNA. His was the most interesting job available when she finished her degree, and also he offered the best salary when compared to those of other labs.

"Yes, as you say, he is strange, and at first it was hard to get used to him and his moods, but by now we have a truce, even though I must admit an uneasy one. I just continue to tell myself when I'm upset, the work is interesting, the pay is good, and I have to adjust to his weirdness. After all, some people in science are introverts and not very friendly. I just didn't pick up during the interview how odd Dr. Steiner really is."

"But, Debra, doesn't it make you nervous working on some of his radioactive experiments? The rumor mill at the hospital says he is dealing with some powerful stuff and not too careful with it either. Not that I would know firsthand because he doesn't exactly share information with anyone and certainly not me. My source tells me that he hates most MDs whom he considers not too sharp and only likes PhDs in the hard sciences, like himself. Tell me, did you ever hear he spilled several flasks of radioactive iodine in the corridor and all the rooms on the floor had to be decontaminated?"

Debra twisted a lock of her hair and admitted, "Well, I suppose those rumors are true enough. I did hear he had a spill of radioactive solutions before I started to work for him, and the authorities had to decontaminate a portion of the fourth floor, but I suppose that could happen to anyone. I must admit I don't even know everything that's going on with his research. I still find the work fascinating even though I only work on a part of an experiment and never see the final results. Dr. Steiner goes over the data in his lab, usually late at night, I guess. I know that because I have seen his lights on when I've driven past the building after I've been out seeing a movie or a play."

Debra took a sip of the wine and asked, "Did you ever hear Jim, that he also has a small private lab in the back of the main lab, which is locked all the time. During my first week of work, I went in there when it was unlocked to try to clean up the dirty glassware. Was I ever reprehended! I was told never, ever to go in there again like I was a high school student."

"That's sure a strange way to run a research operation, and not very professional in my opinion," mused Jim. He reached over to touch her hand and added, "Well, all I can say is I'm glad you are working here in spite of your weird boss and not living in some other city." Then he tried to make a joke by saying, "After all, who would I be able to borrow stuff from if you weren't down the hall?"

When they were finishing the dessert, he leaned over the table, putting his hand over hers, and whispered in an earnest tone, "How long, Debra, have you been divorced? You look so young."

She was surprised by this question also but answered, "Three years, a little over three years actually." And though she didn't like to discuss such a painful part of her life, she decided to tell him about those years.

"I chose to marry someone I had known all my life and dated the last year of high school and four years of college. Unfortunately, he disliked college so much that he quit after one year and returned to our hometown for a job at his family's furniture company. After that, we didn't see each other very much since I was studying at school, and he was at home learning the business. I recognize now that I was more mature than he was, considering some of his behavior. He drank a lot and hung out with a wild crowd from high school. But even though I was worried, I went ahead with the wedding. The church and the country club had been booked a year earlier, and the invitations had been printed. What was I to do?"

"Well, it would have been hard to back out at that point, though I guess some do," Jim added thoughtfully.

Debra sadly looked out a window and whispered, "Almost from the start we couldn't get along. I guess we really changed while I was in college, but neither one of us admitted it at the beginning. After one fight after another, finally we decided by mutual agreement to go ahead with the divorce. So by twenty-four, much to my parents' disappointment, I was divorced with no plans, no husband, no place to go," she answered after pausing painfully.

"But, Debra, you shouldn't feel badly. Many girls get married right after college and then realize they made a mistake. Some girls even go to college only to find a husband. A few of my classmates I knew when I was an undergraduate admitted as much." He laughed. "At least you got your degree. Now you have a Masters in a difficult field, helping to save mankind, no doubt. How did you end up in Nashville anyway, why not go to Atlanta or Memphis?"

"Oh, after the divorce, I didn't know what to do. I was at loose ends, but then I thought why not go back to school, so I moved to Nashville to get a master's in microbiology. I liked the program at the University, and Nashville is closer to my parents' home than any other large city. My degree took two years to finish. After that I went job hunting and was lucky to find a place right away in Dr. Steiner's lab. I've been here ever since. So that's my recent, up-to-date life history, Doctor." And since he had asked about her past, she felt that his was now fair game. "Jim, were you ever married or in a long-term relationship?" For some reason, she hoped the answer was no.

He looked slightly uncomfortable but answered. "Oh yeah, I guess I had a serious relationship during my second year of med school. It ended badly for both of us. She hated the long hours of study that go with the territory. No one gets through med school without spending at least fifty hours a week in classes and labs. Try as she might, she could not adjust to my schedule. I heard later she married someone in banking. I guess she liked his nine-to-five hours better than mine. Since then, there have been a few girlfriends here and there, but nothing major," he said with a weak smile.

The truth is, he thought to himself, *I have been too busy to concentrate on any serious relationship. Not many women would tolerate the neglect suffered with someone like me. Everyone knows the workload at this hospital is hell.*

Jim Tarkington stopped talking and studied the symmetry of his ice cubes in the Coke. *Slow down,* he said to himself. *You like this woman, but don't ruin things by moving too fast and scaring her.* The immediate feelings of attraction he felt for Debra were more intense than his feelings in any past relationship and certainly not with the girl from his second year at med school. Their knees touched accidently under the table, but neither moved away.

When Jim and Debra were walking to the parking lot after finishing dinner, he paused, touching her arm and said, "It's too early to end the evening. Even though I'm on call, would you like to hear some great jazz? One of my patients plays clarinet at a bar about ten minutes from here. Not all the music you hear in this town is country, or so my patient tells me."

Debra gave him a warm smile and said, "I would like to go since I love jazz. But I have a problem because I left my dog in the house. I must run by home and let her out for a few minutes before I can go anyplace else. Could you follow me to my town house and let me take her outside for a few minutes first?"

He agreed with that plan, so she gave him the address for her home ten blocks away. He proceeded to follow her out of the parking lot. As they drove down Hillsboro Avenue, Debra could see flashes of lightning in the distance. Perhaps the heat was about ready to break she thought. Her Volvo sedan, which she and her ex had purchased before the breakup, handled the hilly road easily, but as she turned in her complex, she couldn't see Jim. He was driving a beat-up turquoise Chevrolet that looked like it had been made in the sixties. She decided he must have gotten caught by a red light as she ran in the house and let Annie out on the patio.

The doorbell chimed as she began to pick up yesterday's papers scattered around the couch. She hurried to the door and let him in. Looking over his shoulder, she could tell the rain was beginning to come down in sheets. Shaking off a few drops of water, Jim walked into the living room. "Wow, what a great-looking place," he exclaimed as he admired the eclectic mix of furniture. The room held two overstuffed sofas in dark-brown corduroy and a Victorian love seat covered in a leopard print. A restored steamship trunk served as a coffee table. and over the fireplace hung an oil painting of a horse race.

"Oh, thanks for the compliment. Naturally, I think it's very attractive, but also comfortable. I've spent a lot of time here reading or watching TV. Most of the furniture I found at my favorite secondhand store on Third Street and bought the Oriental rug at a real junk shop. After having it cleaned—it was really filthy—I tried it in the room, and everything clicked in place. I think the rug ties the whole area together just as I planned," she winked with a smile.

They could hear heavy rain falling and rumbles of thunder in the distance, both glad to be inside and out of the weather. There was scratching at the kitchen door, and Debra hurried to let Annie in and introduced her to Jim. She was pleased that he seemed to like her dog, because he even got down on the floor to stroke her silky coat and rub her ears.

Jim looked up and complained. "Here I am thirty years old and still live in a crummy furnished apartment. It's in the house staff building that I rent from the med center. I think they furnished our apartments with the junk they got from either the hospital waiting areas or patients' rooms after they died. When I finish my residency next June, I hope that I can buy some stuff that looks half this good. Maybe when I get ready to settle in a permanent place, you can help me pick out some furniture. Seriously, Debra, I see you have great taste and a sense of style. Maybe you should consider a second career in interior decorating," he added as a joke.

Pleased with yet another compliment, Debra replied, "As I mention earlier, my ex's family owned a furniture store, and while I was still married, I used to work there a few hours each week. I found it to be inspiring just to be there. The furniture in the store was so beautiful that I loved to walk through and pick out my favorite pieces. I even helped decorate one of my friend's home. She ordered a truckload of furniture from my husband. That made him immensely happy. You know, helping the bottom line, that sort of thing was very important to him and his family."

Debra glanced out the window, hearing more thunder and said, "Incidentally, I have a stereo and a perfectly good coffeepot. Why don't we just stay here since it's raining so hard?"

"A great idea, you talked me into it," Jim said. So Debra went in the kitchen to fix the coffee using the percolator instead of the instant she usually drank, while he selected several cassettes to put on the stereo. She returned with two steaming mugs of coffee on a tray with a pitcher of cream and bowl of sugar.

They sat facing each other on one of the couches, listening to the stereo playing softly a Miles Davis melody. His jacket and tie lay on a nearby ottoman. Debra's shoes were on the floor as she sat at one end of the couch with her feet tucked under her body.

Debra walked back in the kitchen to refill their coffee, and upon returning, she unconsciously sat closer to Jim. His arm moved across her shoulders. Carefully he put their mugs on the steamship trunk. Slowly his hand caressed the back of her neck, and he pulled her closer. Lips met lips gently at first then harder as her chest and thigh was pulled toward his in the strength of his embrace. Their lips parted slightly, and their tongues touched. They lay entangled upon the couch. The months of loneliness for Debra seemed to be swept away. A weakness was in the bottom of Debra's stomach as all caution began to ebb. Her body arched toward his as they lay on the couch.

Suddenly the tension was shattered by the urgent sound of a beeper in his coat pocket. "Dr. Tarkington, Dr. Tarkington, please call three north. Please call three north, urgent."

Cursing softly to himself, Jim shook free of their embrace and turned off his beeper. "Where is your phone, Debra?" he asked. She directed him to the phone hanging on the kitchen wall. After a few brief moments of conversation, he reappeared in the kitchen doorway.

"Damn, this is sure a hard way to end our evening. Welcome to my world, baby. A diabetic was recently admitted to three north, and the intern is having trouble stabilizing her blood sugars. Even though this is not my area of expertise, I'm on call for internal medicine tonight for the hospital. So I've got to get there fast and see if I can get the patient stabilized and her insulin levels under control. If not, I guess I can call one of the attending docs for help."

Jim wrapped his arms around her and gave her a brief kiss on the lips, and then he was gone. Debra leaned weakly against the wall. The stereo was playing a love song by Joni Mitchell, whose words kept repeating, "Help me, I'm falling in love again."

Am I? Debra thought as she moved slowly through the living room, turning off each lamp, and then went into the kitchen to put the empty coffee cups in the sink. The rain had temporarily stopped, so she took Annie out the kitchen door to visit the patio again. She thought it was definitely getting colder. She whistled for Annie, and they came back in and went upstairs.

She pulled off her clothes, leaving them in a heap on the floor and found a long-sleeved cotton tee in the dresser to put on. Annie curled up in her wicker bed, and Debra climbed into the king-size bed, a relic from her marriage. The sheets were cold. It would probably be a long time before sleep overtook her. She snuggled up with the pillow and pulled the blanket over her head, still thinking of him.

CHAPTER SIX

FRIDAY MORNING, UNCHARACTERISTICALLY for her, Debra hadn't remembered to set her alarm clock and woke up a few minutes later than usual. She jumped quickly in and out of the shower. While towel drying her long hair, she ran through the house, found Annie asleep under the dining room table, and pushed the poor dog out the back door to the patio. She grabbed a green corduroy pantsuit from her closet and, after pulling it on, hastily applied a minimum of makeup. She then tied her damp hair back in the usual ponytail and coaxed Annie in from the patio, letting her smell a can of favorite Purina dog food, which she used as bait. Feeling guilty, she promised the dog a long walk in the evening to make up for the lack of attention that morning. Debra was thankful she had an arrangement with Harriet Jones, a retired teacher, who lived in a similar town house close by. Mrs. Jones had a key to Debra's house and took Annie out at noon every day for a short walk. Debra knew this wasn't enough exercise for a rambunctious young dog like Annie, so she usually took her on a longer walk or run after work.

Debra made a nail-biting drive to the medical center in order to get there on time. She arrived at the lab short of breath. At her desk while putting on a crisp white lab coat, she began to look over the experiments for the day and waited for Dr. Steiner's appearance. She thought of Jim's remarks the night before about Dr. Steiner. He certainly could be very strange and demanding to work for, but with his national reputation for brilliance in the field of DNA research, he probably didn't care what anyone thought. She knew very little about the man because he never divulged any personal information about himself. The hospital grapevine said that he had never married, had no friends, and no family in the area. Every spare minute of his time was spent in his private lab, which, was always kept locked if he wasn't around.

As she told Jim last night, during her first week at work, that lab door was open, and she went in thinking the area around the sink needed cleaned up. It was a real mess with smelly piles of old petri plates and racks of dirty test tubes on the countertops while in the corner were boxes of dusty journals. Just as she was getting ready to start, Dr. Steiner appeared and asked in a threatening voice what she was doing in there. Debra answered she planned to straighten up the area since the door was ajar, and the lab appeared to really need a good cleaning.

Dr. Steiner grabbed her shoulder, spinning her around, and said in a low, almost deadly voice, "Don't ever go in this lab again. Don't touch any of my cultures or any equipment in this room. The door should have been locked. Anything that I'm working on here has nothing to do with the grant for which you were hired. This is private research that I've been involved in for some time. It has no connection with the University and is no concern of yours. I do not want to see you in here again."

Then realizing how harsh this might sound, he had softened his tone. "Sorry, I lost my temper for a moment, Ms. Chandler. Thanks for offering to clean up, but I prefer to do everything in this lab by myself. Again, you should never go in there. If I get further along with the investigation, perhaps I will allow you to help me in some small way." She still could remember how shaken she had felt after the encounter with Dr. Steiner that day.

So far Dr. Steiner had not shown up yet, so Debra entered a large walk-in incubator located at one side of the lab. She would use this time to take care of the children, as she called the mouse cells. She carried several trays of the cell cultures growing in large flat-sided flasks to a hood in the center of the room.

Switching on an exhaust fan, she began to change the fluid covering the cells. The media contained all the ingredients the cells needed for growth. Working quickly with her hands inserted through the hood's safety gloves, she drew off the spent media, which had changed color slightly from its former healthy red color to a pale rose. This was due to the buildup of metabolic byproducts as the cells grew. Like a gardener tending trays of young flowers, she added fresh media to the sheaths of cells lining the bottom of each culture bottle. Some of the media contained radioisotopes, which would be incorporated into the growing cells with their radioactivity calculated at a later date.

After finishing changing the tissue culture media, she worked swiftly with what was left of the morning carefully weighing the chemicals needed for the next set of experiments. She used an electronic scale that could weigh to the smallest number of milligrams. Distilled water was then added to each flask after the containers were labeled and dated. This part of her work day proved to be tedious as usual.

Dr. Steiner appeared around eleven and went immediately into his private lab and shut the door. What he was doing in there was anybody's guess, Debra thought. At least he had no additional instructions for her.

As she worked, she went over the events of last night in her mind. In the bright morning sunlight, she had to ask herself if a romantic evening had perhaps gone to her head. Granted, he was an extremely attractive man but one who could break her heart and probably be too busy to notice. With a sigh, she lay down the spatula that she was using to transfer the powdered amino acids to the scale's balance pan. Looking at the clock, she was surprised how late it was. No wonder hunger pains were beginning to stab her stomach. In the hasty preparations to get dressed this morning and the mad drive to the medical center, she had skipped breakfast. Two friends usually joined her in the hospital cafeteria for lunch, and it was almost time to meet them.

Debra caught the elevator to the basement and walked into the cafeteria. Although the medical center was known in the United States for its state-of-the-art medical care, its cafeteria was still in the dark ages as far as Debra was concerned. When she was in grad school on the main campus, her classes were close enough to run into one of the campus joints to eat or return home and take care of Annie, but now with a short lunch hour, she was stuck at the hospital. There simply wasn't enough time to go anywhere else. Dr. Steiner usually ate at his desk and probably disapproved of her taking thirty minutes to eat with friends.

She stood in line and glanced over the people already there. Debra saw two third-year medical students walk by. They had just started their ward work and wore their stethoscopes around their necks like prized medals. Then a patient still hooked up to an IV was talking to family members at a table in a corner of the room. He was no doubt giving them a progress report on his condition. In another corner, several tables were pulled together, and a group of ward clerks were eating from brown bags.

Debra chose a tuna and tomato salad, which looked safe enough, and sat down at a table to wait for her friends. Perhaps Jim would show up too, but then she remembered that this was his clinic day to go to Perry, twenty-five miles away. The medical center ran a clinic there and clinics in several other towns. This was for the benefit of the underprivileged, as they were described in the medical center's literature, but the hospital's interns and residents also worked at the clinics and got invaluable experience. The connection was important for both the clinics in the small towns and the medical center's training of the students. She knew Jim wouldn't be returning until later today. Debra thought it was surprising but interesting how she was beginning to learn his schedule.

Her friends appeared and sat down with her at the table. They too were research assistants like Debra and wore similar white lab coats. Linda Stanfield was a classmate from grad school but ten years older than Debra. She was a pleasant-looking large blonde who had gone back to school after her youngest started first grade. Linda only worked until two each day so she could be at home when the children got off the school bus. Funny stories of her children's misdeeds kept her coworkers in stitches of laughter.

The other friend was Michelle Johnston, whose husband was a second-year medical student. Even though she was working in a research lab at that time, Michelle hoped to get a student loan and a grant next year so she could start down the road for a PhD in biochemistry. At times, Debra thought she carried a small chip on her shoulder because of the strain of being the sole wage earner for her husband and herself. Debra overlooked this occasional moodiness for usually Michelle was pleasant company to be with. When her husband was studying on the weekend, which was most weekends, Debra and she would go to a movie or out to eat in a local restaurant.

The lunch conversation began by each of them describing what kind of day they were having so far. Today, they all agreed, was going pretty well. After all, it was Friday, and they would soon have the whole weekend off. They had a fair idea about the general goals of each other's research lab. Sometimes they discussed ways to get around some of the problems that arose in research, but not today. The topic introduced by Linda was health insurance at the hospital, which the other two found rather boring. Linda was especially worried about the hospital's plan to switch to another health insurance company. She thought the coverage might change, and since she and her husband had three children, one of whom was always either having a minor accident or illness and the bills could add up in a hurry.

But while Debra was trying to sympathize with Linda, even though she did not care or even know what kind of insurance the hospital offered, Michelle suddenly interrupted and said, "Debra, I guess you know, but your boss is a jerk, you know, a real jerk and creep." The intensity of the remark startled Debra.

Michelle continued. "Yesterday he was walking down the hall reading a medical journal and walked right into me. It was such a collision that I thought I might be knocked down. Then instead of apologizing, he tried to give me a lecture of watching where I was going as though it was me, not him, who caused the collision. So I just ignored him and walked away. I don't know how you stand to be around him."

Debra knew that Michelle disliked Dr. Steiner for other reasons too. When the radioisotope spill occurred three years ago, some had been tracked into Michelle's lab. Much of her boss's data had been contaminated and caused Michelle to have to work overtime for weeks to correct the mistakes the incorrect data had yielded.

"Gosh, Michelle, I'm sorry. He can be incredibly rude and act as though he is above the normal rules of behavior and civility." First Jim and now Michelle, thought Debra. Did anyone approve of her working for him? Now she somehow felt she should apologize for Dr. Steiner's rudeness while defending his brilliance but didn't know how.

"But you should try working for him if you really want to see him in action. When I show him any test results, he will be very critical and cold. Every figure will be challenged for accuracy for no good reason. After my first few days at work, I would go home in tears, but I just continued doing my job and tried to control my feelings better. Finally, I learned to ignore his outbursts and reminded myself that is how he is. I don't allow my feelings to show. At least he seems to trust me a little bit and leaves me alone for the most part."

Michelle and Linda looked at each other and expressed sympathy to Debra for having to work with such a tyrant. They both agreed that Dr. Steiner would not win any popularity contests at the medical center. Linda then brought up a subject closer to her own heart. Since Debra was the only one of the group who was not married, Linda had been concerned for some time that Debra would never meet anyone suitable to date at her lonely lab job. After all, most of the men were already married who worked in the medical center. So now the budding relationship between Debra and Jim Tarkington was being following closely by Linda and Michelle.

Not able to wait any longer, Linda finally asked, "Well, I suppose you aren't going to tell us how the dinner date went last night. I guess that I'll just have to ask. Did you have a good time, and do you still think he is as marvelous as you did a week ago?" And making an old joke, she added, "At least he is out of med school, and there is no need for you to support him if you get really serious."

Not wanting to discuss any of last night's events with them, especially in the crowded hospital cafeteria, where others might overhear what she was saying, Debra only told them that they had a delicious meal at Molly's Folly, and she had a good time. Then she went on to say that the date had been cut short when Jim had suddenly been called back to the hospital because of an emergency on third north.

"Ha," said Linda. "Now you're getting a taste of what your life would be like if you marry a doctor like him. Your life won't ever be the same or to call it your own. Naturally, he will have to put the patients' needs before yours. And then when you have children, he will be so busy you will have to raise them yourself, just like a single parent. Why don't you try to find an engineer, like I did?"

"Engineers generally have regular hours like most people and usually spend time at home. They won't leave you to do things on your own and will help with the chores," she bragged. Debra began to feel a slow burn begin at the roots of her hair, which spread across her face.

She knew what Linda was saying had some ring of truth to it, but didn't want to admit that to Linda. She could remember the problems their next-door neighbors in Clarksville had when she was growing up. Dr. Murray was always at the hospital or seeing patients at his office, while poor Mrs. Murray tried to run the whole show at home by herself. Debra knew that for a fact because she babysat for the three Murray children when their mother needed to go out. She even went with the family to Florida on a summer vacation to help with the kids when she was fifteen.

Her friends meant well, but sometimes they could be nosy, and Linda could be overbearing. Trying to lighten the conversation a bit, she replied, "Please, ladies, please, we've only had two dates. Don't be planning yet what to wear to the wedding." Then glancing at her watch, she saw it was almost one o'clock. She excused herself and hurried back to the lab.

The afternoon seemed to drag on after she returned from lunch. She had promised another friend, Carolyn Moss, who was head of the microbiology division in the clinical lab, she would play in her bridge club tonight. Carolyn sometimes ate lunch with them, and a week ago, she asked Debra to substitute in her club. Debra really didn't want to play, but Carolyn begged and begged her to come. She was having difficulty finding another player and said she didn't know what she would do if Debra said no. Debra felt she should help Carolyn, so she finally agreed reluctantly to play.

Carolyn lived in Brentwood, which was some distance from Debra's town house and would take a half an hour to get there. But the distance wasn't the reason Debra didn't want to play. Actually, nervousness was the reason, and she was afraid she wouldn't remember enough of the rules to play well in the group.

The club played from seven until ten thirty and met the fourth Friday of each month. Debra knew with those hours it would be a long evening, but at least tomorrow was Saturday. Actually, she used to like to play bridge, having learned when she was in college. In Clarksville, even though her husband refused to learn how to play, Debra had played several times a month at the community center with girlfriends. She had tried to build her own life since he was always busy at the store, and they seemed to have little to talk about.

If he was not working, he would go either fishing or hunting with a group of his high school friends. Sometimes those friends and their wives would come over for dinner. She found that she had little interest in the wives' conversations, which revolved around their young children and neighborhood gossip.

She looked at the lab clock and thought with some concern that Jim had not called her yet. Then she reminded herself there was no reason to think he should. She had to admit that she was more than slightly interested in being with him again. Perhaps she should invite him for dinner tomorrow night. Several times he had commented on the rotten food at the hospital and might appreciate a home-cooked dinner. Steaks usually appealed to men, as she remembered.

If she bought rib eyes at the grocery and added a tossed salad and some sort of potatoes, an appealing meal would be ready in no time at all. Best of all, this choice wouldn't require much effort on her part or need any expert cooking skills. Debra thought of herself as an uninspired cook and became resentful of the time it took to fix anything too complicated. With a possible menu already in her mind, she could just picture the two of them on the patio enjoying a bottle of wine with Jim possibly cooking the steaks on the grill.

Since Jim was working at the Perry clinic today, she decided to write out a quick invitation and slip the note under the door of his lab. Dr. Steiner had left early, saying he was going to a meeting on the other side of campus, so she could walk the note over to Jim's lab right now. Unsure of how to make the invitation sound, she erased the first attempt, but after several more tries, she felt she had captured just the right feeling on paper, not too serious and not too light.

She signed her name and slipped the note in an envelope she found in Dr. Steiner's desk. Then she left her lab to deliver the invitation. *I feel like I'm sixteen again,* she thought as she pushed the envelope under Jim's door.

She finished her assignments for the day, and after putting away the reagents and straightening up the work area, she left, locking the door carefully. By the time she went outside, a cool wind was blowing from the west. It finally seemed like October and not August. The temperature must have dropped ten degrees since she had arrived that morning. Looking at the clock in her car, she saw it was already after five. Debra thought, *I'll have to hurry to get to Carolyn's house for the bridge game by seven.*

CHAPTER SEVEN

THE RAIN THAT hit Nashville Thursday evening passed through Greenwood early Friday morning. Then the weather cleared, and at least the day started off well—a beautiful autumn day. But by early Friday afternoon, a devastating situation began to develop. Soon every living soul in the town would be affected one way or another by the impending disaster. The events of a medical catastrophe unfolded slowly at first, then picked up momentum.

Elizabeth had awakened early that day, thrilled that the weekend had almost arrived. She planned to meet a friend for lunch and would only have to work until four since Taylor closed the office an hour early on Fridays. Then she could relax for the next two glorious days.

The friends had decided to eat at a popular Chinese restaurant called the Oriental Inn. A refugee family ran the restaurant and had taken a beat-up old building in the center of town and turned it into a remarkable establishment, much to the amazement of the rest of Greenwood. The interior of the restaurant was done in colors of red and black with touches of gold. Soft classical music played in the background, and scattered throughout the restaurant were fresh flowers and whiffs of incense. Each table held a small candle, glowing in the dim light, which added to the ambience and mysterious atmosphere of the Orient. While eating there, some customers said they felt as though they were actually in China and no longer lived in Tennessee.

Elizabeth's friend, from high school was Amy Parrish and actually the person who had introduced her to Doug Reynolds. Elizabeth was not sure she wanted to thank her for this favor but knew her heart was in the right place. Amy was a stay-at-home mom, like many of Elizabeth's classmates. She managed to escape from the duties of motherhood for a few hours each Friday. Her three-year-old daughter was always left at a program called Mom's Day Out, run by the Presbyterian Church. Usually Amy put this time to good use to do errands, but occasionally she would treat herself and have lunch with her friend Elizabeth Chandler.

When she arrived, she smiled at Elizabeth as she sat down and explained that she was a little late because she couldn't find any parking places but finally saw one behind a vacant building a few blocks away. Then she had to walk several blocks, pushing the stroller to leave her daughter at the church. Catching her breath, she lapsed into silence while they both spent some time looking over the menu, which the waitress had left on the table. They were several pages long with selections from parts of China, which weren't familiar with either, but all of which looked tempting to try, as Amy commented.

After finally making their decisions, the waitress wrote down their orders and left. Elizabeth took a deep breath and gently told Amy she didn't think she had enough in common with Doug to continue dating him. Amy took the news well and said she wasn't surprised.

"Elizabeth, I could see that you weren't hitting it off with him when we had invited you over for a cookout two weeks ago." She assured Elizabeth that she wasn't offended with the decision, and maybe another man would show up, and they could introduce her to him.

With that problem out of the way, Elizabeth relaxed and began to eat her food with relish. She and Amy had a great time remembering their school days back in the sixties with hilarity and laughter. At the end of the meal, the waitress arrived with fortune cookies wrapped in crisp black paper. Amy read hers aloud with more laughter because it said a stranger would take her on a trip to Europe before the year was over. But when Elizabeth opened hers, a frown crossed her face.

"Well, what does it say?" asked Amy with a smile.

"This is weird, it says my life may be in danger and be very careful. What kind of fortune cookie is this? The owners better change the company whom they buy these weird fortunes from." And she wadded up the paper in disgust and threw it on the table.

Elizabeth glanced at her watch and realized that it was almost one o' clock. "Oops, I've got to go, Amy. The time has slipped away. The office must be opened by one thirty." She called for her check and promised Amy she would see her again for lunch in a few weeks. Then she walked quickly to the office six blocks away.

Taylor had called the office before lunch. He told her he was still at the hospital but had to go talk to his lawyer about the impending divorce before showing up for his office appointments. She had listened in silence, wishing she could comfort him in some way but didn't know how. After getting to the office in record time, she went through the front door and pushed her purse under the desk in her office. All the files still needed to be pulled for a busy afternoon filled with appointments. After finishing those tasks, she went to the supply cabinet to get out the syringes for shots.

The whole office by now looked clean and orderly, and she was checking the files of patients to be seen that afternoon when her thoughts were interrupted by the loud sound of the waiting room's bell. She could hear Peggy's muffled response to a female patient's shrill voice. *Damn, can't they even wait until one thirty when our office hours begin,* said Elizabeth to herself as she hurried to see what was going on out front.

Sherry Whitehouse, the wife of a local accountant, and her five-year-old son were in the waiting room. Both looked ill and uncomfortable. Pallor was on their faces, which glistened with sweat in spite of the air-conditioned room. Sherry's hand shook as she tried to grasp the back of a chair. "I pray it's not food poisoning," said Sherry. "This horrible nausea seemed to hit both of us at the same time just as we were finishing lunch at home. And I feel we are both hot and probably have temperatures. I hope Taylor is in... Oh no, David."

At that point, all control a five-year-old could muster evaporated, and David began to vomit as his small body shook with convulsions. Elizabeth lunged to his rescue, while Peggy ran to get towels in an effort to save the office's carpet. Elizabeth picked the small boy up and carried him to the closest examining room. She was wiping his forehead with a cool towel when the phone rang.

"Hey, Elizabeth, it's Taylor on line one!" Peggy yelled from the front.

"I'll take it in the second examining room, Peggy!" Elizabeth shouted back. "Please come and sit with the Whitehouses while I'm on the phone."

"Hi there," said Taylor over the phone. He was not one who ever wasted time on small talk. "It appears that some alarming illness is beginning to sweep over our community. Several people have come to the emergency room, and plenty others have called to say they are on their way. The symptoms, which you need to recognize, begin like a severe intestinal bug has infected them. The patients already here are running high temperatures. Two of them became rapidly dehydrated due to vomiting and overwhelming diarrhea, and before we could get IVs in them, they fainted. The hospital is beginning to get swamped with too many admissions, and I need to stay here and help. As I recall, we have a light patient load today. Please cancel my appointments and reschedule them for next week. You and Peggy can catch up on paperwork for a little while and leave early since it is Friday."

"Gosh, Taylor," said Elizabeth, "This is odd. Sherry Whitehouse and her little boy are in our office now and may have the same illness as the one that you have described. David has just thrown up all over the waiting room floor. They may not be sick enough yet for the hospital, I must add, in my humble opinion. What do you want me to do?"

"Order some antinausea medication from the pharmacy for them and tell Sherry and David to drink plenty of fluids when they get home so they won't become dehydrated. Then see if her husband can pick them up if Sherry doesn't feel like driving. Tell her that I'll call in a few hours to see how they are doing."

There was tiredness in his voice, and then he paused, as though he was trying to gather his thoughts. "You know, I was looking forward to getting caught up with my work today and seeing my children over the weekend. I think I told you that Claudia was going to Nashville with her girlfriends to do some shopping, and I was to be the babysitter. I think I'll call Claudia and tell her to put the trip on hold. I don't have a good feeling about these patients I've just seen. I wish today was going better. It'll take me part of next week to catch up with the cancellations from today."

Elizabeth felt a lump in her throat as an odd feeling of dread swept over her. She swallowed hastily as she replied, "I wish the day was going better too, Taylor, for you and all of us." And she hung up the phone.

Elizabeth brought Peggy up-to-date on what was happening at the hospital and then went over Taylor's instructions with Sherry. Finally, she helped her carry David to the car. Sherry had insisted that she could drive herself home but asked Elizabeth to call her husband to tell him they were sick and to come home as early as possible. Also, when Elizabeth called the prescription in, she should ask the pharmacy to deliver the medicine as she didn't feel well enough to go in the drugstore and pick it up.

Still in a fog over Taylor's description of the serious situation with many of their patients, Elizabeth returned to her desk and called Walgreens and asked them to fill the prescription for the Whitehouse family. Then she began to pull out a stack of government forms and requests that she was behind in filing. She buried herself in paperwork, while Peggy started calling the afternoon appointments to tell them about the cancellations and reschedule them for the next week.

The ring of the phone jarred them both. A weak elderly voice that Elizabeth recognized immediately was on the other end. "Elizabeth, it is Lucy Van Meter on Hill Street. Annabel and I will not be able to make our appointment this afternoon. We have both been throwing up, and now sister is having chest pains. I don't think I should try to drive her to the hospital. I am very worried about her. What should I do?"

Elizabeth gripped the phone and thought quickly. At eighty-four, Lucy was probably not capable of driving her sick sister, who was eighty-seven, to the emergency room. *Damn,* thought Elizabeth to herself. Then she made a decision on her own and said, "Miss Van Meter, I am going to call an ambulance for your sister, and you should ride with her to the hospital. Dr. Whitney is already there because something is going around, and others have what you and your sister seem to have. I don't want to scare you, but Dr. Whitney would not want you to take any needless chances. I will notify him to meet you in the emergency room."

Just as she was hanging up, Peggy yelled from the reception area, "Elizabeth, it's Taylor on line one again."

"Hey, Elizabeth," a low, strained voice filled her ears. "I'm up to my elbows with sick patients, as are the other docs. More came in than we were told to expect. I've just admitted ten of our patients in the last hour. It's the same type of gastrointestinal problem with all of them. It could be food poisoning, it could be something else, but who knows? None of them seem to have eaten the same food at a restaurant or where they work. At least they all now have IVs and are receiving fluids. Old Mr. Albright was so dehydrated when his daughter brought him in that I'm worried if I can save him."

"Taylor, that sounds so scary. At least Sherry and her son made it home. She called Peggy to let her know. But I was just on the line with Miss Van Meter. She and her sister have been vomiting, and now her sister is having chest pains. I was just going to order an ambulance for them when you called."

"That's good thinking on your part. Go ahead and call the ambulance when we get off the phone. I don't like the looks of this. It could be an epidemic of some sort. The ER nurse has just handed me a note saying that two more of my patients have showed up and are asking for me. I'm going to need more help up here. Jump in the car and get to the hospital as fast as you can after you have called an ambulance for the Van Meter sisters."

Elizabeth explained the situation to Peggy and then got the ambulance company on the phone. Their switchboard operator promised that they would pick up the Van Meters after they made the three runs that were ahead of them. Then Elizabeth, feeling more apprehensive as the minutes ticked off the office clock, ran to her car and started the five-mile drive to Greenwood Memorial Hospital on the other side of town.

CHAPTER EIGHT

BACK IN NASHVILLE Jim had overslept on Friday morning too. He didn't get up until six due to his midnight visit at the hospital the night before. He caught up with a group of residents and attending physicians on three north. They were already making rounds for the day. Feeling like he could never get away from that part of the hospital, he slipped in with the crowd around the nurses' station. Dr. Russell Scott, the department head, was discussing the prognosis of the patient that he had worked on last night. Dr. Scott saw Jim standing in the back of the group of doctors and commented he thought Jim had made the right decision by adjusting the medication and ordering additional lab work. Jim was pleased to hear the patient was improving and that Dr. Scott had paid him the compliment during rounds in front of the rest of the house staff. That type of remark sure didn't hurt his reputation at the medical center.

The head of internal medicine at the medical center and Jim's boss was fifty-nine years old. The years had been kind to him in spite of being a few pounds overweight and his dark hair being thinner than when he had been a resident himself. He was widely admired by all those whose paths he crossed and had not only the respect of his colleagues in the hospital but the nation as well. He was especially known because of his excellent teaching methods for medical students and young physicians in training. Fourth-year medical students eagerly sought positions on his house staff as interns. While sixty-hour weeks were the norm, no intern or resident ever complained. Those who had served under Dr. Scott's direction looked back on their training with great pride. Everyone found his mind was like a steel trap because no small detail escaped him. That kept all the staff, including Jim himself on their toes.

Jim picked up a pile of charts and began to hastily read through them. Besides typical medical cases that he would be seeing with the group, he would be concentrating on illnesses caused by infectious agents, his subspecialty. The general population, as he knew very well, thought most diseases caused by bacteria could be cured by a few rounds of penicillin or some other antibiotic. The truth of the matter was some microorganisms were continuing to mutate, so what might work on them today might not tomorrow. There was a constant battle between new strains of bacteria or viruses and the body's defenses against them.

The natural defenses of people were boosted by pharmaceutical drugs, but drug-resistant strains of microorganisms were frequently being discovered by laboratories across the world. In fact, hospitals were the breeding ground for some of the most deadly bacteria. In spite of the careful precautions and repeated cleaning with strong disinfections, some bacteria still could be found lurking in the cleanest facilities. In addition, a few hospital workers were actually carriers of some strains of bacteria, like staphylococcus whose more common varieties could be found on everyone's skin. Jim's research was concentrated on these resistant strains, and he hoped to have a paper published in the near future describing his findings.

The rounds dragged on for an hour, and first Jim stood on one foot then another, but finally, he was free to go and drive to the clinic in Perry. His 1968 Chevrolet was parked in the residents' lot, which was covered with small branches and leaves from last night's storm. Jim swung around a large branch blocking the drive and hurriedly pulled out of the lot for a trip that would take around thirty minutes if the traffic wasn't too heavy, and he should arrive before nine. By now hunger pains were gnawing at his stomach, so he headed to a drive-in window at a handy McDonald's to order black coffee and an egg McMuffin. This was his favorite breakfast because he could eat with one hand while he navigated with the other. The radio was playing Johnny Cash's latest hit, and with his windows down, Jim felt relaxed and happy as he drove down the highway. At long last, the cooler air in Nashville held a hint of fall, and the traffic was light for a Friday morning, which made the trip even more enjoyable.

He was just finishing his coffee when he entered the city limits of Perry, a small town south of Nashville. The hospital was close to the local high school, which he liked to glance at while driving past. The kids out front reminded him about his own school days in a small Kentucky town across the Tennessee border.

Those days seemed so long ago. Here he wasn't yet finished with his training. He was really sick of the residency program and ready to go out to make a living and repay some of his medical school debts.

He slowed down as he approached the hospital and its attached clinic. It presented a depressing picture because the building's paint, a pale green, was peeling, and the grounds surrounding it were ill kept. The hospital's budget was a testimony to the sad state of affairs in the city, according to some local physicians who worked at the clinic. Unless an increase in the property tax was passed in November, the conditions would only get worse. At least the medical center furnished interns and residents in training to work at the clinic, and there was no monetary charge to the clinic. This was a godsend for the poor in the town who had no other access to health care—plus it gave the house staff from the medical center important experience. A year ago, Jim started his rotation at the Perry clinic and had been there every Friday since then without fail.

He parked in the doctor's lot, and unfortunately, the first person he saw when he came through the side entrance was Sylvia, whom he thought was probably waiting for his arrival. She was a nurse in the pediatric department, an attractive girl in her midtwenties. They had had a brief affair last fall when he first began working there. After a short time of dating her, Jim could tell he would never have serious intentions so quickly tried to break off seeing her. But after ending the affair, he had major problems convincing her that their relationship was over. He told her they had nothing in common, and there would be no more dates or weekend sex at the hospital when he was on call. In his opinion, she tried every trick in the book to rejuvenate his interest, but he held firm to his decision.

Actually, today he was surprised for she only wanted to give a message to him. It was a request to go to the pediatric area of the clinic to see a child who had what appeared to be a severe case of strep throat. The infection was not responding to the usual doses of penicillin, as she told him.

The resident working there wanted his help in suggesting other treatment options for the parents. As she delivered this information, she pressed her shoulder against his. Her white uniform was unbuttoned slightly to show a revealing cleavage. Sylvia gazed at him through large blue eyes lined with blue eye pencil and smiled sweetly. A small clump of mascara could be seen clinging to her left eyelash.

He cleared his throat while thoughts of her arose in his mind. Perhaps he would have been tempted again if he had not met Debra several weeks ago, and last night had not gone so well, at least until he was called back to the hospital. He straightened up and spoke in a professional tone, "Thank you, Nurse Robinson." As he walked past her, he added, "Please let the clinic's secretary know I'll be a few minutes late for my appointments while I check on this child."

He spent about half an hour with the child, a little boy, who was running a high temperature. The child had repeated strep throats, and nothing the clinic doctors tried had any success. There was always the fear the strep infection would lead to a rheumatoid heart or a diseased kidney. An exciting new drug, which promised to hit such bacteria as the boy was harboring, was available through the medical center, and Jim prescribed it after explaining the situation to the boy's mother. Also, Jim had been careful to take several throat swabs to be sent back to the medical center's clinical lab so they could identify the strain. As an added precaution, antibiotic sensitivity tests would be run too in the unlikely event that the new drug would not be effective against the organism. And then after finally arriving at the internal medicine department, the day passed swiftly. A large number of patients were seen, none of whom offered serious problems or required great diagnostic skills except the youngster in the pediatric clinic.

Just as the day was ending, Jim was told about a call that was received by the clinic's switchboard. The operator reported there was a general medical emergency in Greenwood, Tennessee. The information was relayed to the doctors working in the clinic. Jim remembered that Greenwood was a small town one hundred miles to the east of Perry.

It would seem that a large number of the town's population had come down with an undisclosed intestinal illness. The hospital's emergency room and doctors' offices were swamped with ill patients. A cry for help had gone out to surrounding medical communities. Jim knew Greenwood was too far away for the Perry hospital personnel to be involved. However, he could not help but be curious about what kind of illness could be causing such turmoil in the town. He puzzled over what few details he learned from the switchboard operator as he walked to his car.

He had an uneventful drive back to the medical center and arrived there just before seven. In his office, he went over messages he needed to return and requests for consultations. After cleaning up the list of calls, he noticed an envelope on the floor close to the door. It was an invitation for dinner written on the back of a lab sheet and from Debra, no less. She was inviting him to eat with her tomorrow night. He smiled to himself. *A continuation of where we left off Thursday night*, he thought, excited with a chance to see her again, sooner than he had hoped.

He first glanced at the calendar to see if he was on call and was relieved to see he had the whole weekend off. Then he recalled that he had traded with another resident who wanted off so he could go someplace maybe out of town because he had mumbled something about a birthday celebration. Pleased, he picked up the phone, but when he dialed her number, he only got a recording. So he was forced to leave a message on the machine, saying he could accept the invitation for dinner, and would be there at seven with wine.

After hanging up, he could not help but wonder where she was on Friday night. As far as he could remember, he had never seen her with another man, but you could never know about some women, especially someone with her looks. That was a troubling thought, but he shoved it in the back of his mind.

He had first noticed her sitting with friends in the hospital cafeteria a few months ago. He was struck by her classic looks and a figure that was only partly concealed by a ubiquitous white coat worn by all the lab girls. Later, he learned from some interns she was divorced and worked as a research assistant for that weirdo on the fourth floor's research wing. Determined to meet her, he paid a visit to her lab on the pretense of borrowing a reagent for his research that he was out of. They talked only a few minutes on the first visit, but he managed to drop by again to return the first reagent and borrow another. He couldn't help but be intrigued by the interests they seemed to have in common after spending a few minutes with her.

Jim ran his hand through his hair as he now reviewed several patients' charts at his desk. These cases were to be presented at Grand Rounds next week, and he would have to be on his toes and ready for any unexpected questions from the medical staff. All the drugs that the patients had taken in the last five years were meticulously listed, and possible interactions between them were included in his notes. Looking at his clock on the desk reminded him it was time to step next door to check on the gel columns. He was running a serum through them and hoped to extract some human interferon. He planned to test it on some cell cultures of mouse liver that he was growing in his incubator and then infect those cells with a mouse virus.

He spent about thirty minutes in his lab and returned to his office. As his long day was ending, and he was putting additional charts in his briefcase to take home to study, Dr. Scott called. He too had heard about the outbreak of some type of illness in Greenwood. He went on to say that he wanted Jim to drive to Greenwood tomorrow. Due to a possible epidemic that was developing, he thought Jim should investigate the situation. Jim was thinking, as he leaned against the wall, exhausted, *This is a damn short notice, and it's my weekend off too.*

Dr. Scott believed Jim could use the information to write an article for the *Journal of Infectious Diseases,* of which he was one of the editors. Of course, Dr. Scott expressed sympathy for all those sick, but also in the forefront of his mind was curiosity about what kind of possible infection could be causing these problems, as he remarked to Jim. Perhaps, he mused, a chemical spill could be causing the emergency. Then he wondered to Jim if the outbreak could even be caused by tainted meat or vegetables bought at one of the town's groceries. Jim was getting more and more tired holding the phone and wished Dr. Scott would end the conversation so he could go home to bed.

Jim assured Dr. Scott he could be counted on to investigate the problems in Greenwood and would follow his visit up with a call Saturday night when he returned. Before hanging up, Dr. Scott gave him the name of the hospital administrator to contact when he got there and, for additional contacts, the names of several of Greenwood's local doctors who trained at the medical center. Jim tried to figure out how to fit Debra in this change of plans and decided the only way was to invite her to go along too.

He put on his jacket and left, after carefully locking his office door. The sound of the door shutting echoed through the deserted hallway, which was partly dark. On the weekend, the medical center turned off half of the lights in the corridors. This was an effort to save money during the energy crisis on their utility bills because of the large amount of electricity which was needed to run the hospital.

As Jim walked down the hall, he passed a bank of snack machines by the men's restroom. Standing with his back to Jim was a white-coated figure trying to get a Coke from one of the machines. He jigged the machine several times in a fit of temper and was rewarded finally with a can of Coke. As the figure turned, Jim was surprised to see that the man was Debra's boss, Dr. Steiner. Even though Jim spoke to him in what he considered a friendly fashion, Dr. Steiner only grunted and walked away, heading back toward his research facilities, which occupied a different part of the fourth floor. *What an unfriendly bastard*, Jim thought. *I don't know how Debra stands working for him. Maybe I should encourage her to look for another job. There must be a dozen places in Davidson County where she could find a job which would be better than spending time around that guy.*

CHAPTER NINE

EARLIER FRIDAY AFTERNOON, Harry Morgan had sat tapping his fingers on the desk thinking, thinking. Something was terribly wrong. He felt it in his bones. The first suggestion of a problem had occurred about three hours ago when his supply clerk in the storeroom called on the phone. Worried, he informed Harry that he had to leave immediately because an ER nurse had called to say his wife was there very sick, dehydrated, with vomiting and diarrhea. She worked in a local hardware store and had become violently ill after lunch.

The clerk, whose name was Steve Sawyer, told Harry that when he talked to the ER nurse, she was hopeful the treatment his wife had received would stabilize her condition and Steve could take her home in a few hours. The nurse then went on to say that they had had several cases similar to his wife's and some much more severe. An ER doctor was wondering if the cases were tied to some kind of food poison. "That's not likely," Steve had told Harry and added, "Since I'm fine, and we've eaten dinner together all week. She never goes out to lunch. We both bring brown bags to work every day because we're saving money for a house down payment."

After Steve left in a screech of tires in the parking lot, Harry decided to call the ER himself just to satisfy his curiosity. There was a slight uneasy feeling in his stomach. It took him several tries to get through to the hospital as all the lines appeared to be busy. When he finally got hold of the hospital and was transferred to the ER, the phone must have rung ten times before the secretary answered.

Yes, she replied. Everything Steve had told him was true except they had now had even more patients. Did he want to talk to Dr. Taylor Whitney, who had just finished with a patient and was free for a few seconds?

Yes, Harry sure did. He knew Taylor from eating together at Hudson's lunch counter and felt that he would give him an honest appraisal of the situation.

"Hey, Taylor, it's Harry Morgan at the water company. What in the devil is going on? One of my employees just left for the ER where his wife was taken by ambulance. It seems she came down with whatever everyone else seems to have. I heard a lot of people have been admitted there, actually."

"Oh, yeah, Harry," said Taylor in an uncharacteristic strained voice. "Yes, something strange does seem to be happening here. I've just admitted four of my patients in their midthirties. These are people who usually see me only once a year for checkups. So far, we don't have enough information to make even an intelligent guess what they have and what's causing this. Everyone seems to have terrible vomiting, diarrhea, and high fever. Some type of virus, I would guess. But to be on the safe side, why don't you people at the water company run some extra checks to make sure it's not something in the water supply."

"I sure will, Taylor," replied Harry, worry spreading over his forehead. "In fact, that was what I was thinking I should do, even before I talked to you. Now I will tell you in no uncertain terms I don't think we will turn up anything since we perform tests on our water samples very carefully and keep a close watch on all of our controls. Every test has been negative here for months, if not years."

Taylor thanked him for the information but had to hang up suddenly to see a new patient. Harry sat at his desk a few minutes. After more reflection, he decided to call the elementary school where his wife, Joyce, taught third grade and try to talk to her. The school secretary answered.

"Jenny, have you had any kids who became ill today and were sent home with an intestinal problem like vomiting or diarrhea? One of my employees left suddenly because his wife was in the ER, very ill. He said a nurse told him there were others with the same symptoms at the hospital." He asked the question tepidly to the school secretary, almost afraid to hear the answer from her.

"Harry, it's funny you should call, you must be psychic. We have sent around twenty kids home, or others have waited for their mothers to pick them up and take them straight to the doctor. We dismissed early today, at one thirty instead of three o'clock. The health department is here now investigating due to the number of sick kids. Actually, your wife is in our clinic sitting with a few students whose mothers have not gotten here yet."

Oh my god, Harry thought as he hung up the phone. *This town may be in for something very ugly.* Fearing the worst, he then made calls to his various department heads and told them to double the number of samples being checked. Also, he said he would come down immediately to look at the results from the last few days in case anything had been overlooked. Just when he was leaving the office, the deputy commissioner of the county health department called to say there had been an abnormal number of cases reported since noon of an intestinal illness, and he should check the results of the company's water tests. The health department in the meantime was checking the results of restaurant and grocery store inspections.

Right after he finished talking to the health department, the chairman of the board for the water company called. Harry could count on his fingers the times he had ever called his office. The chairman had heard some disturbing rumors around town about a mysterious illness sweeping the town and wanted to know if the water supply had anything to do with it. Harry had been standing at this point, looking out the window, but sat down quickly with that question. He assured the chairman that all the lab tests for the whole week had been negative, but to be on the safe side, he was asking the quality control lab to run more tests, and they would have the results by six. He told the chairman he would be the first to be told if anything came back that looked out of the ordinary and would need additional study.

These conversions transpired earlier in the afternoon, and now it was after five. He could only hope and pray the illness had nothing to do with the water company. All Harry could do was sit now and wait for more lab results at six. He had looked at the data from what had already been collected earlier in the week, and nothing looked suspicious.

At six, Harry went again to the quality control lab to check on the results. He was not satisfied with the new verbal reports he had gotten from the technicians over the phone. Stewart, the chief technician, took some plates out of the incubator, and they both studied them carefully. "You know all these colonies, they look pretty much what we usually see and with an average coliform count too," remarked Harry.

"They sure do, Harry. Don't worry, these colonies are nothing. Whatever is causing the illness up at the hospital isn't caused by our water. Think of all the filtration and chloride treatment every drop goes through before anyone takes a sip. You remember, we had a spike in the coliform count last week, but that was due no doubt to our only rain for the month for October which we got last weekend. You had us increase the filtration time and add more chemicals, and now everything looks normal again."

"Yeah, I know. I remember that. But something is causing the outbreak. I was just thinking that while the water for the city of Greenwood is treated here, the hospital and a few offices and the subdivision surrounding it aren't. That hospital water comes from a deep spring and is treated separately. And of course, most homes in the county use well water dug by the original owners, some probably a century ago. I wonder if anyone who has drunk water from only the separate system or wells or springs have become sick?" Harry added thoughtfully.

Depressed, Harry slowly returned to his office and sank down in his chair. By now, he was deadly afraid the problems somehow could be traced back to his water supply, whose safety he was responsible for. He thought again, could the violent employee he fired back in the summer have anything to do with this problem? No, there was no way a person could contaminate the water of the whole city with the company's safeguards in place, but God help him if there was something wrong with the water. He was proud of the way the company was run and would not want to have to go out and find a job at his age.

Today, as Harry well knew, the people of Greenwood never gave their water a second thought. If the water tasted and smelled okay, nobody had any complaints. They just turned on their faucet for whatever reason when it was needed. And as far as the water's safety was concerned, that was never questioned. On any given day, if a person was at the hospital, he could see the water company's building and its filtration plant standing in the distance as it always had. The water's fine reputation was taken for granted. In fact, most Americans never thought about where their tap water came from or if it was safe to drink, Harry thought cynically.

CHAPTER TEN

After coming home from work Friday afternoon, Debra hoped Jim would call after finding the invitation under his door, but so far there was no word from him. Maybe the envelope blew under a chair and he hadn't even seen it. Then she realized that he was probably still at the clinic in Perry. She quickly ate a peanut butter sandwich and changed into a pair of jeans and a turtleneck. After putting on a leather jacket and taking Annie for a quick walk, she left for Brentwood promptly at six thirty.

It was difficult trying to concentrate on the road while driving because she couldn't keep her mind off how Saturday evening might turn out if Jim showed up for dinner. She hoped he wasn't on call. Thoughts about him brought feelings of excitement, but also apprehension because she was fearful of getting hurt.

Debra began to admire the handsome neighborhood she was passing through, trying not to think too much about a possible next date. Though this part of Nashville was blessed with gently rolling hills, the roads were really winding and a little hard to drive on. Suddenly she pulled the car back to the center line after a sharp curve and realized that she had better pay greater attention to the road and not look at the attractive neighborhoods.

Also in this section of Nashville, the houses were sitting on two or even three-acre lots, all with well-manicured yards. These large yards showed the homes off to great advantage and many were decorated elaborately with realistic Halloween decorations. Though the sun had already set, Debra could still see brilliant cascades of chrysanthemums interspersed with southern pines and red-leafed maples. In spite of the nature beauty of the neighborhood, the whole area felt spooky to her for some reason, perhaps too many ghosts and goblins in front of the houses, she decided thoughtfully.

Carolyn hadn't made the directions very clear because she had been preparing a solution of sulfuric acid as she talked to Debra. Thus, with shaky directions, Debra made several wrong turns before finally pulling up in front of the Moss home. It was a stately-looking Southern colonial with four large columns that ran from the roof to the porch. Debra had heard Carolyn and her husband, a University history professor, had bought the house nine years ago. They got it at a ridiculous low price, according to Michelle Johnston, because it was in deplorable condition after the death of its elderly owner. Since then, the couple had meticulously restored the property, one room at a time. Much of the remodeling they had done themselves rather than hire a contractor. The other lab girls told Debra that Carolyn would come to work at times so tired and sore she could hardly move. But the finished product appeared now to be professionally well done, according to Debra's appraising eyes.

A few months ago, the local newspaper had even written up the home in a feature article describing the restoration. Debra and Carolyn's coworkers read all the details with delight. Debra could already tell that the writer had not exaggerated about the tastefulness of the restoration. She was just admiring the polished brass lanterns that hung on either side of the double doors when Carolyn opened the door.

"Hi, Deb, come on in," Carolyn greeted her warmly, relieved she had shown up. "Thanks for coming. You're a good sport to sub for us when you haven't played in a few years. Let's go back to the family room, where the tables are set up."

Debra quickly looked around a handsome entrance hall before following Carolyn to the back of the house.

The walls of the entrance hall were covered with expensive grass cloth, and polished gray slate was on the floor. A large walnut console stood against one wall. At one end of the console, Carolyn had placed an antique copper bowl filled with yellow chrysanthemums, but that effect was ruined by a hideous ceramic statue of a witch standing at the other end. The witch was twelve inches tall and stirring some sort of green ceramic mixture in a black pot. She had an evil grin on her face, and long black stringy hair was hanging out from a pointed cap. With Halloween less than a week, Debra supposed that the decoration was a concession to Carolyn's nine-year-old daughter, Mary Ann.

Debra shuddered in spite of herself when she passed by the witch. When Debra was six, she had attended her school's Halloween carnival and went with some of the bigger girls through the Witch's Cave. The cave was filled with ghosts and vampires, but it was at the very end of the cave that a great fear struck young Debra's heart. A crackling creature was stirring something evil in a big pot. As she approached, the witch pretended to try to pinch Debra's arm and give her a spoonful of the witch's brew. It was only later that Debra learned the witch was no other than the gym teacher, Miss Jasper. Debra never cared much for her after that.

In the family room, the six other players necessary for two tables of bridge had already arrived. They were sitting at the card tables, waiting impatiently to start the game. Carolyn brightly said, "Debra, I want to introduce you to the other girls." Debra thought to herself that a few couldn't be classified as girls due to lots of gray hair fixed in bouffant styles, but whatever Carolyn wanted to call them was not any of her business. She did make a conscious effort to remember all the names and match them with their faces. The two younger women, close to her age, she already knew since they worked with Carolyn in the clinical lab.

The others were neighbors or friends. A couple of the players with gray hair she later learned were grandmothers.

It seemed to be a different mix of players, what with neighbors and people from the hospital all there together. Debra hoped the women wouldn't do much talking, and she could concentrate on trying to remember the complex set of bridge rules. Regardless, the moment that Debra was dreading arrived: cards were drawn for partners, and the game began.

While it was true Debra used to play bridge when she lived in Clarksville, she had not played in several years. She was nervous but tried not to let it show. She tuned out the conversations about neighborhood gossip and instead studied the cards that had been dealt to her. She was a competitive person by nature and hoped not to make any obvious mistakes. Carolyn had told her yesterday that several of the women played duplicate bridge once a week and were excellent players. That news had made her even more nervous.

A bowl of candy was on each table, and Debra found herself nervously eating several handfuls in quick succession as she looked over her hand, deciding what to do. Luckily, like riding a bicycle, Debra found that she had not forgotten all the bidding rules and how to play the hand was coming back to her a little at a time. She was blessed with a good memory and could recall the most important cards in the pack as the game went on.

They had been playing for about ten minutes when Betty, Carolyn's next-door neighbor, asked Debra what kind of work her husband did. This, obviously, was an effort to make small talk since she posed the question in a friendly, inquisitive tone.

Debra bit her lip at the question that assumed she was married and had no career of her own. She tried to answer in a pleasant fashion, "Oh, I'm not married. Well, that is, not married anymore. I'm divorced and on my own."

"Oh dear," said Betty, who was in her late fifties and somewhat embarrassed by asking what could be perceived by some as a nosy question about a husband when there was none. "I saw that you were wearing that beautiful diamond ring, and I just supposed it was some sort of wedding ring. Ever since the sixties, girls wear all sorts of rings, not just a gold band and a solitaire engagement ring like women of my generation do."

Debra bit her lip again and answered in another polite tone, "Oh, I just decided in a spur of the moment to wear the diamond ring. It was left to me by one of my grandmothers. Actually, this ruby cluster on my other hand was hers also. I rarely get to wear the rings where I work due to the hazardous chemicals in the lab."

"The rings are beautiful, what wonderful gifts to leave to a granddaughter," added Suzanne, another neighbor and Debra's partner for the evening. "Tell me, you've really gotten me curious, what do you do that is so hazardous that you can't even wear rings at work? I hope they pay you well if you work with dangerous equipment."

Debra thought to herself, *Another nosy question that I wish hadn't been asked*, but she answered in a straightforward manner. "I know this sounds strange, but I grow mouse cells in tissue culture and prepare reagents for a scientist doing DNA research who is my boss. Some of the chemicals I use could be dangerous, but I also use radioactive reagents with which I have to be very careful. I definitely would not want to make my rings radioactive," she said with a slight smile.

The women at her table looked a little dumbfounded at what Debra actually did at work. Growing mouse cells seemed like nothing they had ever heard of and a topic for discussion out of their comfort zone. Not knowing where to go with this information, they returned quickly to the game. Debra frowned and thought, *First, Betty asks about my marital status, and then*

Suzanne asks about my job. Now, I am way over my head playing this hand. But somehow, the cards fell right, and she made what she had bid.

After the game went on a few more minutes, Carolyn suggested that they should move to the dining room where there was pumpkin pie and coffee. The pies had been made by Carolyn's housekeeper, Katherine. Since Carolyn didn't have time or inclination to cook, Katherine usually prepared the evening meal before Carolyn got home from work. Knowing that Carolyn would need to buy a dessert at the bakery today for the bridge club, Katherine had made the pies, which were one of her specialties and was waiting in the kitchen to clean up after the dessert was finished.

Carolyn had told Debra she hired Katherine after Mary Ann had been born so she could go back to her job, and she had been with them ever since. Katherine did the house cleaning for Carolyn in addition to the cooking but more importantly waited at the bus stop for Mary Ann to come home from school each day.

Then while they were still sitting around the dining room table eating, Betty informed the group that she had been ill last week, and after lab tests were run, her doctor reported she had had food poisoning. She apparently had gotten the bad food at a church supper she attended a few days earlier. Since quite a few had become ill, the health department had become involved. Their report said some of the chicken served at the dinner had not been cooked properly, and they traced the problem to salmonella bacteria found in chicken at a local grocery.

Some of the women were surprised to hear Betty had been sick and expressed sympathy for her but then began to describe their own experiences with similar illnesses. Debra thought the group started to sound like a bunch of sparrows chirping in fright when a prowling cat wanders by. Would they ever get off this topic? The piece of pumpkin pie in her mouth was beginning to taste like cardboard. Debra thought this discussion was inappropriate at the dining room table and wished they would switch to another subject. She for one would just like to return to the family room, finish playing bridge, and go home.

With these last remarks, Debra could not help but think, *There are some diseases out there, ladies, whose symptoms are so horrible that I couldn't describe them to you here. But I studied about them in grad school. A few other diseases show up from time to time, and we don't even have a name for them or know where they came from. People might think modern medicine has conquered most diseases, but there are still some out there against which we have no defense.* She resisted the urge to mention any of this information and frighten them more.

Finally, the topic of the conversation that Debra found so unpleasant was exhausted, and the group returned to the family room. Unbelievable, considering all the talking that had gone on, the evening ended exactly at ten thirty, just as Carolyn had promised. When Debra was leaving, several players asked her to come back or even consider becoming a member of the club when they had an opening. She told them that perhaps she would and thanked Carolyn for inviting her. She knew her mother would approve of this exhibit of good manners.

Debra was grateful to get outside and escape the stuffy house. When she walked to her car, the air felt crisp and cool. It was fortunate she had chosen to wear the leather jacket and by now wished it was heavier. The odor of smoke from a neighbor's fireplace floated through the air and tickled her nostrils. Dark shadows belonging to the huge trees overhead made it difficult to see. She stumbled on a loose brick in the sidewalk as she reached her car and fell against its side, catching herself from hitting on the ground, somewhat shaken.

On the drive home her thoughts returned to the bridge club. She knew she had been working too hard and missed the company of her cousin, Elizabeth, but wondered if she would have much in common with other members of the bridge club, even the ones who worked at the medical center. They all had husbands, something she definitely no longer had. Some had children to watch over, Friday grocery shopping, and other activities like that. In fact, they all lived normal lives in the suburbs. She had given up that type of life when she chose to leave her husband and get a divorce.

Even though she had enjoyed playing cards and meeting other women tonight, she was not sure she would want to join the club if later they had an opening. She could just hear her mother's voice in her ear telling her that would be a bad decision because it was time to establish new roots and widen her circle of acquaintances.

As she drove home, she looked to her left and noticed a lighted jack-o'-lantern hideously grinning from the window of a stone house which sat on a steeply pitched hill. The kids, whom she presumed lived there, had draped fake spiderwebs across the windows and doors, truly making it look haunted, like a house in a ghost story. Suddenly, the road made a sharp turn, and she jerked her eyes back to the road, putting on the brakes. She shivered and thought about the witch stirring her evil brew at the carnival she had attended many years ago. What if tainted food had been in that witch's pot, like the food the women at the party had described? Now that stuff would really make a child sick and cause terrible stomach aches.

Of course, the organizers of the carnival at her elementary school probably had only colored sugar water in the witches' pot, and no one there got sick unless it was from too much candy. Those distributing childhood memories hadn't crossed her mind in years. Why were such weird thoughts bothering her now? She couldn't explain it as she shivered again and turned up the car's heater to full blast.

CHAPTER ELEVEN

On Friday evening while Debra was struggling to remember how to play a complex card game while fending off inquiring questions about her personal life, Elizabeth was experiencing a completely different type of evening, a devastating evening, in fact. She had arrived at the hospital around four o'clock, after Taylor had called and begged her to come as quickly as possible. Once inside the building, it was as though she had entered another universe. Elizabeth had walked through the hospital noting the mass confusion and chaos surrounding her. It had been a struggle to make her way down the corridors of Greenwood Memorial. After finding Taylor, she had helped him with his own patients and then spent an hour trying to administer to others. By now it was eight o'clock.

Turning down a patient wing to the right of the entrance hall, she saw stretchers lining the hallway. It appeared to her that every room in the hospital was filled. Faint moans could be heard from some of the patients as white-gowned employees dashed around, first in one direction then another, trying to calm those in distress. A ward clerk sat at the nurses' station, and her white hair, normally arranged in a neat bun, now hung down in complete disarray. She was trying to answer the phone, which rang in an unrelenting fashion for as soon as she hung up from one call, another one was waiting. There was also an unpleasant odor in the air that Elizabeth could not quite identify. She interrupted the ward clerk, Evelyn, Johnson, to find out if she knew where Dr. Whitney might be. Evelyn was not sure but had last seen him heading for the emergency room, and she thought that would be the best place to look.

Elizabeth went down the steps and hurried through the hall to find an overwhelming sense of disaster in the emergency room too. It was crowded with patients in various stages of the illness, and all were waiting to see a doctor, any doctor. Those most ill lay on stretchers quietly and appeared to be in almost comatose-like states. A few others were obviously nauseated and throwing up in buckets that they grasped to their chests. The rest of the patients who were not quite as ill as the others sat in the waiting room, holding insurance cards and other papers, waiting to be called. Their relatives or friends sat with them and were nervously leafing through worn-out copies of magazines while sipping on sodas purchased from the machines in the hallway.

Elizabeth caught a glimpse of Taylor inside of an examining cubicle. She stepped over to the side of the walkway and stood in front of the curtain, waiting for him to come out. Elizabeth realized how tense Taylor was when he appeared. His easy smile had disappeared, and his lips were pressed firmly together, a frown on his face. Blood was splattered on his white lab coat, and his tie had been loosened around the collar. The muscles in his neck stood out as he began to read the next chart. He looked up quickly and saw Elizabeth waiting to see him.

"Oh, Elizabeth, an angel sent from heaven and an answer to my prayers once more," he whispered with relief. He motioned for them to move to the corner of the room where there was a large portable x-ray machine. He then leaned against the machine, trying to catch his breath and gain a few minutes of rest, much like a marathon runner who pauses before the final surge to a finish line.

"As you can see, the situation hasn't improved at Greenwood Memorial since last we talked. In fact, one might say that things are going to hell in a hand basket, as my old granddad used to say. By now I must have admitted thirty patients. No one has died yet, but the older Van Meter sister is a likely candidate. As you know at that age, anything can upset her delicate health. A few of my youngest patients are gravely ill too. It seems that this curse, and I don't know what else to call it, is hitting the old and young the hardest."

"But, Taylor, what could be causing this illness? I'm so scared. Is it something contagious or a poison or what?" Elizabeth was desperately trying to understand the reasons for the town's crisis.

"I want to do whatever you tell me to so I can help these poor people, but you look as though you are ready to drop over yourself. Can't you take a small break if only for a few minutes?" Elizabeth asked anxiously as she reached out and touched his shoulder. She couldn't remember touching him like that before.

"Yes, to be honest, I'm very tired and discouraged. I'll consider the break that you recommend, but first, I'll try to answer your questions. No, Elizabeth, I don't think this is caused by some infectious agent that's being passed around from one family member to another. Some family members are ill while others aren't. It's not some type of food poisoning either because no one has eaten the same food or attended the same function in the last seventy-two hours. Hell, it's not like we had a gigantic picnic and everyone ate rotten potato salad. Frankly, right now, I don't know what to think."

"I know everyone here is getting very, very tired, Taylor. What are we going to do? No one can work twenty hours straight without some rest. Some of the nursing staff came on duty at seven, have had no breaks since noon, and are still here."

"I heard that the hospital's administrator has called other towns in a 30-mile radius, and additional help is coming soon. Some nurses should arrive in the next few hours. We also have a call in to CDC in Atlanta to come and check things out. Their investigators should be here by Sunday at the latest and will try to figure out what's causing this mess. But perhaps you are right, Liz, about breaks." And he patted her hand. He always referred to her as Liz when he was relaxing and the office hours had ended. So she was foolishly glad that he called her Liz, even though she had hated the nickname since childhood.

"I tell you what. I'll take a coffee break after I see these last three patients. You can help me by going up to the third floor and checking on Miss Van Meter. I have her in a private room, and it would be a great favor to me for you to see how she is doing. Please try to reassure her sister, Lucy, that we're doing all that we can. They're two of my favorite senior citizens, and I want her to pull through this." Turning around, he wearily walked back to the next patient's cubicle.

Elizabeth climbed the two flights of steps in record time and, after catching her breath at the top, asked a ward clerk for Annabel Van Meter's room number. Luckily there was no one in the other bed yet. Annabel lay in the center of the bed, looking very fragile and as pale as the sheets that covered her. Death seemed to hover in the room. She was hooked up to various bottles and tubes. The only movement that could be detected was the faint rise and fall of her chest as she took shallow breaths of air. Lucy was dozing in a chair beside the bed but woke with a start when she heard Elizabeth come through the door.

"Elizabeth, thank heavens, at last a familiar face," whispered Lucy as she slowly rose from the chair and went to the door to squeeze Elizabeth's hand. "I'm so worried about my sister. She is not doing well at all. Dr. Whitney seems very concerned. She vomited several times after we got here, but now she seems to be unconscious and not breathing well. I'm terribly afraid her heart has been weakened by the asthma attack she had earlier this afternoon."

Elizabeth felt Annabel's wrist for her pulse. It was very weak and erratic. She looked at the chart attached to the foot board at the bottom of the bed and saw that the usual medications had been ordered for the erratic heartbeat after an EKG had been run.

Putting her arm around Lucy, Elizabeth asked, "Lucy, what could be causing all this sickness? It seems that hundreds in the town are ill, and others are getting sick by the minute. No one seems to know what has caused the illness. Could you or your sister eaten some type of spoiled food at a restaurant or gone to a party where you ate something that tasted funny? Maybe you have been around someone who was sick with symptoms like Annabel's? Do you have any idea where she could have caught this?"

"No, Elizabeth, I have no idea, no idea at all. We haven't been around anyone in the last few days. As you know, we live a simple existence at our age and don't go out very much except to church on Sundays. We usually eat the same thing at home and only eat about twice a month at one of our favorite restaurants. Actually, we were planning to go there Saturday night before Annabel got sick. We have the same schedule each week. I cook for two days, and then Sister cooks for two days. I made a pot roast on Wednesday night with vegetables that we had grown from our garden. Last night we had leftovers. I can't think of anything different that she ate than me. It was just good country cooking, if I do say so myself. Sister is always after me to drink eight glasses of water a day like she does, but I never do. I usually get my liquids with coffee and sweet tea."

Elizabeth thought for a minute and then replied, "Well, I don't believe anything you have told me would make a difference. If you think of anything else, please let Dr. Whitney or me know. We were just discussing what could be causing this terrible situation. It's very important that we get to the bottom of the outbreak as quickly as possible. We don't want the illness to spread any further. Some investigators are coming Sunday to try to pin down the cause of the disease, but before they arrive, a lot more people could get sick."

She then went over to Annabel's bed and checked her IV. Her pulse seemed even more weak and erratic. *This is not a good sign*, thought Elizabeth. She brushed the thin white hair back from Annabel's face and leaned down close to the pillow and whispered to her, "Annabel, can you hear me? It's Elizabeth from Dr. Whitney's office. He asked me to come to your room to check on you. Please, please get well. We're pulling for you. Lucy, especially, wants you to get better."

Elizabeth then stroked her head and hugged Lucy before leaving the room. Walking down the hall, she could see more signs of the mounting distress just by glancing in patients' rooms. It appeared that most were in the hospital with the same illness that had stricken Annabel Van Meter, though probably they weren't as sick as she was due to the age difference. Anyone in their eighties could not fight infections as well as younger people.

At the nurses' station, two RNs were huddled together over a chart. Since she knew one of them from high school, she walked over to say hello and ask them to watch Miss Van Meter's vital signs and call her if anything changed. When she got closer, she realized with a start that the nurses and the ward secretary were crying. They told her between sobs that one of their fellow nurses, Marilyn Staple, had a six-month-old baby who had come down with the illness and had just died on the pediatric floor. Grief and shock overwhelmed them, and they were weeping. The baby had been a picture of health only a few days ago. The very young and the very old, just like Taylor had said. Elizabeth remembered his exact words with a chill. She hugged both women and turned around, planning to run back down the steps to give Taylor a report on the Van Meter women.

But as she left the nurse's station, she had a terrible scare because who but Amy Parrish was being pushed in a wheelchair down the hall, following a stretcher bearing the small body of her daughter. Both were hooked up to IVs. Elizabeth ran to them horrified and grabbed Amy's hand. Amy told her they had both become very sick after dinner, and in all honestly, she did not know how she had driven herself to the hospital, but she did. Her husband was out of town on business, so what else could she do.

Elizabeth walked along the side of the wheelchair, holding Amy's hand. Admission was going to let mother and daughter stay in one room, so after helping the orderlies get Amy and the child settled in the beds, she sat with them for a while. Then she knew she had spent enough time in their room and must rejoin Taylor in the ER. He would need some more help with the endless stream of patients. She promised Amy she would be back up later that night to check on them and left.

She followed Taylor's orders to the best of her ability, but everyone was overcome by the sheer volume of patients arriving. It was difficult to get anything accomplished. So far, they were only treating the symptoms since lab reports had not yet been returned to any doctors working in the ER, and no diagnosis could be made. In the background, the screaming of sirens could be heard. More ambulances were making their way up the hill to Greenwood Memorial. It was getting close to ten o' clock. She thought about the hospital's dinner dance that was supposed to be held the next weekend but, naturally, would be cancelled. The gray silk dress left hanging in her closet this morning seemed like something another woman might wear at another time or in another universe. She knew she wouldn't be wearing it in the near future.

Elizabeth had been on her feet since one o'clock that afternoon, but no hunger pains were gripping her stomach, nor did her body feel tired when she moved from one patient to another. She was caught up in the anguish of Greenwood's people who were her people. And she could think of nothing else that Friday night.

CHAPTER TWELVE

On Saturday morning Debra was sleeping soundly when she awoke to the noise of doors being slammed. Those damn neighbors, always getting up early, she thought as she curled up again in the warm bed, forgetting the creepy drive home last night. She opened one sleepy eye and saw that it was eight o'clock. Suddenly she sat up with a jerk. This wasn't a day to go back to sleep. Jim was coming for dinner tonight. When she had returned home from playing bridge last night, Jim had left a message on her recorder. He said he would love to come to dinner and would arrive at seven with a bottle of red wine to go with the steaks.

As pleased as she was that she would see him again, an immediate problem was that there were no groceries in the house to fix this great meal. In addition to cooking steaks on the grill, in a moment of optimism, she hoped to make some type of appropriate dessert to go with the steaks. Now she would have to hunt for a recipe in her only cookbook before she could go to the store.

She smiled to herself as she thought how wonderful it had been the last time he was here. Today, however, her home was a mess and needed to be cleaned before Jim arrived. Yesterday's newspapers were scattered over the floor. Dust lay on the tops of the tables, and the three plants that she had purchased at a local flea market and who resided now in the dining room's bay window were bent over as if grasping for breath. Not a pretty sight, she thought, but one that could be corrected with a little housework. When she listened to the recorder last night, Jim sounded tired and had alluded to the fact that he had gotten little sleep in the last two days. As he was hanging up, she could hear his pager going off, and the nasal tones of the hospital operator saying he needed to call five west about an emergency.

She mused that she knew she had worked hard the past week and had spent little time at her home as the clutter in the house testified; at least she could leave her job at five or six. Jim and the other doctors could not. Even though her boss was not directly involved in patient care, nevertheless, he stayed in the lab for long periods of time after she had left. As she told Jim, she often saw his light on late at night. His hours were almost like those of an intern in the emergency room. Probably those hours were why she had decided not to go on to get a PhD or MD in spite of urging by her faculty advisor.

Cocking an eye at the alarm clock, she saw that it was now 8:15. Sighing, she swung her long legs over the side of the bed and got up. Annie was napping in her basket in the corner of the bedroom and came bounding over to greet her and then ran around in excited small circles. Debra stumbled into the kitchen and let Annie out the back door. She heated a small pan of water for a cup of Taster's Choice coffee and went to the front door to get the Saturday paper. After scanning the front page, she turned to the second section, where a small article caught her eye.

"Greenwood Residents Hit by Mysterious Illness," the headline announced. Debra read on with mounting dismay because this was the town where Elizabeth, Debra's cousin, lived. Some of her mother's other relatives had lived there in the past, but Elizabeth and her great aunt were the only family members who were still there. Aunt Betty and Uncle Jason, Elizabeth's parents, had died in a tragic plane crash twenty-two years ago. That was when Elizabeth went to live with her maiden great aunt, Susan, who had finished raising the teenaged girl when her parents were killed.

After high school graduation, Elizabeth decided to go to Nashville for college and received a B.S. in nursing. Loving the town, she stayed and got a job at the medical center until her aunt's health took a turn for the worse. At that point, she was forced to return to Greenwood. Debra kept in touch with her regularly after she left Nashville and had just called her a few days ago to chat and ask how her aunt was doing. By now, Susan had moved to a nursing home in the country, and Elizabeth still lived in her farmhouse. She told Debra that she tried to visit her aunt several times a week to keep her spirits up. Debra hoped Elizabeth would eventually inherit the farm since she was her aunt's closest relative, and by now, it looked as though Elizabeth might never marry.

Now she knew Elizabeth worked for a doctor in family practice and seemed to love the office job, but in fact, Debra thought Elizabeth might be too interested in her boss who was caught in the middle of a nasty divorce. He was married to a woman from Memphis who had piles of money which she inherited from her wealthy family. Debra had gathered some of this latest information while attending the annual family reunion at a state park in September. As a concession to her mother, Debra went to these reunions, which had wonderful food but were somewhat boring. Debra remembered the air was very hot and humid that day in the park. So hot that even though she had worn Bermuda shorts and a cotton tee, she was soaked in perspiration when she left with her parents to return to Nashville.

Debra and Elizabeth had stood in the shade of a group of trees away from the main group of family members, sipping spiked lemonade. If only her mother had known what they were drinking, Debra thought she would faint. Elizabeth, being much the rebel, had brought along a flask of vodka, which she would generously pour into the lemonade of any relative who asked. Debra had loved talking to her that day and shared updates about medical center people whom Elizabeth also knew.

Debra walked back into the kitchen. She added a teaspoon of instant coffee to a cup of boiling water and put a Pop Tart in the toaster while continuing to read. The article went on to say that local officials were puzzled over the severity of the disease and did not believe food poisoning was the cause. There had already been ten deaths, and local facilities were strained to their limit by the large number of these ill people. The CDC in Atlanta had been alerted and was expected to send a team of investigators on Sunday. In the meanwhile, help was coming from medical personnel in the nearby towns, and if things did not settle down, the large Nashville hospitals would also be asked to send relief workers. The paper then listed the names of the dead, but those names were none that Debra recognized. The ring of the phone interrupted her reading.

It was Jim calling to ask if she had seen the headlines about the illness in Greenwood. When she told him she was just reading about it in the paper, he went on to say that his department head, Dr. Scott, had called and asked him to go to Greenwood to investigate the outbreak. As he told her, this was his field of interest and the area in which his additional research was being done, so it was no wonder that Dr. Scott wanted him to go. Debra could tell by the way the conversation was unfolding that on the one hand, he was concerned about the severity of the disease hitting a whole town, on the other hand, he was excited because this situation offered an opportunity for independent study and research. A paper written about the illness could easily be accepted and published in one of several prestigious medical journals, he added.

After he explained the situation, Jim asked her to put their dinner on hold until next week and invited her to accompany him to Greenwood. "We can't eat at your place tonight, but if you go with me, you could pretend to be my research assistant instead of Steiner's, at least for the weekend. I promise to be a much better boss than he has ever been. Say yes and I can pick you up in an hour."

Debra thought for only one second and told him that she would like to go, especially since her cousin lived there. She could check on Elizabeth then would help Jim if he would first tell her what to do. As she was ending their conversation, she began to pull off her pajamas while walking toward the bath. After a quick shower, she called Harriet to ask if she could keep Annie for the day. Harriet was always a sweetheart, and in a few minutes, Debra walked the dog down to Harriet's house. After exchanging a few pleasantries with Harriet and handing her Annie's leash, she raced back to the house.

After finishing dressing, she was just applying lipstick when the doorbell rang. It was exactly fifty-five minutes since he had called her, but then she had noticed he was always prompt unless he was tied up at the hospital. She opened the door, and Jim pulled her into his arms. He gave her a surprising lingering kiss with his tongue touching the inside of her mouth. She could taste the slightly salty flavor of his lips.

"Debra, I'm so glad you are going with me," he whispered in her ear as he ran his hand through her hair. "It was going to be a damn lonely drive. I felt terrible that we wouldn't be together tonight. Thursday night was special, and it should have ended differently if I didn't have to leave early for that emergency. At least this way, we can have some time together while we're driving to Greenwood, and, honey, the work won't take the whole day. I was told about a cozy inn on the way back, just off the interstate. A friend at the hospital recommended it when he heard I was going to Greenwood. Maybe we can stop there for dinner. Since you are going to help me with data collection, everything will go faster, and we can leave even earlier than I planned."

"Jim, the dinner at a country inn sounds fabulous, but I must remind you that I was trained to do only research work. I don't know anything about patients and data collection." She informed him about this deficiency as they walked toward his old battered car.

Opening the door for her while appraising the tight-fitting jeans and yellow crew neck, he replied, "Baby, you'll do just fine as my assistant. I only have to interview some of the patients and check their records. You can help by copying the records, organizing the files, and stuff like that."

She slid over the vinyl seat, which was warm from the early October sun. He got in on his side and eased the car into gear and skillfully merged it into the Saturday morning traffic on Hillsboro Road. They didn't hit many red lights, and before too much time had passed, they were on the interstate, headed for Greenwood.

While they were traveling, he filled her in on what he knew so far about the illness. It appeared to be randomly striking the town's population, according to Dr. Scott. He had given him explicit instructions on what data to collect from the patients and possible specimens to get from the hospital lab. Jim again repeated that he had a good idea how long the work should take and confidently told Debra they should arrive at the inn for dinner, no later than seven.

Jim asked about her cousin who lived in Greenwood. She told him Elizabeth was thirteen when she went to live with her great aunt after her parents' death in an airplane accident. She had worked in Nashville as an RN and had returned to Greenwood two years ago because of her aunt's poor health. Debra asked Jim if he had known her in Nashville, but he said their paths had not crossed. Debra explained to Jim that while she felt sorry for all the people in Greenwood, she was particularly concerned about Elizabeth, whom she knew from playing together when they were children and more recently from the time they spent together in Nashville when Elizabeth still worked at the medical center, and she was in graduate school.

"Jim, I feel I should ask a few questions, questions I should have asked before I said I would go without giving the trip much thought. Should I be concerned about going to Greenwood, could we catch anything? The article in the paper was not very long, but the conditions it described sounded ominous. I think I still should come to help you and check on Elizabeth and her aunt, but what will we find there?"

"Debra, please don't worry and try not to read too much danger in this trip. We'll be okay," Jim said, and he patted her shoulder with one hand as he negotiated the road with the other. She relaxed and moved closer to him. Then he moved his hand from her shoulder and gently began to rub her knee. She felt herself mesmerized by his touch through the jean's fabric. The reds and yellows of the forest surrounding the road passed in a blur, and she forgot about the rest of the world or where they were headed. She leaned over and slowly kissed his neck where the collar met skin.

Finally, Jim laughed and responded. "Stop or we will have a wreck. Maybe you would like me to find a dead-end road? We could pretend that we are some lovestruck teenagers after the senior prom." This brought laughter from them both, but Debra took the clue, moved away, and looked out her window, trying to remember what she had read about the possible disaster in Greenville that might greet them.

He then mused philosophically. "You know, as a new intern, my first rotation was in the ER. That was really scary for me. You never know what is going to roll in on a stretcher. But wait, this story is funny. One of the first patients that I treated in the ER was a guy with a broken leg. According to his story, his girlfriend was kissing him, or so he said, when he lost control of the car while he was driving on a country road. They hit a tree and totaled his car, but she only suffered a few cuts and bruises." This story brought more laughter, and they both relaxed even more in each other's company.

"Did he recover, and how about the poor girl? Did she get a ticket or a citation for causing a wreck?" Debra laughed. "If I had known a kiss could be so dangerous, I would have stayed on my side of the car and not touched you."

He replied with a grin, "Oh, they both survived, and in fact, I attended their wedding six months later. I heard recently they have a son who is three."

Debra smiled and said, "And I hope they continue to live happily ever after." She decided to stop talking and let him concentrate on the driving. She admired the fall scenery that whirled past the car windows but stole several glances at the man sitting beside her.

In another hour, they reached the outskirts of Greenwood. The road that they were on took them through a poorer section of the town, which was dotted with ill-kept houses and a run-down trailer park clinging to the side of a small creek. The sun, which had been shining brightly, went behind large purple clouds. Dark shadows covered the landscape as if questionable weather was approaching. Some of the happiness they had felt earlier evaporated.

When both saw the city limit sign, they suddenly realized that neither knew where the hospital was located. Even though Debra had visited the town years ago, she had never been to the hospital. Jim pulled into a dilapidated service station to buy gas and get directions to Greenwood Memorial. A tired-looking man in his midsixties came out of the station and began to fill up the tank and clean off the car's windshields. Debra wanted to call Elizabeth and saw a rusty pay phone by the side of the gas station. Stepping carefully over some cigarette butts and a broken Coke bottle, she pulled open a creaky door to squeeze in the phone booth.

After dialing Elizabeth's number and getting only the answering machine, she left a message. "Elizabeth, it's me, your cousin Debra. I'm in town and worried about you. I read in the paper about the epidemic or whatever it is and immediately thought about you and Aunt Susan. I had an opportunity to get a ride to Greenwood. So I took it and wondered if I could do anything to help. Actually, I'm here with a Nashville doctor who is gathering data about the epidemic. Hopefully I will see you at the hospital. If you aren't there, I'll try to call this number again in about an hour."

Jim was just finishing getting the directions to the hospital when she slipped back in the car. Apparently, it was on a road called Big Hill on the other side of town. As they were pulling away from the station, the old attendant hollered after them, "You folks better stay away from that there hospital. I hear a lot of people are sick and dying up there."

Debra shuddered and said, "Jim, I don't know about this visit. Frankly, I admit that I'm still a little apprehensive. I know you have to go. It is your job after all. I'm beginning to get cold feet and wish I was back in Nashville."

Jim squeezed her hand, trying to reassure her. "Deb, we will be very, very careful. We'll use sterile gloves and gowns, masks, the whole works. Just as soon as I collect the data and interview some patients, we will leave, probably no later than five o'clock and have that cozy dinner at the restaurant I told you about, I promise."

CHAPTER THIRTEEN

WHILE ALL HELL was breaking out at the hospital, and he was knee-deep with sick patients on Saturday morning, Taylor Whitney got a call from his wife, Claudia. At first, he was furious that she would call him during such a crisis, until he heard the reason why she was calling. She sounded frantic and out of breath when she cried, "Taylor, it's Denny"—who was the younger of their two children—"He's throwing up and has terrible diarrhea like the others I heard about on the TV news. I took his temperature and it's one hundred and three. A few minutes ago, he was fine, watching some cartoons on TV, and now he is very ill. I am terrified. What do you want me to do?"

"Oh no, not Denny too. I need to check him out immediately. Meet me in the ER in twenty minutes. I'll get some fluids in him, and then we can decide whether to admit him or not. I don't need to tell you how serious the situation is, especially for a ten-year-old. We'll need to keep our fingers crossed and hope he isn't too sick."

Taylor finished up on the second-floor ward and ran down the back stairwell to enter the ER just as his wife and son arrived. Claudia was holding their son's hand as she spoke to the nurse. Taylor quickly started an IV, while Claudia held Denny, who shrieked first at the sight of the needle and then the pain when its point pierced his skin. The saline started to drip into his vein, and Taylor then administered medication to lessen the nausea and a mild sedative to calm him down. Taylor felt a lump rising in his throat as he surveyed his son, so pale and small lying on the bed, and his beautiful but so difficult wife, collapsed on her knees beside the bed.

"Oh, Taylor, please, please don't let anything happen to him. For the love of God, you've got to save him," Claudia whispered as she looked up at him through eyes wet with tears.

Taylor pulled her to her feet as he motioned for the nurse to move the bed that was on wheels out of the room and head toward the children's ward on the second floor. Taylor patted Claudia on the back as she clung to him, and more tears flowed down her cheeks.

"Is Jessica all right?" Taylor asked as they followed Denny's bed down the hall toward his room. He was supporting Claudia at the elbow, and his other arm was wrapped around her waist. He was afraid that she would fall on the slippery marble floors due to her distraught condition.

"So far she's fine. I asked Barbara, the babysitter I've been using lately, to come over and stay with her." She smiled weakly at him.

"I don't know what in the hell is going on. I feel so helpless and worried for all my patients. Now our son is one of them. I wish I had some answers, Claudia, I don't. I'll treat his symptoms just like I'm doing for everyone else. Stay with him in his room, and I'll be back in half an hour to see how he is doing."

Claudia threw herself upon Taylor and kissed his neck. "Thank you so much, Taylor," she whispered in his ear. "I'm sorry that I've been such a bitch. I wish I could undo these last five months."

Taylor hugged her back but only slightly. He could smell the scent of the Chanel No. 5 she always wore. The curls of golden hair brushed his face as he stepped away from her. He turned to go and see more patients waiting in the ER. He had been at Greenwood Memorial since yesterday afternoon and had only grabbed a few minutes of rest in the doctor's lounge on a hard cot around two that morning.

Elizabeth silently appeared in the doorway of a patient's room and watched Taylor and Claudia holding each other in the hallway. After Claudia turned and got on the elevator, Elizabeth caught up with Taylor and walked with him to the nurses' station. He briefly told her about his son's illness and how Claudia would be sitting with him while they both would pray the worse symptoms of the illness would spare their child.

"I'm so sorry to hear about your son's illness, Taylor, and I'll pray for his recovery too. Now I hate to mention this, but I must tell you some more sad news. The nurse, Marilyn Staple who works on the third floor, lost her six-month-old baby early last night. I went to high school and college with her."

Taylor set his mouth in a thin line and muttered, "I am afraid this is going to get much worse before it gets better." He patted Elizabeth on the shoulder and left to visit patients who had been admitted over the last twenty hours. There were now thirty or possibly forty in the ER waiting to be admitted. The hospital's rooms normally held two beds, but by now a third bed had been squeezed in by housekeeping. Relatives of the sick trying to help their loved ones were also in the rooms adding to the congestion, and making it difficult for the nurses and doctors to even get to the patients.

Most of the victims as described by Taylor had high fevers and were first covered with sweat then shaken by chills. Dehydration was present in some, and those were receiving fluids by IV. Other patients were nauseated and had relatives holding pans for them to be sick in since the nursing staff was pushed to their limit, and there were no more private duty nurses available to help those able to afford their services.

The hospital had not yet instigated any policy about visitors, and the whole building was overflowing with people. The staff was so overwhelmed they could do little to stop the flow of visitors. More and more people poured into the building to check on their loved ones and friends. So far, no one had said the illness was contagious, so passing it to one another wasn't considered yet.

The news media were on high alert. TV cameramen from Nashville and Knoxville were stationed in front of the hospital, hoping to get an up-to-date report from the hospital administrator. Most of the phone lines were jammed. Rumors were flying from one end of the county to the other as concerned residents called each other to talk about the spreading sickness. Everyone working at the hospital was praying the CDC would soon arrive and get to the bottom of the mystery.

While she was helping in the pediatric ward, Elizabeth got a call from her friend Doug. He was afraid that he too was coming down with the illness since he had been up most of the night vomiting. Many of his employees at Kmart were also ill. The store was open but operating with only half of their clerks. After listening to his symptoms and getting him to calm down, she suggested he should come to the ER, providing he felt like driving. Elizabeth promised she would check on him once he arrived. *Is there no end in sight to this tragedy?* she thought.

Walking briskly down the hall, she reminded herself to call his mother in Knoxville, who would probably like to know about her son's illness. Elizabeth had met Mrs. Reynolds once when she was in town visiting Doug. He took both of them to lunch, wanting his mother to meet Elizabeth. The lunch went very well, and Elizabeth enjoyed talking to Mrs. Reynolds. But it seemed to Elizabeth that mother and son were very close, maybe too close. Doug told her that he talked to his mother usually every morning before he went to work.

Once when Elizabeth and he were on a date, he gave a detailed description on what his mother's opinion was on an event that had happened earlier in the day. Elizabeth, at that time, thought whoever married him would have to be best friends with the mother too.

Elizabeth returned to the floor where Annabel Van Meter was located and went into her room. She lay on the hospital bed as white as the sheets that covered her. Her pulse was very weak, and her breath came in short gasps. She appeared to be no longer conscious. Elizabeth held her hand for a few moments while trying to speak encouraging words to her sister, Lucy. Then, not knowing what else to do, she left, making her way down the hall crowded with patients lying on stretchers, some comatose, to find her friend Amy, who had checked in the room yesterday and was still there, sharing it with her daughter.

At least, things were going better for mother and daughter, even though both were still hooked up to IVs. By now Amy's husband had arrived and was holding her hand, almost in state of shock having his wife and child in the hospital at the same time. Amy had been trying to cheer him up. She told Elizabeth, Dr. Whitney had said they might leave tomorrow and free up beds for others if they continued to improve.

Elizabeth then went to the ER and found the cubicle where Doug lay on a stretcher with his eyes closed. He sat up and grasped both of her hands, his eyes misting over with the thought she had come by to see him.

After checking his vital signs and reading the notes on his chart, Elizabeth said, "Doug, I feel encouraged about your situation. Please just be patient and let the medicines which the ER nurse has just given you take their course. Unlike so many of the patients that I've seen, you aren't as sick as some of the others."

"I guess I have a lot to be thankful for then. The only good part of being in this cubicle is seeing you standing in front of me. I need to ask another favor. Could you call my mother, Elizabeth, and at least give her the news that I'm not too ill?"

"Of course, Doug, I was planning to do that anyway." And she patted his arm and left to find a pay phone to call his mother. After getting hold of Mrs. Reynolds, who was understandably upset, Elizabeth tried to reassure her that Doug was not as ill as many of the patients and according to the ER doctor whose notes she had read, he might be able to go home in a few hours.

Finally, she stopped by a coffee station that the hospital auxiliary had set up in a hallway. She needed a caffeine fix and hoped that would keep her going for what might be another long day. She carried the cup of coffee to the cafeteria and sat down with the head nurse from the ward where Annabel Van Meter was.

The nurse held her hand briefly and then said, "Elizabeth, I hate to give you this upsetting news, but Annabel died less than an hour ago. Not only that, but now her sister is showing more signs of the disease and has been admitted as well."

"Oh no! Annabel was such a wonderful person and taught many of us in school." Wiping a few tears off her face, Elizabeth promised the nurse she would be up to check on Lucy before the day ended. Then, she finished her coffee in the silence that surrounded everyone in the cafeteria.

CHAPTER FOURTEEN

MEANWHILE, JIM AND Debra drove up the steep, winding road to Greenwood Memorial. They could see the hospital sitting on top of the mountain overlooking the town, not unlike some pagan temple from another age. It had been built during the Great Depression by the Conservation Core and was still an impressive structure made of maroon brick. The design was neo classic with a steeply pitched roof covered with charcoal slate. Smoke curled from one of its several chimneys, and marble pillars rose from either side of its two-storied entrance. The grounds of the hospital totaled four acres, much of it left in a natural state, but around the entrance were groups of towering hollies and red-leafed dogwoods. The circular driveway in front of the hospital was lined with cars and trucks, some spilling over onto the grass. While there was ample parking for visitors on normal days, plus a large lot for staff, all were filled to capacity today.

Their romantic mood quickly evaporated when they saw hundreds of cars spilling over the parking areas. Jim was shocked at the number surrounding the hospital and told Debra it would seem that the situation was more serious than he and Dr. Scott had realized. Jim went through the employee parking lot, looking for a spot, but finally gave up there. He drove through a separate doctors' lot that had a few spaces left. He quickly whipped into one and jumped out immediately, his adrenaline levels high. Debra helped him pick up the supplies piled in the back seat and followed him to the main entrance.

The first thing that hit Debra as they walked through the front door was the terrible smell. Debra was used to bad odors, working in biology laboratories, but this smell took her breath away. It gagged her so much she searched through her purse to find a Kleenex and covered her nose.

The number of people standing or sitting on the floor in the entrance hall waiting to get into the ER was unreal. Most seemed filled with various degrees of despair and had frightened relatives clinging to their arms. Jim grasped Debra's elbow to give her fortitude to plow through the crush of people and reach the hospital's offices. At the intersection of two corridors, they split up, with Jim heading toward the administration offices, while Debra pushed through more people to get to the women's restroom. She hated to go in there, because if there was an epidemic in the town, there was no telling what diseases lurked in the restroom, but after the long drive, she had no other choice. After leaving the restroom, she literally bumped into her cousin Elizabeth in the crowded hallway. Elizabeth was wearing a stained lab coat over her nurse's uniform and looked exhausted but said she thought she would faint more from surprise than exhaustion after running into her cousin in Greenwood Memorial's hallway.

They hugged each other tightly and then sat down on a bench close by the restroom while Debra tried to explain why she was there. Elizabeth held Debra's hand and listened to a roundabout story of how she came to be sitting with Elizabeth that Saturday morning since Elizabeth hadn't picked up Debra's message on her recorder.

"Actually, I rode with one of the head residents, Jim Tarkington, who works at the medical center. His department head told him to go to Greenwood today to investigate the reports of a serious illness that might be breaking out. While he's here, he's supposed to collect information and interview patients so he can write a paper for a medical journal. Jim thought I could help him with the data collection. But I came along not only to assist him gather material for his department but also to see if you were okay and check on how Aunt Susan was doing," Debra added with a smile.

Elizabeth absorbed all this information but was puzzled and could not help but ask, "Debra, I thought you were working in research at the medical center and not involved with patient care. I'm glad you came, but it seems like Dr. Tarkington would need a nurse to help him and not someone like you, who has only worked in research."

Debra didn't care for the remark, "Only in research" but answered in an even voice, "Elizabeth, I still work in research. I just came along to help Jim. Actually, I think I'm only going to copy patient files, and you don't need any experience dealing with patients or an RN degree to do that. Anyway, I suppose you would say Jim and I are dating, at least we've had two dates. I had invited him to dinner tonight, but he called early this morning to say he had to cancel the date because he had to go to Greenwood. He asked me to ride here with him.

And as I told you a year ago, I have been working in research for Dr. Joseph Steiner since I got my master's degree. I have to add, he is not the easiest person to work for, but I'm proud to be associated with his lab because of his reputation. In fact, he's a world authority on recumbent DNA."

A strange look came over Elizabeth's face. "Steiner, Steiner… That name is sure familiar. You never mentioned your boss's name before. There was a Steiner a few years ahead of me in school in Greenwood. He was considered a very brilliant student and probably never got anything but an A in his life. All the kids disliked him. He was the school nerd and teased unmercifully especially by the older boys who were always picking on him. I remember once being on the school bus with him. He was reading a book, oblivious to the world, and some of the boys crawled under his seat and tied his shoelaces to the legs of the bus seat. When the bus came to his stop, he could not loosen them and fell on his face. The school bus driver had to come in the back and untie his laces. We all laughed and laughed, but now I know how mean that really was. I heard that after graduation, he went east to an Ivy League school… Could that be the same guy?"

Debra sat quietly, trying to think. "I can hardly believe that person could be him. Dr. Steiner never talks about himself. Really, I thought he was from California. I just know he got his PhD at Harvard and moved to California to do postdoc work. Then he spent several years working at a California Medical Center before he took the position in Nashville. Our administration loves him because of the large grants he lands and the national publicity his research generates.

As I said before, I really admire his intelligence, but he's very difficult to work for. He has a cold personality, never smiles or discusses anything other than what's required for the experiment we are going to do, but that's okay with me. He's not someone I would want to be friends with anyway. It's a good job for me and the best one I could find when I finished grad school."

"What a coincidence if he is the same man I knew as a child, Debra. It is hard to believe he could be from Greenwood and never mentioned that he grew up in Tennessee to you."

Debra shifted in the hard bench and continued speaking, "Well, who knows where he came from. I guess it's not my problem. Anyway, as I said before, I'm only here to help Jim collect samples and copy patient charts for his research. Then he and his boss will try to solve the reason for the epidemic back in the Nashville lab. So we plan to leave later in the afternoon, and it can't be too soon for me. Elizabeth, I have never seen a hospital with so much chaos and so many sick patients. I can't help but ask, what do you think is going on here? Is the hospital doing anything to prevent the spread of this disease, and do you think we could catch whatever it is?"

Elizabeth sighed and answered, "It doesn't seem to be contagious in the usual sense, but as you can see, everyone is wearing gowns, masks, and gloves around the sick. Obviously, something terrible has stricken the whole town. The doctors don't know what it is and are only treating the symptoms so far. It seems to be hitting people in random fashion, and not all members in a family get ill. The first cases started appearing Thursday afternoon. By now the illness has affected many of our people. Terrible vomiting and diarrhea and high fever seem to be the major symptoms. In the worst cases, severe dehydration develops and then organ shut down and, for some unfortunate few, death follows swiftly.

We have already lost eleven patients, and probably there are thirty in critical condition. At least the CDC officials will be here Sunday afternoon, or so I have been told. The health department can't find any reason to pin this outbreak on spoiled food. I heard that the water company hadn't turned up anything either after retesting the water."

"I know everyone will breathe a sigh of relief once the cause of the illness is discovered. How do you feel, Elizabeth, and is Aunt Susan all right?" Debra asked in a worried tone.

"Oh, I'm alright for the most part except for being exhausted, Debra. Aunt Susan and the others in the nursing home are okay too. The nursing home where she stays is out in the county. Maybe they are too isolated to catch whatever this is."

Just then, Jim came out of the administration offices and headed toward Debra, who was still sitting on the bench with Elizabeth. After introductions were made, Elizabeth excused herself and headed back to the ER. Before she left, Debra promised to meet for coffee before they left for Nashville. Jim remarked as she walked away that the two cousins resembled each other even though Debra was a brunet and Elizabeth was a blonde. He could not help but add with a smile that he was partial to brunets.

"Now please come, Deb, with me. We are going to get patients' records and make copies in the hospital office on their Xerox. The hospital administrator just gave me the okay. He seemed glad to meet me and said anything we can do to help end this epidemic will make him grateful. While you are doing the copying, I plan to interview some of the patients, if I can find some not so ill and willing to talk. The lab already has plenty of swabs from the fecal samples and will let me have some of their extras. I'll put them on ice in the cooler that I brought from Nashville. They also have some cultures from Thursday that are already grown out and are going to give me some of those too. Please wear this lab coat and gloves while you are working here, even though you won't be that close to any patients. We can't be too careful in this situation." And he squeezed her shoulder as he handed her the lab coat and gloves.

Debra followed Jim quickly down the hall. They went to the nurses' station on first floor south. He told the head nurse what he wanted, and she insisted on calling the administrator to get his permission before she would hand over any patient files.

When that was approved, Jim was all business and said to Debra, "Ms. Chandler, please take these files and make copies in the administrator's office on their Xerox machine. I will in the meantime talk to the healthiest patients. When you are finished, we will move to the next ward and repeat the procedures."

"Yes, Dr. Tarkington," answered Debra using her professional voice. She picked up the pile of files and retraced her steps to the front of the hospital while leaving him behind reading additional patient files.

Jim headed to the first patient's room, a Miss Mabel Hall in room 11A. She was to be his first interview. After putting on a protective coat and gloves, he added a mask then knocked gently on the door and entered. After introducing himself and mentioning that he was from the medical center in Nashville, he explained why he wanted to do an interview. Miss Hall, who wasn't as seriously ill as most in the hospital, seemed pleased that someone had taken an interest in her case.

"Dr. Tarkington, in answer to your questions, I work as the personal secretary for the school superintendent. I have little or no contact with the children who could have passed the illness on to me. Also, I live alone and have not eaten out or gone to any party or church services since last week. Jim, I must add that I'm grateful to be on the road to recovery and pray that some of my friends, whom I haven't heard from, will be as lucky as I and recover as well."

Jim thanked her for the cooperation and information. Then he proceeded down the hall to see another four patients on the floor. None had any common denomination linking their illness to the others except they were all Greenwood residents. By then, Debra returned with an armload of copies of the case files. Jim and Debra moved on to another ward, following the same procedure, and finally to the ICU, where he could only talk to the patients' relatives. Debra continued to make more copies of files, which were placed in alphabetic order in a large cardboard box that she had found in central supply.

After she had copied the last group of records, Debra bumped into a medical technologist coming out of the administrator's office. After introducing herself, she told the woman that she worked in a research lab in Nashville and was there only for the day to help a friend gather data for his research project. The woman, Helen Sexton, seemed thrilled to meet her and asked if she could help them in the clinical lab for two or three hours because of the desperate situation the hospital was in.

"What a lifesaver you could be if you could just plate out some of the samples. We're overwhelmed with all of these specimens. We've got hundreds of them, and the floors and ER just keep sending us more."

Debra replied that she could help but had little experience in clinical work. Helen told her that didn't matter and grabbed her hand to lead her down a set of back stairs to the lab in the basement. Like the rest of the hospital, the odor in the lab was overpowering. "Perhaps you can help Judith Ann. She is sitting over there in the back, working under the hood. There is room for two at the bench, and you can see the stack of plates and swabs. We are trying to smear the swabs from the patients on the plates as quickly as possible since more samples just keep on coming. But first, put on a mask, even though you already have on that lab coat and gloves before you go over there."

Debra dutifully did as she was told and then sat down on the lab bench by Judith Ann, who showed Debra the procedures to follow. Debra worked as fast as she could for two long hours, streaking out new plates from the patients' swabs. But after putting multiple trays of bacteria plates in the lab's huge walk-in incubator, she told Judith Ann she had to go meet Jim and her cousin.

By then the time was 4:30, and a weak autumn sun was setting over the mountain. Cool mountain air descended around the hospital. Dense fog could be seen rising around the lower areas of the hospital grounds. Debra glanced out a window and shivered. So she caught up with Jim on the pediatric wing, who said he definitely needed a break. They headed to the cafeteria for coffee.

Elizabeth was sitting in the back of the room where she had suggested they could find her. Debra observed that her cousin looked even more tired and forlorn than when she had seen her earlier. Debra bit her lip when they sat down at the table to keep from making any comment. Elizabeth said that the director of nursing had told some of them to go home for eight hours of sleep before coming back early Sunday morning. A group of volunteer nurses from nearby towns was expected to arrive any minute to take over for the night shift. All of the hospital's departments were being stretched to the limit. Patients were still being admitted with no end in sight. And all the beds were full. The phones were ringing nonstop, some with no one to answer them.

Jim and Debra filled Elizabeth in on how the data collection was going and Debra's work in the hospital lab. Jim admitted it was a strange outbreak, and so far, he had no clue to its cause and could easily spend a week working on the mystery.

After putting down her coffee cup, Elizabeth looked out the window at the descending darkness, thought for a minute, and asked, "Debra, do you and Dr. Tarkington want to spend the night at my house? It is already getting dark, and you would have to drive over some treacherous curves before you reach the interstate. A heavy fog appears to be rolling in to make matters worse."

Debra looked at Jim in confusion, not sure how she felt about Elizabeth's invitation. But he answered quickly for them both, "Sure, that's a great idea, Elizabeth. I still have some more work to do, and it makes me just tired thinking about a two and a half-hour drive home in the dark. Deb, why don't you leave now with your cousin? I'll join you in a couple of hours. Elizabeth, all that I will need are some good directions to find your home. Debra told me it is in the county, but it's a big county."

After they persuaded Debra to agree to stay and not try to drive back that night, Elizabeth drew a map on a paper napkin for Jim so he could later find the house. Debra left with Elizabeth, while Jim returned to the wards for a few more interviews. He then hoped to discuss treatment plans for patients with what doctors he could find and corner the hospital administrator again to answer some questions. He was actually pleased that he and Debra were going to stay because it would give him time to gather more information.

CHAPTER FIFTEEN

AUNT SUSAN'S HOME was on a lonely country road about ten miles from the hospital. The narrow road had pockets of mist and fog rising around it, making the driving treacherous for Elizabeth, who was forced to slow the car down to a crawl. Averaging only twenty miles per hour, it seemed to take forever to reach the house. Finally, Elizabeth told Debra they had arrived and turned into a long gravel driveway that led to the house. A white wooden fence surrounded the property, and dried corn stalks and a few shivered pumpkins lay beside the open gate. Debra looked around curiously, because even though she had been there as a child, she could remember little about the visit.

As the car approached the house, a white-frame Victorian with large windows and dark-green shutters could be seen through the mist. Running across the width of the house was a wide porch. At one end, a swing hung from hooks in the ceiling, and a group of wicker furniture, turned upside down, was at the other end of the porch. While Debra could visualize how attractive the house must have looked in the summer, it unfortunately appeared neglected now. The porch was covered with leaves, and two dead ferns sat by the front door. The grass appeared as though it had not been cut or raked for several weeks.

Elizabeth, realizing how shabby everything looked, said, "I must apologize for the yard's appearance. Due to everything that has transpired in town, I've not even had time to sweep the leaves off the porch. The boy who cuts the grass returned to college weeks ago, and so far, I've been unable to find a replacement."

After pulling into a garage behind the house, they went in the back door, and Elizabeth turned on the lights. There, much to Debra's astonishment, was a beautiful kitchen complete with modern appliances and custom cherry cabinets. Debra rolled her eyes in surprise at seeing a kitchen like this and told Elizabeth it looked as though it came straight out of a *Southern Living* magazine.

After smiling over Debra's comments, Elizabeth replied, "Oh, thanks, yes, it's a wonderful kitchen to cook in. Even you might be inspired. I guess I never told you about the remodeling, only that we were replacing some appliances. I talked Aunt into redoing the whole kitchen after I moved in with her. You can't believe how antiquated it was. The stove was new in 1930. We decided to split the cost fifty-fifty. To pay my half, I used some of Dad's insurance money I had in a CD, and Aunt put in the other half. Since she and I both loved to cook, having a new kitchen to work in was wonderful for both of us. To tell you the truth, remodeling the kitchen was about the most exciting thing she had done in years."

Elizabeth went into the pantry and got out a can of chili and a box of crackers for their dinner. She decided that looked skimpy and prepared some grilled cheese sandwiches too, which she made using an iron skillet on top of the stove. Debra set their places on a round pine table in the breakfast room in front of a brick fireplace. Then following Elizabeth's directions, she found a bottle of wine in the pantry and poured two glasses. They ate slowly while warming their toes by the gas logs, still feeling tired and depressed.

Elizabeth started a conversation by complimenting Debra on her choice of a boyfriend. She told her that she already liked him better than the ex whom she had never cared for but had never mentioned those feelings to Debra. Then she shifted gears and began to talk about what had been on her mind all afternoon.

Pushing her blond hair out of her face, she began, "You know, Debra, I've been thinking about your boss, the guy in Nashville, while I was helping with patients this afternoon. I'm almost certain the boy on the school bus I told you about and your boss is the same person. He must have been around ten years older than I was then. And even though I was only seven, I will never forget how he cried at their joke when he was finally able to get off the bus."

Debra took in all this additional, information. She found it hard to believe the gossip about her boss's childhood, and sat silently for a moment. The thought that Dr. Steiner really was from Greenwood shocked her.

"Gosh, Elizabeth, he never suggested that he was from Tennessee and gave everyone the impression he was from California. But there are stranger things about him than where he was from, that's for sure."

"Well, you never know about anyone really, only what they want you to know." Elizabeth yawned and stretched slowly. She said Debra must excuse her so she could go to her bedroom on the first floor and get some sleep.

Before she left, she added, "You and Jim take any of the bedrooms you want upstairs. There are some of my summer things stored in the hall closet, so perhaps you can find a gown and a robe to fit you. I even have shampoo and extra toothbrushes and toothpaste in the bathroom's cabinet, which you can have. I probably won't see you in the morning because I plan to leave before six. If you come by the hospital again, please call me before you leave town. Debra, you don't know how much your visit has meant to me. I feel a little more hopeful that we will all get through this alive." And then Elizabeth hugged her and retired to her room.

Debra had seen a phone on a table in the entrance hall and decided to call Harriet in Nashville. After reaching her on the phone, she asked if Annie could stay until Sunday afternoon, explaining she was needed here and should plan to spend another day. Then she sat down by the fireplace and leafed through some magazines, waiting for Jim's arrival.

At last, she heard his car in the driveway. When Jim came in, he said he was very tired and collapsed in a chair by the fireplace. Debra warmed up the chili and sandwiches and put them on the table in front of the fire. Finding a bottle of Jim Beam under the kitchen sink, she poured two stiff drinks and then sat down across from him. Refreshed from the dinner, Jim said that he planned to talk to the manager of the water company tomorrow before they drove back. He went back to his car to get his overnight bag, which he told Debra he always carried in his car as he never knew when he might have to stay at the medical center. His schedule was unpredictable, to say the least.

"What are you going to do, Deb? Obviously, you did not bring a suitcase, no toothbrush either, baby?" he asked with a raised eyebrow and slight grin on his face in spite of being exhausted.

"Well, I certainly don't carry an overnight bag along, like you. After all, I was told we would be back early and even have dinner in a country inn. It's good for me that Elizabeth and I are about the same size. I can just borrow some things from her. Oh, and, Jim, she told me there is extra shampoo, toothpaste, and toothbrushes in the bathroom cabinet for guests in case you need anything." And she stuck out her tongue at him.

They went up the staircase to the second floor. Debra showed Jim his room, which was next to hers, and then she went into the bathroom to take a shower, hoping to wash off all the germs and grime from Greenwood Memorial. In the linen closet, she found a blue summer robe that fit perfectly. The hot water felt so refreshing, and she let it wash over her tired body for a long time before getting out. Her hair was wet after the shampoo, so she combed it back into the usual pony tail and walked back to her room. Voices came through Jim's partly shut door. He was talking to his boss back in Nashville. "Yeah, yeah… None of this makes any sense, Dr. Scott. Some who are sick appear to have nothing in common with others who are, but it's definitely not food poisoning. Maybe it's the water. I don't know. All the docs that I've met seem competent enough, and they're trying as hard as they can. Thank God it does not seem to be contagious. I'll call you when I get back tomorrow." And he hung up the phone.

She then heard him go in the bathroom and turn on the shower. The guest bedroom's bed looked very comfortable with its white comforter and big goose-down pillows. There was a small bedside table next to the bed, and the only light in the room was provided by an antique lamp with a rose glass shade. She stretched out across the comforter on the still made-up bed. In spite of herself, she felt her eyes becoming heavy, and then they closed.

She began to dream. In the dream, people were stumbling down a mountain outside of Greenwood. Their hair was wet from the heavy rain coming down in sheets, and their knees were bloody from falling on the rocky terrain. Jim and she were trying to help them up when she awoke to a slight noise outside her door. Jim was standing there in the dark hallway. He had on a white T-shirt and boxer shorts. A gold chain hung around his neck and dark stubble of a beard outlined his face. He was holding a blanket.

"Deb," he whispered, "I thought you might be cold, so I brought you this." He pushed through the doorway. Suddenly they were in each other's arms, as the blanket fell to the floor.

He kissed her hard as he pulled her even closer. His hands ran over her back and her hips. They fell onto the bed, while Jim loosened the tie of her robe and jerked it open. He began to kiss her neck and then her chest. She could feel the strength of his erection as she ran her fingers through his hair.

"This time, no telephone, no interruptions, Debra," he said as he reached to turn off the bedside light. The moon shining through the sheer curtains gave the room a pale-white light as all thoughts of the tensions and ugliness of the day disappeared.

The lovemaking was tender at first but became more urgent as their kisses and caresses built to a peak. Debra felt as though she was stretched out on a cloud, somewhere in the heavens, where no one could reach them. All other parts of earth were far below. Their bodies and souls seemed to mingle together. It was as though she had always been waiting for Jim and finally they found each other. At last her universe seemed complete, and tears flowed down her cheeks.

"Why are you crying, darling?" he asked gently.

"I didn't know anything could be so beautiful," she answered in a whisper. And she brought his fingers to her lips and kissed them gently. *Yes, he thought, beauty and love here but chaos in the town.*

Dawn was breaking when Debra raised her head from the pillow. She could see that Jim was still sleeping with one leg hanging outside of the bed. Her watch on the bedside table said 6:10. It was hard to believe that they had slept so long. The first rays of the sun passed through the sheer drapes and struck the headboard over her head. The sound of Elizabeth's car going down the gravel driveway was the only noise to be heard in the otherwise silent house. She made her way to the bathroom, nude, clutching her clothes in her hands.

After emerging from the bathroom, she went down the steep stairs and made coffee in the kitchen. By the time she had finished a cup, Jim came in the kitchen and gave her a familiar and lingering kiss, which brought exciting memories back from the night before.

Elizabeth had left some bananas and a box of cereal out on the countertop with a note asking them to touch base with her before they went back to Nashville.

They sat at the breakfast table, while Jim outlined what he had figured out so far about the mystery illness. "I know, Deb, that I said last night it probably isn't food poisoning, and an intestinal virus hasn't caused it either because of the random nature of who comes down with the illness and who does not. Nor does it look as though you can catch it directly from someone else. I'll be excited to see if the Nashville lab can grow out anything from the culture swabs, which, by the way, we are going to pick up at the hospital on our way out of town."

Debra washed the few dishes from breakfast, while Jim went out to his car to get the cooler for the lab samples. He then filled it with ice from the refrigerator and carried it and his overnight bag to the car. He got his old, temperamental car finally started and pulled around in the driveway to the back porch to wait for her. She glanced around to see if everything appeared in order in the kitchen before she left the house. She could not help but turn to look at the house one more time in order to etch its appearance in her memory. *A night I'll never forget for the rest of my life*, she thought.

CHAPTER SIXTEEN

ARRIVING AT THE hospital, Jim and Debra went in the side entrance and down a flight of steps to the lab to pick up the patient samples. The hospital seemed to still be in a mess. A dozen carts loaded with specimens to be processed were parked outside the lab's door. Jim went in the front office to talk to the lab director, while Debra used this time to borrow a lab phone and paged Elizabeth over the PA. When she came on the line, Debra thanked her for letting them stay overnight and asked how everything was going.

Elizabeth told her she had her fingers crossed because she still felt well and had no symptoms of the disease. Maybe the worst was over. Elizabeth said this in a hopeful voice because they had had only twelve deaths during the night. Some of the sicker patients were starting to improve, slightly, but perhaps it was too early to tell. Debra was relieved over the possible good report and promised to call tomorrow before hanging up.

Jim came out of the lab, and they left the hospital and drove toward the water company, which was fairly close to the hospital. Even though it was Sunday morning, Jim had arranged to meet with its manager, Harry Morgan. Jim believed it would be useful to get the man's opinion on the purity of the water supply and the results of any quality control test run in the last few weeks. In the back of his mind, he could not help but question if the water had anything to do with the disease.

Debra thought the plant looked as though it had been built fifty, maybe sixty years ago, though there appeared to be one part added on more recently. She accompanied Jim into the administration building, which was located in front of the actual treatment plant. Mr. Morgan appeared immediately and introduced himself to them. Debra found a chair in the lobby close to a counter where a large sign hung saying Accounts Payable. She picked up a worn magazine to look through, while Jim and Mr. Morgan went back to his office to study lab data and bacteria plates.

Jim followed the manager into his office and was impressed by the clean and meticulously organized room. There were several plaques hanging on the wall that stated Greenwood's water company had won national awards for quality. Also, there were Mr. Harry Morgan's bachelor's degree in microbiology from the University of Tennessee and professional designations from several National Water Associations hanging above his desk. Sitting on a leather chair, Jim faced Harry, who looked as tired as the lab techs from the hospital he had seen earlier that morning. The thought crossed Jim's mind that the town's medical community might collapse from lack of sleep if not from the unknown disease.

Clearing his throat, Jim began the conversation by asking if there had been any changes in the data collected from recent samples compared to those a month or two ago. The tests looked for pathogens in the water supply taken before and after purification. At first Harry assured him that nothing had shown up that could even remotely be linked to the illness that had hit the town.

"You know that the CDC is supposed to arrive this afternoon," Harry stated. "I sure as hell hope those guys can track down the cause of this disaster. My own wife is not ill, but some of the teachers she works with are, as some of our own staff. A few of her students, third graders, are very sick and in the hospital," he added with a frown.

Jim continued to ask probing questions but could not get any more useful information from the manager. Just as he was picking up his briefcase, preparing to leave, Harry spoke up.

"You know, there was something that was out of the ordinary which I almost forgot to tell you about." Jim paused, his hand almost in midair as Harry continued. "The coliform count was rather elevated recently. We had had a heavy rain a week ago, and also a lot of campers were here to see the autumn colors, so I attributed the increase in bacteria to runoff from their campsites. When that happens, we just up our treatment methods so the count will come down, which we did a few days ago. Additional chemicals and more filtration will do wonders for getting rid of any junk in a water supply."

Jim asked if he could see some of the plates that held the new *E. coli* isolated from the past week's collection. Harry said, "Well, let's go back to the lab and take a look."

They went back a long hallway to a walk-in incubator. Harry pulled out a tray of plates and held one plate up to the light for Jim to see. The colonies looked like any other Jim might have seen in any lab in the state. They did seem, however, to have a slight rosy glow on their surface, which could be seen as Harry rotated the plate to catch the light from the overhead bulb.

Jim could never remember such a color on a bacteria colony and asked Harry about it. Harry, at first, could not see anything different but then saw what Jim was referring to as the faintest rose blush.

"Well, now I see what you mean. At least, I think I see what you are talking about. Any such faint tint could be caused by the new type of media we are using. We changed companies the first of the month. I don't think it's anything to be worried about, Jim," he added in an authoritative tone.

"Harry, would you mind if I took a couple of plates back to our labs in Nashville? I'm sure it's probably nothing too, but my boss, Dr. Scott, will chew me out if I fail to bring a few sample plates from the water company. I've already collected swabs from the patients at the hospital, and their lab gave me extra plates with patients' bacteria growing on them. I'll run analysis on them too. Perhaps I could have some luck at solving this riddle and even beat CDC in finding an answer to the mystery."

Harry thought sarcastically, *Sure, this guy still in training will solve everything for us*, but only replied in a polite way. "Of course, Jim, please be my guest. In fact, take half a dozen. We have more of these darn plates than we need. I have been having the techs run everything in triplicate. They will be held for three more days and then, after the bacteria are destroyed in an autoclave, dumped."

Jim selected six plates and placed them in a special carrier that Harry furnished. After shaking Harry's hand, he went back to the front of the building, where Debra was patiently waiting for him, still reading the worn-out copy of *Time* magazine. They got into the car and started to drive back to Nashville. Jim caught her up with what he had learned at the water company and his developing suspicions about the three-day-old plates with the rose-tinted colonies given to him by the director.

"Deb, you never know what may turn up. They look like harmless coliform colonies, but maybe they are some different organism. The color can only be seen in certain lights. This is a huge case, involving all types of patients, rich, poor, young, old, male, female, you name it over the whole county. I must check out all avenues of infection. No one can rule out any possibility dealing with such a deadly situation."

"But, Jim," Debra replied, "we all know that modern water supplies will always have a certain low number of *E. coli* or other types of harmless coliform, and that number from the previous week is acceptable. Modern plants adjust the levels of disinfectants and extra filtration for safety if the number is a little high. After that high count, it sounds as though they did add more chemicals, and everything is okay now, according to state guild lines. The water is safe to drink. Besides, who ever heard of innocent coliform bacteria causing an intestinal plague?"

They both sat in silence while perplexed over these contradictions involving the illness in Greenwood. After leaving the outskirts of Greenwood, Debra pulled out two Cokes and packages of Nabs from her purse and suggested they stop to eat. She had purchased them from machines in the employees' break room at the water company, while Jim was talking to the manager. Jim said he didn't realize he was getting hungry and pulled off the road, where he saw several picnic tables. While they were eating, Debra asked if she could compare the plates of colonies from the hospital and the water company.

"Sure, Deb, let me get both sets out." They examined the colonies, and Debra suddenly exclaimed, "Jim, all of the colonies have this pink tint and not just those from the water department, which you told me about. Look here what I mean." And she showed him the hospital plates whose colonies did indeed glow slightly in the sunlight as did those from the water company.

"Damn if you are not right, Deb. This could mean that the same bacteria found in the patients' specimens is growing in Greenwood's water supply. If that's true, this is really scary, and the epidemic is, in all probability, a water-borne disease. This is something you would expect to find a hundred years ago, not today."

"And you know, I've seen similar tinted colonies someplace before, but I don't remember where," added Debra, deep in thought.

CHAPTER SEVENTEEN

THE GREENWOOD HOSPITAL ran at full steam the whole weekend, with all available staff working twelve-hour shifts. While some patients died, others clung to life. The staff itself was hit hard by the mysterious illness with doctors and nurses both collapsing now from the disease or exhaustion. Fifty personnel from the surrounding counties had shown up to help, but it was still not enough. But now real help had just arrived, when at precisely one o'clock on Sunday afternoon, Penny Cox, the secretary for Greenwood's hospital administrator, knocked on his door.

"Mr. Montgomery," she said in a trembling voice, "the official from the CDC in Atlanta is here and wishes to see you."

"Please show him in, Penny, and notify the doctors on the staff, at least those who are still able to work and not ill to come to my office immediately for a meeting. I want them to hear what the CDC official has to say."

Dr. Todd Marcum, a tall thin man in his midfifties, was shown in by Penny. He wore rimless glasses perched on his noise and had an air of reassuring authority. The cut of his brown tweed suit suggested perhaps an English influence in his past. He pulled out a pipe, which he lighted before speaking with a slight British accent.

"Mr. Montgomery, let me assure you that we will get to the bottom of this unfortunate situation for your hospital and the people of Greenwood. We will do our investigation quickly and carefully. We will need new samples from the patients and autopsy results from those who have died. I will also require a few rooms from which to operate and several of your employees to assist us. My team consists of three technicians who should be arriving any minute in our equipment truck. They will run tests and collect data. Monday afternoon or possibly Tuesday I will send a courier to Atlanta with what early findings we have for further analysis."

Just then, most of the doctors, including Taylor Whitney, arrived and filed silently into the room. Some sat in chairs, while others leaned against the wall in the back of the room as did Harry Morgan from the water company. Dr. Marcum went over his plans in more detail and discussed how he proposed to handle additional quarantine measures in the hospital. As he said, it was of the utmost importance to prevent the disease from spreading.

Taylor spoke up, "Dr. Marcum, how will we know if this disease is caused by an infectious agent? It seems that patients arrive here sick, but some of us working with them haven't become ill."

"A good question, Doctor, uh, Doctor Whitney," he replied as he struggled to read Taylor's name badge in the back of the dimly lighted room. "However, we do not know the incubation period of this pathogen. So some of the hospital staff could yet become ill at any moment. Do you agree? The only protection is diligent sanitary methods at all levels of the facility. This includes, of course, gloves, robes, disinfectants, frequent hand washing, and so forth." As he continued speaking, a doctor whispered to Taylor, "I heard he did all his training at a big London hospital and then got a PhD in infectious diseases at Duke. He must think we are all hicks up here in the mountains."

"Could our water supply be the problem?" A question came from the back of the room.

Taylor answered the question quickly. "Hey, we checked that possibility out early. It was one of the first things we did. We asked the head of the water company, Harry Morgan, about his quality controls over the last few days. The coliform count was up slightly, but of course, no pathogens were detected. Harry was going to run more tests immediately considering what has now happened, right, Harry." From the back of the room, Harry nodded in agreement.

Dr. Sam James, the hospital pathologist and head of the clinical lab, thoughtfully added, "You know, I wonder if everyone who is a patient in the hospital and those who died lived in the city and not in the county, where the water comes from wells." A hush descended on the room as the group thought over these possibilities. "At least I'm pretty sure that could be a possibility, but I'll have my secretary check the addresses of all patients to determine where their water came from or where the water at their place of work came from."

Ben Montgomery spoke up and volunteered his secretary, Penny, to help Dr. James's secretary check records where the victims lived.

"Just what I've feared," mumbled Harry under his breath, while several people assured the CDC official their water had always received the highest rating from the state agencies.

Dr. Marcum asked that the CDC be assigned several rooms next to the lab to conduct their research so that they could coordinate their work with the results from the clinical lab's tests. The CDC team was planning to stay at the Holiday Inn but would be in the hospital for the majority of the time until the mystery was solved.

It was decided, after there was more concrete information to report, a news conference would be held perhaps tomorrow morning in front of the hospital. Newspaper reporters and TV stations across the state were badgering the administration for information. After a few more questions, Dr. Marcum told the staff they could return to their patients and the pressing business of saving lives. Then he adjourned the meeting.

When Ben Montgomery returned to his office, the superintendent of the public schools called and asked for information about the current situation. After hearing the latest tally of the large numbers of sick or dead, he decided to close the schools for the following week. Then the commissioner of the city's health department, Dr. Hilliard, called and asked whether or not a boil water alert should be issued. Ben replied he should check with Harry at the water company because as far as he knew, nothing had been proven yet to implicate the water.

But when Dr. Hilliard reached Harry on the phone, Harry assured him all the tests that had been run were negative, and as far as he knew, the water was safe, but the final answer about boiling water should come from the CDC. At last the commissioner got Dr. Marcum on the phone, who decided it would be an excellent idea to get everyone to boil the water, just in case, and a boil water order should go out immediately. He told Dr. Hilliard the city would need help from the staff at the health department and the media to publicize and implement this plan.

The bureaucratic wheels spun slowly, and the notifications to everyone in the town took an agonizing amount of time. And in the meantime, precious hours were lost as more and more victims showed up at the hospital's doors.

By now, everyone in the whole town was frightened, and neighbors did not even want to talk to those next door, with lifelong friends avoiding each other in fear of catching what the others had. Many of the stores and restaurants closed even before they heard about the boil water order, with the possibility of the water being the cause of the illness.

Not everyone took this position though. The area churches reached out to help the sick that were still at home, especially if it was known that they had no one to care for them. The elders of the Presbyterian Church at first thought they should open a food bank in the space where Mom's Day Out usually met because the grocery stores had closed. Then the minister decided that was a bad idea because the one thing no one wanted at this time was food, even though it hadn't been proven what had caused the outbreak. So they decided instead to have bottled water and cleaning supplies on hand to give to any one requesting them.

All the area ambulances were several hours behind in picking up patients, so police cars were designated to retrieve more victims and take them to the hospital or the health department, which was now designated a station for those not seriously ill. There they received fluids and antinausea medicine from the public health nurses, and if their condition stabilized, they were allowed to go home in a few hours.

By Sunday evening, most of the families in the town either had a relative being treated for the still unnamed disease or knew of someone in the neighborhood or at work who was sick or, worse yet, dead.

CHAPTER EIGHTEEN

WHEN THEY FINISHED their meager lunch at a roadside table, Jim turned onto the interstate's ramp and cautiously edged the car into traffic to head back to Nashville. In spite of the golden beauty of the mountains and the wonderful night at Elizabeth's house, the drive was made in a tense atmosphere. Both were wrapped in their own thoughts over the turmoil they had witnessed the day before. At times, Jim broke the silence to describe some patients' distress or a few deaths he had seen. When they reached Nashville, Jim dropped Debra off at her town house. After thanking her for the help and exchanging a brief kiss, he promised to get back in touch with her later in the evening.

He skipped going to his apartment and instead drove immediately to his research lab at the hospital, weaving expertly through the traffic. But his mind was not on the road as he concentrated on how he would go about the problem of identifying the cause of the epidemic. He would have to be careful how he used the samples that he had collected. Perhaps after he got new growth, he should call the head of microbiology in the clinical lab since he sure as hell wasn't an expert on bacteria identification.

He entered the hospital, carrying the Greenwood plates and swabs, and went to his lab on the fourth floor. Putting on sterile gloves and working under a hood in the back of his lab, he ran each patient's swab over a blood agar plate, which he had previously labeled with the patient's name and today's date. The blood agar medium was used because it was conducive for bacterial growth of pathogens present in human tissue. The plates were about four inches in diameter, and he placed them on trays, which were then placed in an incubator. The incubator was held at a temperature of 37 degrees Celsius or 98.6 degrees Fahrenheit, the temperature of the human body. Jim turned his attention to the three-day-old plates from the water company and the hospital lab. Most had the same tinted colonies growing on the media, and again he was amazed that the same type of colonies appeared an all the plates. Apparently, no one had yet thought to compare the two groups.

He lit a burner and sterilized a platinum needle in the burner's red-hot flame. A few colonies from each plate were picked by the needle and streaked out on new blood agar plates in order to get fresh growth from Greenwood's original colonies. He once more noted the similarity in appearance between those colonies from the hospital and those of the water company. Finishing up, these additional plates were also placed on trays and put in the same incubator.

Jim next went to his office next door and reviewed his notes from Greenwood. It was still very confusing to make sense out of patients' symptoms, doctors' opinions, and lab results. He ate a package of peanuts, washed down with a Coke, while puzzling over the data. Finally, he called Dr. Scott at his home to go over his preliminary findings and the suspicions he had drawn from them.

* * * * * *

After Jim let her out in front of her door, Debra walked down the complex's driveway littered with fall leaves to her neighbor's home. She rang the doorbell, anxious to retrieve Annie. Even though she thanked Harriet Jones profusely for keeping her dog overnight, she chose not to go into the reasons for her sudden change of plans to spend the night in Greenwood and not come back until Sunday.

Miss Jones, full of curiosity, asked if Greenwood was not the same town where some type of epidemic was going on. She had read about it in the paper that very morning and had innumerable questions to which Debra gave some vague replies. Debra preferred to lead her to believe that the sole reason for her trip was to check on her cousin, Elizabeth. She was afraid that Harriet would be tempted to gossip about the trip if she knew Debra had gone there with Jim. Promising that she would pass along any news on the epidemic, she and Annie left.

Once inside the house, Annie dashed around the kitchen, chasing her ball like a puppy, happy to be home. Debra fed her the usual can of Purina and then went upstairs.

She filled the tub with hot water and added a cap full of scented oil for good measure. Debra climbed gingerly in the tub, hoping to wash away the unsettling memories, the smells of the hospital, and any germs she might have picked up there Sunday morning. Annie seemed exhausted too from her stay at Harriet's and lay down on a bath mat by the door and was soon asleep. Debra's long hair floated out in the warm water as she smiled to herself, thinking of Saturday night at her cousin's house.

The time got away from her, and she realized she had soaked enough. After drying off, she pulled on a sweater and a clean pair of jeans and went down the stairs. It seemed a simple and fast supper was in order since by now, it was six. Actually, the thoughts of the patients' gastrointestinal distress she had witnessed had ruined her appetite. She fixed a poached egg and toast, which seemed safe enough, and sat at the kitchen table to read the paper while she ate. Today, Greenwood's troubles made headlines on the front page of the Nashville *Tennessean.* She thought, as bad as the paper made it sound, the situation was much worse for those living there. She could still remember the terrible smells throughout the hospital, and by closing her eyes, she could visualize the trauma and illness in the emergency room.

At seven, Jim called from his office, sounding very tired. He told her he had plated out the hospital swabs and the plates from the Greenwood Water Company in his lab, and then he caught up on his hospital work. He spent a little time describing the appearance of the various colonies, and finally, after running out of things to say, he asked if he could stop by to see her. He could be there in about an hour after he went by his apartment to take a quick shower and put on clean clothes.

"Of course, unless I get another emergency call," he added, trying to make a joke. Debra smiled to herself and answered it would be great if he would come by. She was still very tired but not too tired to see him. Did he plan to spend the night, she wondered. *I hope so,* she thought.

Promptly at eight, the doorbell rang, and she opened the door to a cool blast of autumn air that took her breath away. Then she was smothered by a warm, comforting hug.

"Debra, guess what? I brought along the red wine we never got to drink Saturday night. We probably need it now more after that weekend in Greenwood."

He showed her the bottle, holding it over her head so the streetlight illuminated its rich red color. She took his coat and led him into the kitchen, where she retrieved two wineglasses. They were on the top shelf of her kitchen cabinet with other wedding gifts which she used infrequently. She climbed on a kitchen chair to reach them. He helped her off the chair and gave her a deep, passionate kiss. Taking the glasses from her with a smile, he expertly removed the bottle's cork and poured the merlot to the brim of the crystal glasses.

When they returned to the living room, they sat curled upon the sofa while sipping the wine and reliving the troubling experiences from the weekend. It was hard to let go of the scenes of the disaster they had witnessed and impossible to make any sense of the disease patterns of the epidemic. At first, Jim tried to discuss some of his plans for laboratory experiments with the samples, but soon exhaustion overtook both of them. Debra took his wineglass and placed it on the table. Holding his hand, she led him up the steps to the bedroom. Unlike his first visit to her home, no emergency calls were received, and they slept in utter exhaustion in each other's arms.

The next morning, he was gone by the time she woke up; only a crumpled pillow was left as a testimony to his presence. He had told her he had to leave by five in order to get to the hospital to prepare for rounds at seven plus check on any new patients who arrived overnight. The time seemed ungodly to her because most of Nashville was still asleep. Debra herself only had to get to the lab by eight, so she could at least sleep another hour. She still felt very tired and hoped today she could leave early, unless Dr. Steiner had a special project that would hold her longer. She wondered what Dr. Steiner would think of her visit to Greenwood. But wouldn't it be something if he was originally from Greenwood as Elizabeth had suggested?

She probably shouldn't even mention the trip to him. Dr. Steiner never seemed interested in what she had done over the weekend or anything else that happened to her in Nashville for that matter.

A case in point was last spring when she had been out four days with a bad case of flu. When she finally pulled herself out of bed and came back to work, he made no mention of her illness or asked how she felt. Rather, there was a much longer list of reagents to prepare for the week's experiments. He had pointed to the list at her desk and urged her to start on them immediately. She had thought again at that time what a cold and demanding person he was.

Debra took Annie for a quick walk around the complex's parking lot and left for work. The traffic was not too heavy on the usual busy Hillsboro Road. The day was crisp with a clear blue sky. Many leaves were still clinging to the trees on either side of the road. Halloween would be tomorrow, and usually the holiday was followed by a long Nashville fall with warm days and cool nights. When daylight saving time ended and the days became shorter and shorter, Debra would leave the hospital at five and drive home in her car, surrounded by a dark and frosty city.

She thought about the arrival of the holidays, by then there could be snow showers and icy rains. She wasn't looking forward to that, and while Nashville was usually spared a heavy snow like cities farther to the north, ice could be a problem. Her drive to work could be slippery, even dangerous, as she found out last year. But Nashville was beautiful to behold at Christmas, decorated with a million sparkling lights.

And even though lonely last December, she put up a small tree in one corner of her living room and invited her hospital friends and husbands over for a Saturday brunch, buying most of the food from the grocery deli in Hillsboro Village.

If things were normal, she would be excited just imagining spending the holidays with Jim, perhaps introducing him to her parents. But driving through the traffic, her thoughts kept returning to Greenwood and the misery there. She said a silent prayer for those suffering and wondered if things would ever be normal again in that town. Turning the car onto a side street, she pulled in the employees' parking garage. Fortunately for her, there was one space left, and she squeezed the Volvo into the tight parking place close to the stairwell.

After hurrying to the lab on the fourth floor, she hung her cardigan on a hook in the coatroom and slipped a freshly starched lab coat over her gray blouse and slacks. Peeking around the corner, she could see that Dr. Steiner was sitting inside his glass-walled office in the back of the room. Debra approached him and smiled weakly while mouthing a greeting, which he did not seem to notice at first. He finally curtly acknowledged her presence as she stood in the doorway of his office and gestured to her workstation, where there was no doubt a list of instructions for the day's experiments. He then lowered his head and continued to read the front page of the morning paper.

Debra had already skimmed it while she was trying to wake up by having a second cup of coffee in her kitchen. She knew the article contained more frightening information about the epidemic in Greenwood and wondered again if it was where he grew up.

Before proceeding to her desk, she could not help but notice the line of dirt on the cuffs of his not-so-white nor clean lab coat. If she had to give an estimate, she would say he had probably been wearing it for at least the last three weeks. *Oh well,* she thought as she sat down at her desk, *the Nobel Prize committee does not disqualify on appearance, I guess. I can just see him accepting the prize in a dirty and ill-fitting tux.*

CHAPTER NINETEEN

THAT MORNING, WHILE working diligently under the lab hood weighing chemicals and preparing solutions, Debra tried to remember where she had seen colored colonies similar to the ones Jim had brought from Greenwood. She didn't think she had studied them during course work for her master's degree. Rather, she felt she had seen them more recently, where had it been? Then for no reason, her gaze shifted to the back of the room and the door to the locked lab. She took a deep breath, and her eyes opened with amazement. Suddenly, she knew where her path had crossed that of the strange colonies. During the first week at her new job and before she had been chastised by Dr. Steiner, she had tried to clean up his private lab. The door was unlocked and partly open. Stacks of dirty petri dishes were in the sink, waiting to be autoclaved and then discarded. Those had held the same colored colonies as the plates from Greenwood.

Dr. Steiner interrupted her thoughts by silently walking over to the hood and announcing he was going out for an early lunch. He then said he was scheduled to attend a meeting across campus and would probably be gone for several hours. She should answer his phone, taking down any messages correctly, and place them on his desk. Debra looked at him with nervous anticipation, waiting for him to leave so she could call Jim.

Jim was standing at the nurses' station on third north when Debra got through to him. "Jim, Jim, I know where I saw colonies like the ones from Greenwood. They were right here next to me in Dr. Steiner's private lab. Remember, I told you when I first started to work for him, I went in there to clean up the mess. He saw me in there, got very angry, told me that lab was off-limits, and never to go in there. The colonies he was growing there looked like the ones we got in Greenwood, same pink color. I'm sure I'm right." She spoke with an excited rush of words.

"What, holy shit, just a minute, Deb, what you are saying? Hold on and let me transfer the call to our staff office's phone so we can talk privately," he said in an excited voice. Several nurses gave him inquiring curious glances after hearing him yell in the phone but said nothing. He quickly moved from the nurses' station to the office and shut the door.

Picking up the phone, he spoke in a low voice so no one could hear him. "Debra, I have to sit down just to absorb what you said. This is unbelievable, are you sure you're absolutely right? You say you have seen the same colonies in the lab he keeps locked up. What does this imply about Steiner, and what kind of research is he doing on the sly?" He paused for a minute and then said, "Let me finish here and then I'll come up to your lab and see exactly what you are talking about."

"Please come as soon as you can, Jim. We've got to get to the bottom of this. Dr. Steiner has just left for lunch. He said he would then be attending an afternoon meeting and be gone for several hours."

In twenty minutes, Jim arrived breathlessly and tried to calm Debra, who was frightened, as she stared at the locked door with anticipation and fear. "I must have some of those plates you are talking about, Deb, to compare them with the ones from Greenwood. Can we open the lab to get them?"

"Yes, we can, Jim. Actually, I knew where an extra key was. One day Dr. Steiner thought he had lost the key to that lab and asked me to call maintenance to make a new key. Later he found the first one, and I saw him hid it in his desk drawer as a backup. I made a mental note where I thought he put the key in case I ever needed to go in there. I just found it in the back of the drawer before you showed up."

She showed him the key with a weak smile. "I must admit I'm terrified of what we are about to do." Debra hesitantly went to the door and opened it so she and Jim could enter the small lab.

They went in. Jim took in the stacks of used petri dishes, racks of test tubes and notebooks scattered around the room, and exclaimed, "This place is a disaster. The health department could make a raid here. Let's take a look at those plates, but let's do it quick in case he decides to come back."

Debra shuddered at even the thought of Dr. Steiner reappearing but opened the door to one of the incubators and carefully removed several petri dishes. Jim took one of them and, holding it to the light, observed the familiar pinkish tint glowing from its colonies. "Deb, I've got to take these back to my lab and compare them with what I have growing. Are you okay with this? I think what has happened is too serious for us to do anything else."

She thought for a few seconds about the implications of their actions then took a deep breath and told him to take them and leave quickly. Jim placed the plates in an empty box that he found in the trash can by the sink and left the lab. He rapidly walked down the hall to his office, looking over his shoulder as he turned the corner. Fortunately, he met no one else in the hallway.

Debra locked the lab door and returned the key to the desk drawer. She leaned against the desk, barely able to get her breath and decided to escape by going to the cafeteria. It was important to not allow herself to think about what they had just done. If Dr. Steiner found out, her job would be gone and perhaps the chance to ever have another one in research. She dreaded eating lunch with her friends because, being Monday, they always wanted to hear what each other had done over the weekend. She would need to put up a good front and especially couldn't say anything about her visit to Greenwood with Jim. With these thoughts rolling around in her head and her hands still shaking, she locked the door and took the elevator down to the cafeteria in the basement.

And then talk about bad luck, the first person she ran into was Carolyn Moss, who was just coming out of the cafeteria. Carolyn seemed to want to talk and discuss the bridge club in great detail as they stood in the hallway leading to the cafeteria.

"Debra, honey, thank you so much for being a substitute Friday night. All the girls thought you were so sharp and hope you would come back again and play with us."

But after looking at Debra more closely, she could not help but remark on how pale and exhausted she looked. Carolyn then inquired if she was feeling well or had been ill over the weekend. Debra brushed the questions off and told her she was feeling fine. She promised to call her soon and escaped to the cafeteria. After waiting in line for a few minutes, she picked up the first sandwich she came to, not even noticing what kind it was.

Her friends were sitting at their usual table, laughing and having a good time. After joining them, she picked at her food and didn't enter into the animated conversation. The others didn't seem to notice her quietness since they were too busy discussing how their own weekends had gone and planning for Halloween, which was tomorrow. She thought, *If you only knew how I spent my weekend, you wouldn't believe what I would tell you.* After spending thirty minutes listening to them talk, she quickly left the cafeteria and returned to the silence of Dr. Steiner's lab in the research wing.

Debra worked slowly that afternoon. Frightening thoughts about Greenwood kept reoccurring in her mind. One patient had even hemorrhaged through his nose while she was standing by the emergency room, and blood had sprayed over the nurse working on him. Debra had turned away nauseated after witnessing the incident.

Around four, Dr. Steiner made an appearance and, without saying a word, unlocked the private lab door and went in. She looked at his back, and suddenly everything that had happened in the past three days clicked in Debra's mind. It was a perfect deadly scenario, and he was in the evil center of it. She stared in horror at his door, putting down her pipette, her hands shaking. He was a murderer, and the Greenwood deaths had been his doing.

For that matter, what was he capable of doing to her? If he knew she had given Jim the plates, she would be in great danger. She did not even finish her work or put away the reagents. Grabbing her sweater, she left, not saying a word to him, planning never to return. She could not get to her car fast enough and drive to the safety of her home.

CHAPTER TWENTY

After he left Debra and in the safety of his own lab, Jim compared colonies on Steiner's plates to those from Greenwood. He used a magnifying glass to study the colonies that had been grown from last night's work when he used patient swabs and old water company plates to streak out additional plates. All the new plates from Greenwood patients and the water company showed healthy growth. Some from the patients were consistent with bacteria found in the human intestine. But others looked different, and their colonies had the characteristic pink tint. The water company's media was also selective for human bacteria and showed some typical colonies and some with that pink tint. Unfortunately for Steiner, Jim thought both groups also resembled the colonies he had just taken from Steiner's lab.

Quickly he made and stained slides from all three groups and examined them under his microscope. Again, they appeared to be the same organisms. He would call them gram-negative rods, the kind found in the human intestine for sure. By then the clock on the wall said it was almost one o'clock. A department meeting in Dr. Scott's office was scheduled at one. He took the steps two at a time to get to the fifth floor and to the meeting with three minutes to spare.

Before he took a seat in the back of the room, Jim spoke briefly to Dr. Scott and told him in no uncertain terms he needed to speak privately about an urgent matter at the end of the meeting. Dr. Scott was surprised, but his courtly manner and appearance was always that of a Southern gentleman, so he made no comment or appeared curious about Jim's statement. He was always meticulous dressed, and today, under his white lab coat, he wore navy suit pants and his signature bow tie, this time in navy silk. Dr. Scott started the meeting promptly at one and spoke slowly while reviewing the month's most interesting cases for the benefit of the staff and medical students rotating through internal medicine.

The meeting went on and on to Jim's chagrin but finally ended a little after two. Jim waited patiently for Dr. Scott to finish talking to an intern who at last left by a side door. He turned his attention to his chief resident to see what urgent private matter he wanted to discuss.

Jim swallowed and nervously began. "My trip to Greenwood over the weekend, you know, I didn't mention this to you, but I took a girl along, someone whom I have been dating. She has relatives in Greenwood, and believe it or not, she is a microbiologist here. I thought she could help me gather data. You may even know her, tall, with long brown hair. Her name is Debra Chandler. She works for Joe Steiner on the fourth floor in the research wing."

"That fellow, a bad egg in my book. I don't know where this story is going, Jim, but I know who your girlfriend is. Very attractive, and I heard she was an outstanding student in graduate school. I wondered at that time why she was working for him, none of my business though. I guess it doesn't matter that you took her along, but perhaps you might have mentioned it to me."

"Uh, yes, sir, I am sorry. I didn't think to tell you she went along, but I must say I wondered the same thing about her job and why she was working in his lab. I even told her I felt having a job with him was not a good idea. Well, anyway, she was a great help to me in Greenwood. Since it took a lot longer than I had anticipated gathering the data and everything, we stayed Saturday night at her cousin's home. Elizabeth works for one of the family practitioners, a Taylor Whitney, whom I met at the hospital."

"Well, after we finished up Sunday morning and were on our way home, I showed her some of the plates the people at the hospital and the manager of the water company in Greenwood had given me. The first thing she noticed in the sunlight was that plates from both places looked very similar. They all had some funny unusual pink-tinted colonies growing on the media. I guess at this point the hospital and the water company had not compared the two groups. The CDC was scheduled to arrive Sunday afternoon, so I suppose by now they have seen the similarity too. But, Dr. Scott, the most interesting thing about all of this is Debra thought that the colonies looked familiar but could not remember where she had seen them, that is, until today."

He hesitated now, hating to go on with what had happened that morning in Steiner's lab when he took the plates from Debra, but knowing he had to finish the story, he cleared his throat and continued. "Dr. Scott, I believe I have some information about the possible source of the bacteria causing the outbreak in Greenwood. I have in my possession some plates of colonies that appear to be identical to those we got from Greenwood. And they were obtained here from a locked lab one story below us."

"What in the hell are you talking about, Jim, and what lab below us?" exclaimed the usually calm and reserved Dr. Scott as he jumped from his chair.

"Please calm down, sir. I think I can explain everything, Dr. Scott just before lunch, Debra called me and said she thought Steiner was working with the same bacteria. She remembered the weird color and believed he had some growing in his private lab, one he always keeps locked. As soon as I could get away, I went to see for myself what she was talking about.

"We were able to get in the locked lab because Debra knew where an extra key was kept. After looking at the colonies on his plates, I thought they resembled the ones which I brought from the Greenwood labs. Then I made a decision for which I take full responsibility, sir. I took several of his plates back to my lab. I made slides from each group, and after examining each under the microscope, I would say they appear to be the same gram-negative bacteria."

"You did what, Jim? Damn, do you know what you just told me? You and your girlfriend went in a locked lab and stole research material from another person, one who works here and is highly regarded by this institution. What do you think he is going to do if he finds out? Do you know how serious this sounds?"

"I fully know, Dr. Scott, how this looks and what the authorities would say if they knew about it. However, can you deny that I had to take a chance if Steiner is in any way involved in the Greenwood epidemic? Personally, what I now know about him, I think he could be capable of doing anything."

"Jim, that is too strong a statement, and don't repeat it beyond this office. The identification of the bacteria is beyond my area of expertise. I don't remember anything about the finer points in microbiology. I believe I should call Mark Rosenthal, the head of the microbiology department on campus, and see if he will come over this afternoon. Maybe he can identify the bacteria and shed some light on what you are suggesting. Needless to say, this situation is a very serious matter, and we must proceed cautiously. Do not, and I repeat, do not breathe a word about this to anyone. If what you say is true, we will have to get the chancellor, the medical center attorneys, and the Nashville police involved."

With that said, he picked up the phone and, after getting Dr. Rosenthal on the line, asked him if he could meet them in Jim's lab at five. He did not go into any details other than to say he felt one of his residents might have some information concerning the illness in Greenwood, and they needed his help in evaluating the data.

After hanging up the phone, he said, "All right, Jim, Rosenthal said he could come over at five. Now let's pray none of this is true. Go back to the floor and try to finish up seeing your patients. Then at five, we will meet in your lab."

Jim finished seeing his patients in record time and managed to get to his lab a little ahead of schedule with minutes to spare. He needed to clean off the lab counters, put away some reagents, and go over his notes before Dr. Scott and Dr. Rosenthal arrived. When they came in the door, Dr. Scott made introductions. Dr. Rosenthal was an articulate man around fifty with salt-and-pepper hair and a trim, athletic body. He wore black horn-rimmed glasses, which made his eyes appear large and inquisitive.

Actually, Jim had a freshman biology course from Dr. Rosenthal years ago which he immediately mentioned to the professor. Debra previously had told him they had the same instructor in common for microbiology, a big coincidence in her book. She had taken two courses from him while she was working on her master's degree and, in her opinion, thought he was a great teacher and researcher.

Jim remembered he had the reputation of being very popular with campus undergraduates by making science exciting for students in his classes. Even those not interested in biology enjoyed his course, and last year, he received the prestigious Excellence in Teaching Award. The University was equally impressed with his research grants and his popularity as a teacher.

After a few pleasantries were exchanged, Dr. Scott got right down to business. "Mark, I want to thank you for coming over here on such short notice. I didn't tell you very much over the phone because the information we want to share with you is unbelievable and could be highly dangerous." With that opening statement from Dr. Scott, Mark Rosenthal put down his pipe he had started to light and turned to Dr. Scott, giving him his full attention.

"I know you have read in the paper about the illness in Greenwood. I was troubled and intrigued by the situation myself and sent Jim there this past weekend to investigate what was going on. I hoped he could collect enough information to write a paper for publication in a medical journal. The *Journal of Infectious Diseases* would certainly consider it. You may know I have been the editor of that journal for the last two years."

"Yes, Dr. Scott, I knew you were the editor. And may I say, it is an honor for the University to have you at the helm of such a prestigious publication," Dr. Rosenthal said with a slight smile.

"Well, yes, thank you, Mark, for saying that. I will tell you Jim's trip went as planned, and he is now in the process of growing out bacteria from patient swabs and new colonies from the old plates he got from the hospital. The head of the water company also gave him some old plates, and he's growing new bacteria from those too. Now the story becomes more involved. Ms. Debra Chandler, who is a personal friend of Jim's, also went along to help him with his data collection. I believe you know her as one of your former graduate students."

"Oh, yes, I remember her well. She was an excellent student, and I enjoyed having her in my classes," replied Dr. Rosenthal, puzzled and not sure how his former student and Jim were connected with Greenwood's epidemic.

"Well, before their drive back to Nashville, Jim showed Debra the plates he had obtained. When they examined some of the colonies, she thought those from each source looked identical and also thought she had seen similar colonies before because they have a certain characteristic pink tint. She could not remember where she had seen them, at least not until today.

Now she thinks that her boss, Dr. Joe Steiner, has been working privately for some time with what appears to be the same bacteria."

"Good lord, Russell, how could a person at this University have the same bacteria? I know Steiner. We are on the same committee for undergraduate science education. What would he be doing with pathogens from a little town in Tennessee? He has a national reputation on recombinant DNA, as you well know. Pathogens are not his interest. All this blows my mind." With that said, he rose from the lab stool where he was sitting and turned to Jim sitting behind the lab desk.

"What have you uncovered, Jim? My God, this seems like a can of worms. Obviously, I want to help in any way I can, Russell. The newspapers and TV stations are covering the story and sending it across the whole state. What would happen to the medical center's reputation if the media gets wind a medical center employee is involved? Jim, show me the colonies you are talking about. I don't know how you got Steiner's cultures, and please don't tell me. I don't want to know."

Jim removed all the plates from the incubator and silently handed them to Mark Rosenthal, who studied each one carefully with a magnifying glass and made notes about each. He also looked at Jim's slides under the microscope before making new slides himself from the colonies taken from Steiner's lab. In less than half of an hour of study, he was finished and took a deep breath before speaking carefully.

"First, I will tell you I have never seen gram-negative colonies with a pink tint. I can also tell you that the hospital bacteria, the water company bacteria, and Steiner's bacteria appear to be the same organism, but of course, chemical analysis would help confirm that. We can run those tests and will. A better and newer idea would be to check the DNA of each organism. That would prove beyond a shadow of a doubt their relationship.

My research group has developed a rapid DNA analysis, and possibly we could have an answer in twenty-four hours, maybe even less."

Dr. Rosenthal whispered, "Gentlemen, this is a horrible scenario if they are the same, I don't know what the next step should be. Steiner could be responsible for the deaths in Greenwood. The police will have to be called in. I am trying to wrap my head around this and all the terrible implications. The only thing that is obvious is that time is of the essence, so I'll get two of my post docs to start on the analysis as soon as I get back to the lab."

The men sat around the lab table for a few minutes longer, discussing various possibilities of how Steiner could have the same bacteria as that isolated in Greenwood. Hoping it was a coincidence but having no answers, Dr. Rosenthal carefully placed several plates from each source in a carrier and left, promising to call Dr. Scott tomorrow the minute he had a definitive answer about the bacteria's DNA.

Dr. Scott glanced at his watch in alarm because by then it was almost six. He told Jim he and his wife were hosting a fund-raiser for underprivileged children who were patients from the hospital's pediatric wing. He had to leave immediately. The party was being held at their Belle Mead home and started at six. The traffic on West End Avenue would be heavy, ensuring he would be late and his wife would be upset. She was counting on him for support, even though caterers were preparing the food, and several other doctors' wives from the medical center were also serving as hostesses. Mumbling, he left in a rush but first told Jim to expect a call early the next morning. If the results from Rosenthal's lab were positive, he planned to call the chancellor of the medical center and possibly set up a conference call tomorrow with the Greenwood hospital. He felt by now they must share the Nashville developments with them.

CHAPTER TWENTY-ONE

JIM SHORTLY LEFT the building also and drove to his apartment on West End to get a change of clothes. The University actually owned the six-story building and rented it out to the house staff and other employees. It was cheap, clean, and convenient, but that was all he could say for living there. After a quick shower, he headed over to Debra's to bring her up-to-date on the latest news.

It was reassuring to think about the time they spent together in Greenwood, and he would be with her again in a few minutes in spite of the crisis. He hoped they were falling in a pattern of spending many nights together, though last night, there was too much talking about what had happened in Greenwood, a real killer for romance in his book. In the end, at least, they finally made love. Remembering the evening, Jim felt he might never tire of seeing her silken body or kissing her soft skin.

Jim glanced up and down the street as he was driving. Even though tomorrow was Halloween, a few larger kids were out on the streets a day early, collecting candy. Tonight was known as Beggar's Night and was popular in some parts of the South. It occurred the night before Halloween and allowed kids to get even more candy. Jim could just picture the new cavities developing from the sugar they would be gobbling down. At least there seemed to be none of the beggars in Debra's neighborhood, which was quiet.

When he arrived at her home, he was surprised to find a frightened woman, which wasn't characteristic of the Debra he knew. Her face was streaked with tears, and her body was trembling. Talking rapidly, wiping her eyes with a tissue, she told Jim she was now completely convinced Dr. Steiner was involved for some sinister reason in poisoning the Greenwood water supply by creating a pathogen that could slip by water treatment systems. The existence of the bacteria in his lab was no coincidence. Although she defended him in the past for rudeness and strange behavior, she now knew intuitively he was guilty. As she said, there was no other possibility to explain the evidence.

After coming to this frightening conclusion, she spoke decisively, "Jim, I plan to quit my job tomorrow. I'll leave a message on his recorder early in the morning and follow that up with a registered letter in writing, stating my resignation. I'm terrified to be in the same room with him. If he could poison the water of a whole town, what's he going to do to me if he finds out I gave you the plates?"

"Deb, please calm down, don't do anything rash yet. I agree with you that he is a very dangerous man, but we may need your help to get in his locked lab. You know where the extra key is and could help us identify various things in the lab. I think you should just call in sick and wait to see how the situation unfolds." He then explained about his meeting with Dr. Scott and afterward how Dr. Scott had called Dr. Rosenthal for help in identifying the bacteria.

"They both met at my lab at five. When Dr. Scott explained the situation and I showed Rosenthal all the plates, he said they appeared to be the same bacteria, but to be on the safe side, he would run chemical and DNA analysis. Let's see what kind of results Rosenthal gets before you do anything rash, Debra. Try to be patient. I believe the Nashville police will be called in if the DNA tests confirm Steiner has the same bacteria, and he will be arrested. Then all hell will break out for sure."

Jim finally got Debra to agree to wait for Rosenthal's results before resigning. She promised that she would only call in sick tomorrow as he suggested. He poured two generous glasses of wine and handed her one while he leaned on the kitchen island while she heated a can of soup and pulled a jar of cheese and a box of crackers from a cabinet to go with the soup.

They sat down to a meal on trays in front of the fireplace. She had started a small fire, which was burning in a cheerful manner, unlike their thoughts. The local TV news gave an update on the crisis in Greenwood, which they both watched in glum silence and, after they had finished eating, they tried to make sense out of what had taken place. Even though he did not tell her, Jim was more worried about Steiner's behavior than he let on.

They both slept fitfully that night, tossing and turning. He finally pulled her in his arms and held her in a tight embrace until daybreak. That day, October the thirty-first, broke cool and rainy. Once again, Jim left early in the morning before Debra awoke. Somehow at four o'clock, she had managed to fall back asleep and didn't hear his departure.

At the hospital for once, the morning seemed to go slowly for Jim, but at ten, he had a break in his schedule. He thought for a few minutes, and he then decided to take matters in his own hands. First, he went to his lab to pick up a reagent bottle and then headed for Steiner' lab.

The door was closed, but after knocking persistently on the door, he heard a curt "Come in."

Jim stepped into the lab and spoke in a confident manner, "Hello, Dr. Steiner, I'm Jim Tarkington, the chief resident in internal medicine here. I believe we have spoken in the hallway a few times but have never been formally introduced. Besides being a doctor, I also do a small amount of independent research with infectious diseases. My lab is on this floor too. I needed a bottle of silicone gel, and your lab assistant, Ms. Chandler, was kind enough to lend me some weeks ago. My supplies came in, and now I can repay the loan. This is an unopened bottle that I was going to give to her, but I don't see her now."

"That girl," Steiner said with a snarl and put down a graduated cylinder filled with a white liquid that he had been pouring into a larger flask. "I don't know what she was thinking of, lending out my reagents without permission. If she loans out reagents here and there to anyone, soon I will have nothing left to work with. I can't depend on her either. She called in sick today just when I needed her to help with an important analysis. Last spring, she missed a whole week with the flu, or so she said."

"Well, yes, sir, I am sorry if she wasn't supposed to lend me anything. I guess she saw no harm in doing it since I promised to pay her back when more of my supplies arrived. And let me say, I am sure it is stressful not to have your assistant here today. It is difficult to find reliable help in research, or so I've been told." He delivered these words with a slight smile even though his hands were clenched.

"You don't know the half of it, Tarkington. Even though I'm upset she loaned you the reagent, I will accept your apology. You say the bottle has never been opened?" Steiner seemed pleased with the reagent since it was in a large bottle and expensive to order. He took it from Jim's hands, waiting impatiently for him to leave.

But Jim had other plans and changed the subject swiftly. "Dr. Steiner, I was wondering what you think about the illness that is in Greenwood. It appears that a possible epidemic was caused by an unknown pathogen in their food chain or their water supply. I heard some people have died, and many more are sick. Actually, I went there this past weekend at Dr. Scott's suggestion. After investigating the situation and collecting data, I am planning to write a paper for his journal. I was wondering if I could get your opinion on what could have caused the epidemic." He clasped and unclasped his fists as he spoke, wanting to hit the scientist.

At this point, Steiner paled slightly and looked up. A lock of black hair hung over his forehead. He stared at Jim with eyes that were cold and unblinking. Carefully he put down the flask. "I don't know about anything that has happened in Greenwood, wherever it is. I am far too busy with my own research to worry about people in a little town. I would advise you to take care of your own patients here and forget about problems elsewhere in the world."

As Steiner was saying this, Jim looked over his shoulder and could not help but notice the newspaper lying behind him on the lab counter. It lay open to the story about Greenwood, so Jim persisted in his questions, pushing Steiner to see what he would say.

"But, Dr. Steiner, do you think the epidemic could be caused by some crazy virus or maybe a chemical contaminant in their water? I would really appreciate your input. Your opinion would mean a lot to me."

"Dr. Tarkington, I have told you once and will say it again. I don't know anything about Greenwood, nor do I care what happens in that town. Now get the hell out of my lab. I have experiments to run."

Jim left quickly at this point and hastily returned to the internal medicine floor with sweat on his forehead. He sat down at a desk and pretended to look at some of his notes, his hands shaking. A nurse looked curiously at him but said nothing.

CHAPTER TWENTY-TWO

MONDAY, AT ONE o'clock in Greenwood, the CDC had some tentative but devastating answers to the puzzle about the illness that had infected so many in the town. Dr. Marcum had called a meeting for key staff members in the hospital library to go over early results. Those attending included Dr. Sam James, chief of staff and the head of pathology; Dr. Richard Blake, head of surgery; several internists; and Taylor Whitney and three other family practitioners. Before the meeting started, several friends gathered around Taylor to ask how his son was doing and gave him updates about their own families.

Ben Montgomery, the hospital administrator, walked in accompanied by the hospital attorney. Just as the meeting was starting, Harry Morgan from the water company slipped in, carrying a pile of reports from his quality control lab. The meeting was closed to the local and state news media in spite of their protests.

Dr. Marcum rose and started the meeting with theses opening remarks, "Gentlemen, there is no use in making this news sound any better or make it palatable to you. Our investigation has found there is an unfortunate correlation between the bacteria isolated from the hospital's patients and some atypical bacteria found in the town's water by the water company's quality control lab. Our field lab, which you know was set up next to the clinical labs in the basement, ran quite a few tests on the samples. We also have spent time interviewing hospital personnel, Greenwood physicians, and the technicians at the water company. We came to these conclusions carefully and find the results extremely serious. The disease is a water-borne one and has implications for this whole area if not for the state."

Those in the room were dumbfounded and almost paralyzed by this news. Sweat broke out on Harry Morgan's forehead. A deadly silence seized the room, and then several gasps could be heard. Finally, Taylor Whitney spoke out, "And what kind of illness can this bacteria cause? Does the disease have a name?"

"Well," Dr. Marcum answered slowly, "the illness is not dissimilar to typhoid fever seen here a century ago or that which infects populations today in third world countries. To refresh your minds, there are billions of bacteria in our intestine not harmful at all, in fact very beneficial to us by helping to digest food, produce vitamins, and the like. These are usually called gram-negative due to their inability to absorb Gram's dye when they are stained in preparation for slide making.

But a few bacteria in this class are not innocent but are pathogenic to us. These include the bacteria that cause typhoid fever and other types of infections. Our modern methods can pinpoint and identify these devils quickly, but today of course, we never have the opportunity to study them in nature because the water systems in the States and Europe purify their water, making it extremely safe to drink.

"Your water company's quality control lab diligently searches each day for such pathogens but never finds anything suspicious, that was, until last week. At that time, an increase in the coliform count was noted, but that was contributed to a heavy rain that occurred a few days earlier and overwhelmed the purification process. Harry ordered extra chemicals and filtration methods to be used to correct the problem, which always worked in the past." Harry at this point could be seen visibly squirming in his seat as Dr. Marcum continued.

"However, the bacteria colonies from this increase in numbers didn't look quite right to the water company's people. But they ignored the red flags and decided the bacteria were harmless and said nothing to Harry. The lab people would tell you as they told me yesterday that the colonies appeared to be like all the other coliform colonies but for one exception. They exhibited a slight and peculiar pinkish tint that had not been seen before. The water company had just changed companies that supplied their media a few weeks before. After calling the new manufacturer of the media that they had ordered, they were told the tint could be caused by a different dye being used in the media. So they passed the color off as harmless. But it turns out that the hospital lab had isolated the same tinted bacteria from the victims of the illness here. But no one thought at that time to compare the two. Now we have a dynamite situation. Is this a coincidence? I do not think so. Though these new bacteria at first appeared to be some form of *E. coli* and passed the basic test for such, they are not true *E. coli*. Rather after running more chemical identification tests, we found that they appear to also pass the muster for the identification of the typhoid bacteria."

Gasps of horror could be heard throughout the room. Typhoid fever brought terrible images of people from the last century dying in pain and whole communities being isolated.

"How could that be, this makes no sense!" shouted Dr. Blake at the end of the table. "They are two completely different bacteria. They must be one or the other."

"Yes, you would think this doesn't make any sense, but it would appear that we have a strange mutation which is growing in Lake Crystal, the source of your water supply. It also multiplies much faster than bacteria found in nature. These bacteria seem resistant to the usual methods of water purification and are only killed when much stronger methods are used. This is causing a typhoid fever–like illness in the city's population but not for those in the county because those people use well or spring water. This hospital itself has a separate water supply fed by a spring, as does a close-by subdivision, and both appear to have safe water. We can only speculate that those who have not become ill but have drunk city water have some type of genetic protection against the bacteria. And I repeat, others who have not become ill have only drunk water from other sources like wells out in the county."

Dr. Marcum reassured them that they would soon have everything under control since a boil water alert had already gone out, and perhaps no one else would be infected. Then he began to list treatment methods approved by the CDC for those already hospitalized and preventive measures for the rest of the county's population. Now that the disease was identified, the correct antibodies could be administered along with the use of more IVs to correct electrolyte balance and fluids to fight dehydration. He noted few deaths occur with modern drugs, but some patients with typhoid fever take several months to recover. Therefore, for some, a long convalescent period was anticipated.

Someone in the back of the room asked in a worried tone, "What about Typhoid Mary, you hear about her sometimes?"

"A good question, I must remind you that a few people never completely come down with the disease but neither rid themselves of the bacteria. Those may be able to infect others if good hygiene is not practiced. A case in point was the story of Typhoid Mary, who was a cook in the New England area before the turn of the century. She caused many to develop the disease though was never sick herself."

He told the group they needed to call a press conference in one hour to go over the findings and assure the public that soon everything would be under control.

"Harry, that brings us up-to-date to the way the water company must respond to rid the waters of Crystal Lake of this pathogen. Our tests indicate the mutant is more resistant to normal chlorination than other pathogens. But it can be killed more easily by exposure to ozone, which is a new method in water purification not used here yet, but the system can be set up quickly."

Harry answered quickly, "Actually we have been planning to try an ozone treatment method out, so we are already in the process of thinking how to use it as a test in addition to the normal chemicals and filtration methods." This information was digested, giving most in the room a sense of relief. It was decided to announce information about the new plan at the news conference.

At two, the news conference started. The hospital had set up a hastily assembled platform with a microphone and table and chairs at the front of the building. There were reporters from several papers around the state and TV cameras from Nashville and Knoxville. In addition, three to four hundred residents were crowded in front of the platform, anxious to get information. Dr. Marcum ran the show, but Ben Montgomery and chief of staff, Sam James, were there also to answer questions from a frightened audience. Dr. Marcum told the group that a strange new bacteria had been discovered growing in their reservoir, and it resembled somewhat the typhoid bacteria and somewhat *E. coli*. Though deadly, due to improvements in modern medicine, most of those sick could expect to recover, and with care, no one else should become ill due to the boil water order.

Dr. Marcum went on to say the water company was planning to treat the water with new methods to be sure all the damaging bacteria were killed before it left the plant. Until all the tests were negative for pathogens, the people should drink only bottled water or that which had been boiled. He then patiently answered questions, trying to assure the audience that the town would survive, especially now that their physicians knew how to treat the illness.

"What about the Aberdeen Scotland epidemic? Are we to become like Aberdeen?" This question was posed by Dr. Hill, a retired UT professor and somewhat of a history buff. This question startled everyone at the news conference. They turned to each other with surprise on their faces. What kind of connections were there with a town in Scotland and the problems Greenwood was experiencing?

Dr. Marcum too was surprised at the question and the man's knowledge about Aberdeen. He searched his memory and slowly answered, "Yes, you are speaking about the unfortunate incident which took place in Aberdeen in 1964. I may know more about the story than some because I had two cousins who lived there at that time. An outbreak of typhoid fever occurred there and was traced to corned beef sold in Aberdeen by a chain store owned by the Scottish grocer William Low."

"So in Scotland, it was not contaminated water that caused an outbreak like is the case here?" asked another person in the audience who was standing next to Dr. Hill. Ben Montgomery strained his neck and thought he recognized the speaker to be another University professor who also had retired to Greenwood.

Dr. Marcum cleared his throat and spoke again, "No, it was not exactly a water supply issue, but the problem was due in a roundabout way to bad water. The corned beef came from South America and was packed by a firm called Fray Bentos. It would seem that infected and untreated water from a local river in South America seeped into the cans of beef during the manufacturing process. In Aberdeen, the grocery's cutting knives became contaminated in slicing the shipment of infected corned beef, and many who bought the meat became ill. I believe four hundred people in the town were infected, but there were no deaths. Some of the patients were hospitalized for several weeks, but most made a full recovery, actually in a short time."

Dr. Hill persisted. "Yes, but didn't the town suffer economically by loss of tourist trade plus lower orders for their farm supplies and industry products? Much of our town's economy depends on tourists visiting our area to camp and fish. How will this epidemic and the existence of a strange mutation in our water system affect our livelihood? Would anyone want to vacation here? The media will have a field day out of this."

These statements brought a frown from Dr. Marcum, but he answered quickly, "You are correct, sir, in that the illness did affect their economy for some time, but not to the degree for the company who produced the meat. It eventually went bankrupt. The William Low grocery store in Aberdeen closed after a few years, but they opened other stores in Scotland, so overall their reputation was not hurt. I can understand your concern, but this is 1979 and not 1964. We understand much more about disease now than even fifteen years ago. We hope to get this unfortunate incident under control in the next few weeks, and all these events will be a distant memory by next spring when your tourist season begins."

The mayor and the director of tourism looked particularly worried on hearing this news since they knew much of the town's revenue came from the tourists. After all, if people stayed away from Greenwood out of fear of the water supply, what would happen to the many businesses that depended on their visits?

The CDC director moved right along, however, and after spelling out all treatment plans for the patients and prevention options for those not ill, he turned the microphone over to Harry Morgan. Harry told the audience about the new ozone method for water purification at the reservoir and promised the plan would be implemented immediately. A sense of relief swept through the worried crowd. After a few more questions from the media and concerned citizens, the news conference ended.

After leaving the conference, Harry went back to his office and scrutinized once more the water company's lab reports but could find no new information. Finally, he gave up in despair and drove home at seven o'clock. His house, a simple brick ranch, was located on a dead-end road about four miles out in the county. Ironically, his own water was supplied by a well in the backyard. There were no lights on in the front of the house when he pulled up, but he found Joyce stretched out on their bed with a wet washcloth over her eyes, trying to recover from an upsetting day.

A single lamp glowed from their chest of drawers, painting the room in shadows. It was hard to say who was more depressed at the moment, but Joyce sat up when she heard Harry, relieved he was there with her. She told Harry that since the schools were closed all day, she tried to help her friends and fellow teachers as much as she could. Harry was brought up-to-date on their conditions. At least none of her friends had died, as had many others, and she could take comfort from that, she told him.

Harry sat down in the armchair by the window and put his head in his hands. "Joyce, I've tried to be so careful all these years using the best equipment, having our water checked and rechecked for purity. Now I feel I have failed, but I don't know why. I'm afraid the water company, unfairly, is being blamed for this tragedy. The chain of events is unbelievable, like a bad dream, but I guess it really happened. All our problems were aired on live TV, and I'm sure more of the story will be covered tomorrow in the papers."

Joyce got out of bed and came over to Harry. She squeezed his hand. "Harry, please don't be so hard on yourself until we know all the facts. Maybe there's much more to the story than we know. Could the man you fired back in the spring have poisoned our water? You told me he was very angry and might cause trouble later."

"Joyce, there is no way one person could poison the whole water system. We have too many checks in place for anything like that to happen. Besides, that guy was not the sharpest knife in the drawer, and it would be impossible for him to figure out how to do anything to our water. At the time, I was more concerned that he would try to harass me or burn down the plant, but I never considered he was capable of poisoning our water."

"I understand what you are saying, Harry. But, please try to put these problems on hold until tomorrow. Your job is still secure and your reputation is still intact I'm sure. The people in the town and everyone at the water company think a lot of you. You look terrible though. Some food and a good night's sleep will make you feel better. Earlier today I made chicken salad to take to our friends who are ill, but I saved enough for your dinner. Your plate is on the second shelf of the refrigerator. Please go eat your supper and then come to bed." And she gave him a swift kiss on the cheek and pushed him toward the kitchen.

CHAPTER TWENTY-THREE

At three o o'clock, Mark Rosenthal called Dr. Scott at the medical center and spoke tensely over the phone to give him the bad news. "Damn it, Russell, it's the same bacteria. Steiner has the exact same bacteria in his lab as they have in Greenwood. We have checked and rechecked our data, and there is no other conclusion. Also, I could hardly believe it, but it's some form of the typhoid bacteria resistance to water purification. I'll send you a written report with more information, but I thought I should call you as soon as possible. Now I just heard on the radio a news report from Greenwood saying the CDC had isolated some type of typhoid mutation from both the water supply and patients' samples, so their findings confirm ours. They said they have no idea where the mutant came from, but we sure do. God knows what Steiner was planning and if or how he managed to infect their water."

Dr. Scott let out a long sigh and said, "Yes, I heard the same report over the radio. I'm afraid we could have a madman working in the building with us, Mark. I'm going to call the chancellor and tell him everything we know about the situation, including your report. There is nothing else I can do at this point. I'll let Tarkington know too because if it were not for him and Debra Chandler, no one would even have suspected Steiner. Of course, I'll check first with the chancellor, and if he thinks this is a good idea, I'll call the folks at Greenwood and let them know we may have some information about what caused the illness there. We could do a conference call tomorrow, but of course, I need to wait to see if the chancellor gives me the go-ahead before I do anything."

Dr. Rosenthal agreed with the plan and hung up. Dr. Scott opened his desk drawer and took out two Tums. The food that the caterer had prepared the night before was much too spicy for his stomach. Unfortunately, he had eaten more than his share of everything.

Several guests had cornered him at the buffet table to get his opinion about the epidemic in Greenwood, but he pleaded ignorance and escaped to another room. In addition to his upset stomach, he was exhausted because two of their neighbors stayed until eleven o'clock even though the party was supposed to end at ten. He made the sarcastic comment to his wife when they were getting ready for bed that the last two to leave appeared to be more interested in the den's Scotch than Nashville's needy.

He looked out of the office window, hardly seeing the traffic below on Twenty-First Street. This entire scenario was unbelievable anyway. A prominent researcher at the medical center was somehow involved in causing an epidemic in a town a hundred miles away, and his own chief resident and girlfriend had stolen research material from Steiner's lab to prove his guilt. Now, whether he wanted to be or not, he too was involved in the tangled web of intrigue. As he was getting ready to pick up the phone and call the Chancellor, there was a knock on the door. He looked up to see Jim Tarkington standing in the doorway, looking apprehensive.

"Come in, Jim, have a chair. I'm just getting ready to call the chancellor. Let me tell you too, Rosenthal called and confirmed the DNA analysis showed all of the bacteria were from the same source. I must add, I was expecting this answer, as bad as it is. Now not only that, but it's some mutation of the typhoid bacteria which could be harder to treat. That's really a bombshell."

Jim digested all the information. After asking a few questions about the bacteria, he confessed he had gone to see

Steiner that morning to try and get more information out of the scientist.

"You did what, Jim? Don't you know by now that man is very dangerous? I believe your girlfriend has more common sense than you do. At least she refuses to be around him anymore I have been told."

"Yeah, I know I was stupid to do that. After confronting him, I realized he was more frightening to deal with than I realized earlier, and I was glad to leave his lab. I went there because I was furious at what he has done, and I thought I would push him a little to see what his response might be. As it was, he said he knew nothing about the Greenwood situation, but he was lying. A newspaper open to the story about Greenwood was right behind him on the lab counter, what a piece of lies.

Anyway, I advised Debra to call in sick today, which she did, and plans to quit as soon as we finish the investigation. She never wants to be around Steiner again. He scares the hell out of her."

"I can understand completely Debra's feelings about Steiner. I am beginning to feel the same way myself about him, Jim."

"Yeah, I agree with you. Now I've got some important information. Get this, Dr. Scott, Debra remembered to tell me, last night her cousin Elizabeth thinks Steiner may have grown up in Greenwood. There was a guy ahead of her in school who had the reputation as the town nerd. She had never heard of what happened to him after he went away for college. After Debra told her about her boss with the same name. She thinks he may be the same guy."

"Well, it will be a strange coincidence if it turns out he's from Greenwood. It may explain why he picked Greenwood as a guinea pig for his experiment. We will have to check out and confirm that Greenwood was where he was raised. Now, listen closely, Jim. I am ordering you to stay away from Steiner and his lab. We will eventually have to get the police involved. Our attorneys wouldn't want you to compromise any criminal investigation or, worse yet, get in a fight with him. Go back to the floor and finish seeing your patients. We will probably have a conference call to Greenwood tomorrow. I'll let you know the time."

Jim left quickly to go back to three north, not used to a reprimand from his kindhearted boss.

Dr. Scott then asked his secretary to get the Chancellor, Dr. Duncan Katter, on the phone. The head of the medical center had been there for five years, coming from John Hopkins with the blessing of the board of trust and prominent Nashville alumni. Dr. Scott had a few dealings with the chancellor over the years but nothing of this magnitude. He was worried what he should say to best describe the horrible situation. The chancellor's secretary transferred him immediately to Dr. Katter. Dr. Scott swiftly told him the upsetting story concerning one of the University's top researchers and skipped none of the unpleasant details.

At first, Dr. Katter couldn't even comprehend what Scott was trying to explain. "But, Russell, why would he have those bacteria in his lab and what was he doing with them? Why would he even have a locked laboratory? None of this makes any sense to me. I only hope nothing he has been up to has anything to do with his grant through us and the federal government."

Dr. Katter paused, thought for a minute, and continued, "His actions are definitely breaking his employment agreement. I know he has some personality problems and is somewhat weird, but nothing so bad to explain this. I'll have to call the University attorneys and get their opinion before we even think of talking to the police. You say Ms. Chandler is terrified of him and has taken sick leave, good idea. It sounds like if all of this is true, he is capable of doing anything and is extremely dangerous. We don't want her or any other medical center employees for that matter to get hurt. I want him off our property as soon as possible."

"Yes Duncan, I hear you. Jim Tarkington was even worried about her being around him before any of this turned up. You know that is just what I thought when I heard she was working for that nut, she could get hurt. I wouldn't want him around any of my daughters.

But now that Rosenthal has made a DNA identification of all three samples, there is little guesswork left. Perhaps when you talk to the attorneys you could ask them if we could call Greenwood and let them know about Steiner's possible involvement in the situation. I think that is very important information they need in treating their patients. If the attorneys agree to this idea, I could make a call to the hospital and set up a conference call for tomorrow morning to tell them what we know. A few of the doctors working there trained under me. I could contact one of them and would feel better setting up the meeting with a former resident rather than with some complete stranger."

One hour later, Dr. Katter called back and said he had spoken to the University attorneys. "They said for you to go ahead and set up the conference call for nine tomorrow morning. We will all attend, and it will be held in my office. Needless to say, don't mention a word about Steiner when you talk to them today. Tell Rosenthal and your resident Tarkington to be at the meeting too, Russell."

Dr. Scott asked his secretary to locate the number for the Greenwood Hospital and get Dr. Sam James on the line. James had done his training at the medical center about twenty years ago, and they still kept in touch occasionally.

Shortly, Dr. James was on the line, surprised to be hearing from Dr. Scott, who spoke in a friendly but hesitant voice. "Sam, it's good of you to take my call, and let me thank you for allow-ing Jim Tarkington to investigate the situation in Greenwood last weekend. I want to express my sympathy to you for the terrible problems your city has experienced. Now it looks like we may have some information that could be of help."

But before Dr. Scott could continue, Sam told him how relieved everyone at the hospital was when the CDC arrived and identified the bacteria even if it was some natural mutation of the typhoid bacillus that had infected the town's water supply. At least he felt they knew how to treat a known pathogen and weren't dealing with some unknown microorganism.

Dr. Scott interrupted the conversation. "Yes, yes, I know, Sam, it's a great sense of relief to you to have the CDC identify the bacteria even if it may be some form of natural mutation. And hopefully, the disease can be treated like any other case of typhoid fever. As I said earlier, we may have some information that could be of help to you, but I think it would be better to wait and discuss everything tomorrow morning."

"Well, okay, Dr. Scott, I must admit I am very curious what people in Nashville could possibly know about our water and the situation here to help us."

"Yes, I can understand that this sounds very strange, Sam. But regardless, here is what I would like you to arrange. I propose a conference call for tomorrow morning. Everything said will be held in the greatest confidentiality. Ask the head of the CDC investigation to be there and also get as many of the doctors in town as you choose to attend too. You better add the hospital administrator and of course the head of the water company. I think they all will be interested in what we have to say." Sam, though mystified, agreed to arrange the conference call for nine.

Anything would be a help, Sam thought as he hung up. If the medical center in Nashville had any suggestions, he was all for it. Some members of the staff themselves were recovering from the infection and finding enough nurses to staff the emergency room, and intensive care was a real headache. In fact, other emergencies and any surgery cases were being sent to the closest town, about twenty miles away. The once-proud regional hospital was being held together with determination and prayer.

CHAPTER TWENTY-FOUR

LATER IN THE afternoon when he finally got off work, Jim stopped by his favorite Chinese restaurant and ordered some carry-out. The sun was setting as he drove to Debra's house. He could see the streets were overflowing with kids busy with trick or treating. Small ones and large ones were in groups of three or four running from house to house while anxious parents followed at a discrete distance. Jim was beginning to get a headache and hoped Debra's doorbell would not be ringing all evening. If that were the case, he should have stayed in his apartment. The day had been very stressful, to say the least. The worst part was when he decided to visit Steiner in his lab. Maybe he too would be on the hit list along with the Greenwood residents.

In a way, he did not know why he went to Steiner's lab. When he walked in the door, he had to catch himself from punching Steiner in the face and remembered gripping his fists tightly. Perhaps he went there to confront him or get some explanation of what Steiner thought was going on and maybe trick him into saying too much. But of course, nothing like that happened. Steiner was one cool, scary customer, he had to admit. When Dr. Scott had jumped down his throat for going near Steiner's lab, he guessed he had a point. It had been crazy for him to try to take matters in his own hands, but at least Debra was going to resign and would never have to be around that guy again.

His thoughts jerked back to the present. The whole complex of town houses was lit up as though a gigantic block party was being held. He parked in front of Debra's town house, between two groups of parents waiting for their kids and ran up the steps, dodging two little girls coming down. One was dressed like a witch and the other as a fairy princess. Both were carrying large sacks of candy, as were the rest of the kids running up and down the street.

He stepped inside, and before he could even kiss her, the doorbell rang with three kids wanting candy. As she passed out the candy, Jim told Debra he was on call, but he wished it would be a quiet night as he handed her the sack of Chinese food. "I brought this so you wouldn't have to worry about fixing anything for dinner. I hope you like sweet and sour pork. Deb, you appear to be in better spirits than you were last night," he added encouragingly, as she gave him a slight smile.

Just then the doorbell rang again, and Debra, dutifully, went to the door to pass out treats, accompanied by Annie, who was jumping up and down, barking her head off. Jim could hardly believe his eyes because he didn't think Debra was the kind of woman who would care anything about Halloween or bother to buy candy at the grocery. Besides, he was anxious to go over details of the day's developments with her if the doorbell would ever stop ringing.

Almost losing his temper, he complained, "Debra, this year is not the year to celebrate Halloween. I want to tell you what happened today, and I can't even talk with that damn bell ringing. Please put the candy in a bowl on your steps and don't answer the door anymore."

She looked at him in surprise and said, "I'm so sorry, Jim, I guess the noise was getting a little much. I know you need some peace and quiet." Reproached, she put the candy on the porch as he suggested and locked Annie in the utility room with water and fresh food. She got out some paper plates, and they started to eat the Chinese dinner. Over the sweet and sour pork, Jim explained that Dr. Rosenthal had identified the same DNA from all three samples and then told her about Dr. Katter's decision to hold a conference call with Greenwood tomorrow morning. Since Debra had also heard the afternoon news report that a bacterium resembling the typhoid bacillus had been isolated in the city's water supply, this news did not surprise her.

Then reluctantly Jim told her about going to Steiner's lab that morning and Dr. Scott's angry reaction to the visit.

"Why, Jim, did you go in that man's lab? By now, you know how crazy he is. I have been trying to figure out all morning the reasons he would put a pathogen in their supply water. There had to be a reason that he picked Greenwood. Did he want some type of revenge on people living in the town, or was he just testing the mutation's properties for heaven knows what purpose and Greenwood was a convenient choice?"

Debra gathered up the paper plates and empty bags, tossed them in the trash can, and continued. "So I called Elizabeth at lunch today. It has been bothering me that maybe Dr. Steiner was really from Greenwood, and if so, that could explain the connection between bacteria found in their water and that growing in his lab. Elizabeth naturally was horrified to hear that the illness could have been deliberately caused by another person, but she promised to go immediately to the high school and look up any records for a Joseph Steiner, not letting them know the reason for her visit. I asked her to find concrete proof he had lived in Greenwood as a child, and guess what? I got a phone call from her later in the afternoon. She had gone by the school and looked his name up in their collection of yearbooks and found his picture. Steiner graduated there in 1953. She also talked to some of the teachers who had been there a long time. Those stories which Elizabeth remembered about kids teasing the town nerd were about him."

Jim looked at Debra in disbelief. The pieces of the puzzle were starting to fit together, but he was not sure how the story was going to end. They talked a little longer about the circumstantial evidence, then Debra unplugged the electric candles she had set in the window sills for the children, and hand in hand, they went up the steps to bed.

As usual, the next morning Jim left very early for the hospital. Since Debra had called in yesterday pretending to be sick, she was still in bed at eight o'clock and half asleep when suddenly, she was startled to hear Annie barking and growling at the front door. The bell rang, several times in a persistent manner. She collected her thoughts, thinking who could be at the door at this hour. A salesman, no, they wouldn't be out until later, and Harriet Jones never got up until after nine.

She crawled to the front window and tried to peer down and see who was at the door. Because of the way the roof hung over the small porch, she couldn't get a view of who was there. With some sixth sense kicking in, she decided not to answer the door in spite of the constant ringing. Annie continued to bark. She hoped the visitor would finally give up and go away. Finally, the ringing stopped. Still peering out of the window, she glanced at the cars parked along the curb and did a double take. The dark gray Plymouth in front of her house seemed to look too familiar. Just then, the person at the door apparently decided she was not home and walked back to the gray sedan. Horrified, she realized it was Dr. Steiner. Fear once again grabbed her by the throat as she watched him get in his car and drive away.

Why was he stopping by her house? Could he be concerned that she told the authorities about his research and wanted to check her out or even kill her? But really, he had never discussed his long-range plans with her other than ordering her to keep out of the locked lab. Terrifying thoughts raced through her mind. *Maybe he thinks I know too much and have associated him with the epidemic in Greenwood. Or even that Jim and I have put two and two together and know he is guilty of poisoning the town's water supply.* Debra slowly went down the steps, clutching a robe to her chest. A note had been slipped under the door. She recognized his strange handwriting immediately.

"Ms. Chandler," it began, "I was surprised to hear your message over my recorder. You stated you were ill and could not come back to work for several days. This way of communication is most unsatisfactory. I dropped by to discuss such a serious matter with you in person. I don't know if you are at home or not, but I could hear your dog barking. I have several important experiments planned and needed your help for their execution. Call me to discuss this so-called illness immediately and in addition to your future employment with me. Let me know when you return if you have gone to a doctor, then I will come back to your house."

Horrified, Debra thought, *He could have just called me yesterday when he got my message on his recorder. Instead he came by here. Now he knows where I live.* True panic hit her. *I will never feel safe again. Was he coming by my house to find out how much I know or hurt me?* With this final thought, she called Jim at the hospital and was lucky to reach him between patients.

"Jim, if I wasn't frightened before, I'm really frightened now. He came by my house and left a note saying that he wanted to talk to me about my job. If he could poison a whole town, what's he planning for me?"

Jim thought for a minute. "I don't know what is in that sociopath's mind, but here is what I want you to do. Take Annie and go straight to my apartment, take enough clothes to stay a few nights. My place should be safe. I will call the building's janitor and tell him to let you in. I'll make up a story about a broken hot water heater at your house or something like that and you need a place to stay. There is no reason to take any chances when dealing with someone like him, Debra, now that he knows where you live and has stopped by your home. At least he doesn't know about us or that you went to Greenwood with me."

Frantic, Debra threw some clothes in her overnight bag and grabbed food for Annie. She flew out the back door, dragging Annie on a leash behind her. She backed the car out of the carport in a reckless manner but then threw on her brakes in front of Harriet Jones's house to run in and tell her that she was going on vacation and would not need help with Annie for a few days. She looked behind her to make sure Steiner's car was not following her and then drove straight to Jim's apartment building on West End Avenue.

The building was made of yellow brick, stained gray by gas fumes from the hundreds of cars that traveled down the street each day. Jim had told her it had been built before World War II, and she believed him. She parked under a tree behind the old building and followed a sign telling visitors to go to the front entrance and ring the bell.

The janitor, an elderly black man, answered the door and took her to Jim's first-floor apartment. He had no comment other than to say he had received a message from Dr. Tarkington to let her in.

The apartment was as small as Jim had described it. There was the cheap oak furniture that the medical center provided since Jim had said he had none of his own. The apartment had a combination living room and kitchen with a small table and two chairs at one end of the living room. Apparently, Jim was using the table as his desk. Behind the kitchen was a really tiny bedroom, barely large enough to hold a double bed and dresser. The bathroom was equally cramped. All the walls were painted an unappetizing shade of pale green.

However, by this time, Debra was so grateful to be in a safe place she didn't care about the surroundings. Instead she found a jar of dried-out instant coffee in the kitchen cabinet and a pan under the sink. She struggled, her hands still shaking, to light the gas stove but finally succeeded and heated the water for a cup of coffee. The apartment seemed to have very little heat, so she put on a heavy cardigan she had brought with her and sank down into an old couch whose center was noticeably lower than either end. It was hard to relax after such a morning, but already she was feeling better. Annie watched her anxiously, unsure of the strange place, but finally curled up in a ball by the door.

CHAPTER TWENTY-FIVE

Dr. Katter's office was located on the top floor in a new section of the medical center. It was built six years ago after a University fund drive had raised sufficient money for an ambitious building project. The spacious room was decorated extensively in the University's colors of navy and red. Floor-to-ceiling windows revealed a brisk fall day in Nashville. The windows themselves were richly draped in red velvet and trimmed in dark navy. Patches of white clouds could be seen drifting slowly by in a brilliant blue sky. On the street seven stories below, Ginkgo trees lined the circular driveway of the medical center. Their bare branches moved slightly in the breeze, while golden leaves shed the night before lay in heaps around the trees' stately trunks.

Inside, the floor of the office was covered with a navy carpet, so thick that one sank into it with each step taken. The great seal of the University was woven into the carpet's wool, and the chancellor's desk was placed imposingly behind it. To the right of the desk was a large mahogany table, and arranged around it were eight leather chairs, ominously waiting for the meeting to begin.

Two Nashville police detectives, looking somewhat intimidated by the surroundings, were admitted to Dr. Katter's office by his secretary at 7:30. Already there were University attorneys, Mason Pope and Ted Ellis, plus Dr. Scott. The lawyers had insisted on calling the earlier meeting after hearing more about the crisis from Dr. Katter and believed that the Nashville police should first be included for a briefing. They told Dr. Katter, of course, everyone was concerned about the people's fate in Greenwood, but if it turned out a medical center employee was involved in the situation, it was extremely worrisome about the University's liability, not to mention the reputation of the University.

Dr. Katter asked the policemen to have a seat at the table, and then he and Dr. Scott told the police in great detail about the current situation at the medical center and its possible connection with the Greenwood illnesses. They emphasized that while they had a smoking gun, there was no concrete proof of Steiner's guilt. Lt. David Cooke, the detective in charge of the investigation, wrote all the information down on his notepad, trying to keep up with the two doctor's comments. He wrote as rapidly as possible, but this situation was so foreign to the typical crime scenes he was used to dealing with he was not sure if he had taken all the details down correctly or what his next move should be.

He cleared his throat and asked, "Let me get this straight, gentlemen, you think a scientist working here has developed some type of a bug and put it in the Greenwood reservoir. That same bug caused the typhoid fever the Greenwood people have come down with. I have been reading about all this in the paper, and the TV coverage has been nonstop. I've gotta say, this is unbelievable and sounds more like a science-fiction movie than a crime in Tennessee."

Mason Pope spoke out. "That's right, Officer, I admit the whole story does seem weird, but let me assure you, we haven't made it up. Dr. Steiner has the reputation of being an odd bird, but no one in their wildest dreams would have thought he was up to anything like this! He has no friends here, and nobody knew anything about his personal life, nor had a clue what bacteria he had created in his secret lab.

"We do know that he was working with the bacteria in his lab long before the outbreak in Greenwood. At least that is the information we have gathered from his research assistant, Debra

Chandler. This fact is worrisome and incriminating. Also, we've just found out he actually grew up in Greenwood, which he didn't disclose on his job application, not that it would have made any difference at that time. Dr. Steiner has a national reputation in DNA research, and when he was hired, the University felt they were lucky to get him."

Detective Cooke continued to be puzzled and asked how they could know that the bacteria found in his lab matched the bacteria in Greenwood and was responsible for the epidemic. For that matter, how had the medical center even obtained the samples from Dr. Steiner's lab? He did not think that Dr. Steiner had handed the cultures over voluntarily and would admit to poisoning the water.

Dr. Scott hesitated and answered, "Uh, yes, Detective, this is an involved story. You see, my chief resident, Dr. Jim Tarkington, under my direction went to Greenwood to investigate the epidemic. Ms. Debra Chandler, who works for Dr. Steiner and is a friend of Jim Tarkington, went along. When she returned from the trip, she became worried about what she thought was a connection between Steiner's work and the epidemic. She asked Jim to come to her lab and examine the plates of bacteria Dr. Steiner had growing in a locked area of the lab. After studying them some more, Dr. Tarkington took Dr. Steiner's bacteria plates to his lab to see if they were the same as he got from the folks in Greenwood. He examined them in his lab and decided they were probably the same bacteria. He then came to me. Jim and I discussed the situation in detail and called Dr. Rosenthal, who is head of the microbiology department on campus. We thought we needed his help in identifying the bacteria."

Dr. Scott cleared his throat and continued, "Upon Dr. Rosenthal's recommendation, we decided to have a DNA analysis done by the microbiology department to see if what we found in his lab matched what Jim brought back from Greenwood. Dr. Rosenthal found the bacteria taken from Steiner's lab two days ago had the same DNA sequence as the bacteria found in Greenwood patients and Greenwood water supply. That match terrified us, and it was at this point I called Dr. Katter."

"Yes, that must have scared you to death, finding the match, but also there is a legal problem right here because something was taken from his lab without permission, in other words stolen. You did not have a search warrant to go in there. How would that hold up in court? His attorneys could claim they weren't his cultures and were planted in his lab by someone else."

Dr. Scott answered hotly, "Yes, I can see that legally now, playing Monday night quarterback, but we couldn't just stand by and let him continue to operate and harm more people. Perhaps he was planning more experiments to test on other water supplies or God knows do what else."

Mason spoke up, trying to inject some calmness in the conversation, "Officer, when we heard how the University obtained the bacteria, we too as attorneys were worried about the legality of the situation, but I believe we can get around that, after all, Dr. Steiner is a University employee. His superiors have the right to inspect the University property, especially if wrongdoing is suspected. Perhaps we should go ahead with the conference call at nine. We can find out from the CDC how they came up with evidence for the mutation theory and how they tied the mutation to the epidemic in Greenwood. We don't want to move too swiftly because if our premise is incorrect, he could sue the University. But we all agree he is a dangerous man, and if all the evidence points to him, he should be arrested."

Dr. Katter slammed his fist down on the table and said, "We have talked long enough. I've decided after listening to this discussion to go ahead with the call. We'll first get the information just mentioned from the CDC, and if that proves to point to Steiner, we can go ahead and tell the people at Greenwood about him and our suspicions. We also will promise to give them all the information and data from his lab once we recover it. Perhaps that will help the CDC prepare a vaccine against this atypical typhoid-like illness. After the call ends, I'll ask the police to prepare a search warrant so we can get what information we need from his lab."

"Heaven help us," said Dr. Scott under his breath.

The police were asked to wait in a small office located close to Dr. Katter's office. The medical center technical department worked quickly to finish their preparations for the conference call. They hooked up a phone system to handle the conference call and tested all the equipment to make sure everything was operational.

Detective Cooke and his assistant, Andy McClure, had been sitting in the small room and were sipping coffee which Dr. Katter's secretary had brought them.

"Well, who would have thought this is what we would have heard when we were asked to come to the medical center. Never in my worse nightmares did I think they would give us information about one of their researchers causing an epidemic a hundred miles away," David Cooke remarked as he shook his head in disbelief. He looked around for an ashtray for the cigarette he was planning to light but, not seeing one, stuffed the package back in his pocket.

"Yeah, this whole situation gives me the creeps just thinking about someone who works here is crazy enough to try to poison a town's water supply," replied Andy. He then took another sip of his coffee and turned to a magazine on the table beside his chair.

"To tell you the truth, David, I feel much like a patient myself, sitting in a doctor's waiting room, hoping to hear that the cancer has not spread."

CHAPTER TWENTY-SIX

THE CONFERENCE CALL was still set to go at nine. A few minutes before nine, all the participants were assembled in Dr. Katter's spacious office. Dr. Katter sat at one end of the rectangle table. At the other end was Dr. Scott with a phone directly in front of him. Jim and Mark Rosenthal were to his right, and the two University attorneys were to his left. Dr. Katter's secretary had placed a sheet of paper in front of each participant, listing the agenda and points to be covered in the conference call. The operator's voice came on at exactly nine o'clock and announced the connection to Greenwood had been made, the speakerphone should be turned on, and the call could begin.

In Greenwood, the other participants were gathered in the hospital library around a table not as polished as the one in Nashville. The group included Dr. Marcum and his assistants from the CDC, Jason Blake, Sam James, Taylor Whitney, and many other attending physicians standing around the sides of the room. Ben Montgomery and Harry Morgan also were there. Everyone was perplexed for the reason for the call yet eager to hear what the Nashville Medical Center had to say.

Dr. Scott was to be the mediator and spoke first. "I hope you and the rest of your colleagues can hear me, Dr. James." Dr. James answered to the affirmative, so Dr. Scott introduced the men sitting beside him, and Dr. James followed by introducing those people in Greenwood.

First Dr. Scott said that his people in Nashville wanted to know how the CDC came to classify the bacteria isolated from the water supply as a mutation of the typhoid bacteria. In response, Dr. Marcum went over many of the same points he had discussed with the hospital staff Monday, including the chemical and physiological identification of the strain. Again, he empathized that it was not completely like the typhoid bacteria and had many characteristics of *E. coli*, which allowed it to escape the water company's screening and purification processes. That and its more rapid growth in a variety of media made the CDC decide to classify it as an atypical strain and probably a natural mutation.

In fact, he added, the Greenwood strain appeared to be even more dangerous than that found in nature, judging from the severity of the symptoms and the number of deaths. But today the CDC thought they had found the right combination of antibodies to give patients, who, for the most part, were responding well.

The CDC in Atlanta also hoped to sequence the bacteria's DNA and were in the process of developing a vaccine to give everyone in the town as soon as possible. Since the boil water requirement had gone out, hospital admissions had dropped dramatically. The number of deaths had decreased too, fortunately.

Dr. Scott looked at Dr. Katter, who gave him a nod as if to say "Go ahead." Clearing his throat, he spoke, "Gentlemen, after hearing how the identification was done in Greenwood, we can confirm that our Department of Microbiology on campus also identified the samples from the hospital and the water company as typhoid. Not only that, but they recently developed a means for the rapid sequencing of the bacillus' DNA, and those tests also showed they were the same bacteria."

"That's good news to hear the University got the same results as we did. Not only that, but the rapid sequencing of bacteria DNA is something I am not familiar with. Congratulations to the University on this breakthrough," added Dr. Marcum.

"Well, yes, that was an exciting development for Dr. Rosenthal's lab. But moving on to the real point of this call,

I'm sorry to have to tell you this, but I must. We believe one of our researchers at the medical center developed this mutation you have isolated. He did this by the use of recombinant DNA techniques he personally developed. Then later he may have infected your reservoir with the bacteria for some unknown reason." Gasps were heard around the table in Greenwood, and angry comments reached a peak in the background.

Dr. Scott continued, "We now know that he had ties to your town because he grew up in Greenwood. He never mentioned the fact to anyone here about his Tennessee background when he was a boy, not that we ever asked. Why he would do such a thing to your town is beyond anyone's imagination. We have two Nashville policemen in the building, and after we go over all the details of this terrible event with you, we plan to ask them to seek his arrest."

Dr. Katter then broke in to add, "I'm the chancellor of the medical center, and let me assure you how devastated we are about these events. The individual was operating in secret, unknown to us. This work had nothing to do with his University contract or the grant he received from the federal government. Obviously, he must be mentally deranged to have planned such a thing. Of course, we do not have absolute proof yet of his guilt. In this country, no one is guilty until proven so. Therefore we and the police must follow all the correct procedures."

Then Dr. Scott tried to calm down the furious group in Greenwood and answer questions on how the medical center had made such a connection.

"The evidence against him is overwhelming. Bacteria from his lab have been matched exactly to those samples given to our resident last weekend by the Greenwood hospital lab and, in addition, samples from your water company. And as I said earlier, the DNA analysis and match was done by our campus research facility. That is all I can tell you now, but I hope when his lab is searched, more information will be forthcoming."

The group in Greenwood was at first dumbfounded in hearing this information. Rage then took over as they tried to comprehend why anyone, especially a scientist, would do such a thing. One doctor said surely, he was mentally ill. Another said it was as if he was using the town of Greenwood as a guinea pig in an evil experiment and must not care about the deaths and suffering he had caused.

"What is his name?" finally Dr. James yelled as angry voices could still be heard in the background.

"Keep the information in the utmost confidence because first we have to have absolute proof to his guilt before he is arrested, but his name is Dr. Joseph Steiner," answered Dr. Scott in a low voice. "He got his PhD at a well-known eastern University, worked in California for a while, and has been here four years. His national grant is probably the largest a medical center employee has ever received. His national reputation is huge, with his research being published in some of the country's most reputable journals. We are all sick over this possible betrayal by a scientist in our employment, by one who is supposed to be helping heal mankind, not killing them. In addition, we feel terrible for the distress in your town."

"I remember him," Taylor Whitney spoke out suddenly. "He was a few years ahead of me in school. He had a reputation for being a very odd duck. The kids loved to tease him. No one seemed to have felt sorry for him or tried to stop the teasing."

"I remember him now too," added Harry Morgan. "The guys on the football team especially liked to pick on him. Some of those are my friends, the ones who now hang at the Lodge on the weekend. I can hardly believe that he could be so filled with hate for something that happened here when he was a kid. Why would he do something so monstrous now?"

Dr. Marcum listened to the discussion with amazement. It was hard to believe that someone would even be able to poison a water supply, and then shockingly, some in the library remembered him from high school. He cleared his throat and asked that after Steiner's arrest would Dr. Scott make sure they got the data from Steiner's research as quickly as possible. That information should be sent to Atlanta immediately to help in developing of a vaccine. He assured Dr. Scott that everything said on the conference call would be kept quiet until the Nashville police made the arrest. The conference call ended with the promise to hold another one, possibly the next day.

Dr. Katter asked his secretary to show the two Nashville detectives back to the room. "Gentlemen, after talking to officials in Greenwood, we believe that Dr. Steiner probably did infect the water supply. Their results mirror ours. In addition for needing evidence so an arrest can be made, we must recover the bacteria and research notes from his lab to give to the CDC in Atlanta. They can analyze the data and prepare a vaccine for the Greenwood citizens. Of course, I realize this means you need a search warrant and some papers prepared to arrest him later. Whatever that takes, please do it."

"I can get the search warrant, but I'm not sure we have enough evidence to actually arrest him. That is for our district attorney to decide. Also, how do we search a research lab when we are not trained scientists and won't know what we are looking for?" asked Detective Cooke.

Dr. Scott spoke up and said, "Dr. Rosenthal could direct the search, if that's all right with you, Mark. And I think we should ask Ms. Chandler and Dr. Tarkington to help. I think it's necessary to add them because Debra works for Steiner, and Jim is familiar with the bacteria. Now how are we going to get around Steiner if we want to get in and search his lab, Detective Cooke?"

Detective Cooke answered, "It looks to me like you have two choices, either you can wait until you know he has left for the evening, even if we have to search in the middle of the night. With this plan we could conduct the search without him knowing about it, but we would have a search warrant as a backup with us if he returns. The other possibility is that we could present him with the search warrant in the lab while he is still there. Read him his rights, and conduct the search in front of him. Either way, I can have the search warrant ready in a couple of hours."

Ted Ellis, the other attorney spoke up, "Of course, if we choose the latter plan by going to the lab while he is still there, he will try to destroy any incriminating evidence if he has any common sense. Then he will hire a lawyer after we tip him off that we suspect him in the Greenwood epidemic."

Mason Pope added, "I vote to do the search when he is not there and suffer the consequences, if any. After all, his lab is University property, and everything in it belongs to the University or the federal government through the grant. Nothing belongs to him. If the University suspects him of any wrongdoing, it has every right to check out their property and how he is behaving as an employee."

Dr. Katter then weighed in and said, "I agree and think too we should search the lab when he is not present. Of course, we will need Dr. Rosenthal, Ms. Chandler, and Jim to help us. If enough evidence is there, the authorities can arrest him immediately. We will either put him on leave without pay or fire him outright. We need to sever our association with him as quickly as possible."

The attorneys and police agreed to this action. The group decided to meet in Dr. Scott's office at seven to go over final plans for searching Steiner's lab. They would all be there except the attorneys and Dr. Katter, who said he would defer decision-making to Dr. Scott but asked him to keep him informed.

Jim went over to Dr. Scott and whispered, "Dr. Scott, I haven't had an opportunity to tell you this, but Steiner came over to Debra's house early this morning. When she wouldn't answer the door, he left what I would call a threatening note about her future employment and said he would come back when she returned. Naturally this terrified her. There is no telling what he is planning next. Because she was so frightened what Steiner would do, I suggested she stay in my apartment in the house staff building. She has taken refuge there and is still there, safe from harm."

Dr. Scott told Jim he was relieved she was at his apartment. Like Debra and Jim, he considered Steiner to be very dangerous.

CHAPTER TWENTY-SEVEN

WHEN THE CONFERENCE call ended, Jim went back to the internal medicine floor and tried to catch up with his work, but his head was spinning from the morning's developments. In addition to the large number of patients already there, several new ones were admitted overnight. All these seemed pretty sick to him and needed complete workups. Just before noon, he realized he should go check on Debra and asked another resident to finish seeing his patients, pleading a family emergency. This request surprised the other resident who knew that Jim had no family in Nashville but agreed without making any additional comments. Jim immediately got his car and drove rapidly to his apartment. Knocking softly on the door, he said, "Deb, it's me, baby, please let me in."

He could hear the dead bolt's lock turning, and then Debra threw herself in his arms, with Annie whining at their feet. He kissed her and got her to relax as they sat on the couch. Then he gave her a blow by blow account of what had transpired in the chancellor's office that morning. He hesitated for a second then said, "Debra, we will need your help tonight to enter the locked lab and go through Steiner's research papers and notes."

Debra gripped his hands, sickened by the thought of having to go in his lab again. But remembering the suffering and deaths she had seen in Greenwood, she knew she could do no less and reluctantly agreed to help.

"Good girl, I plan to pick you up around six, and we'll go in my car to the medical center since Steiner doesn't know what it looks like. I don't want to take the outside chance that he would see you driving there. We are hoping he won't be working late tonight, but if he does, I guess we'll just hang around until he leaves and then enter the lab. We'll be looking for any records that tie his work with the Greenwood epidemic. I guess he could have some cultures he has marked as deadly or something like that." And he laughed at his attempt of humor.

Debra told him she really didn't know where his private notebooks were or what they would find in them. The ones he used in the research connected with the federal grant money were very detailed, as required by the medical center and the government. At least she could read his handwriting easily and was familiar with his style of research. Hopefully, they would find incriminating evidence so the authorities could quickly arrest and prosecute him.

Jim then added that at some point during the search, they would report back to Dr. Scott and Dr. Katter, who would decide if there was enough evidence to confiscate his research and ask the police to arrest Steiner.

By now Debra had recovered her courage and replied, "All this sounds well and good, but how it will play out who knows. I'm going in the kitchen to find some food to eat in the meantime before I collapse from hunger."

Since no morsels of food could be found in the apartment and both were starving, Jim volunteered to walk to the local deli and buy sandwiches. Annie needed a walk by now, so he took her along, hooking her leash to a bike stand when he went in the deli. Jim had never had a dog because of his mother's allergies but decided he had better get used to the idea because Deb seemed crazy about Annie.

While he was ordering the food from the girl at the counter, the owner hollered from the back, "Say, Doc, I didn't know you had a dog." Jim just waved as he paid for the food and hightailed it back to his apartment.

Back at the hospital, Detective Cooke asked Dr. Scott's secretary on what floor he could find research and the room number for Dr. Steiner's lab. She told him research was on the fourth floor, and Steiner's suite of labs was 425. He decided to stroll down the research hall before he returned to headquarters, leaving Andy to wait upstairs. This way he would be familiar with the layout before the search team's entry tonight. Not seeing anybody in the area as he passed by room 425, he made a note of the lab's location. Everything in the corridor seemed normal, with polished floors, neat appearance, maybe a few bad smells, like hydrochloric acid, which he could remember from his high school chemistry days. He did not know what he was expecting, perhaps signs saying Dangerous Work in Progress.

Just then a lab door opened behind him, and he turned around as a man in a white lab coat fitting Dr. Steiner's description walked down the hall toward him. He stopped in front of David and in a curt voice said, "Sir, you seem to be lost. No visitors are allowed on this research wing. Go back immediately to the main part of the hospital, or I will call security."

David improvised and said, "Gosh, I'm really sorry. I must have gotten off on the wrong floor. Do you know what floor surgery is on? I have a cousin here who had his gallbladder removed today, and I wanted to visit him."

"I think it is on two. But do I look like a hospital directory? I'm very busy, and I must say I'm not interested in your family's problems," replied Dr. Steiner in an even more unfriendly voice. Then he continued to walk toward the men's restroom.

David mumbled an apology and immediately turned around to head back toward the row of elevators. The encounter told the detective two things about their suspect. One, he was a very cold and authoritative person. The other thing he noticed about Steiner was hard to define, but he observed a look of detachment and an emotional void in his eyes. As he got on the elevator, a slight shiver went down his spine. Some of the doctors thought Steiner just lacked a pleasant personality and was a little weird, but two years ago, David had some of the same feelings after interviewing a serial killer in the Nashville jail. Intuitively, he knew Steiner could be the person responsible for the deaths and disease in Greenwood, feeling no remorse over the chaos that he caused.

* * * * * *

Arriving at the hospital after six, Debra and Jim bypassed the elevators to avoid meeting Steiner and climbed the stairs from the ground floor to the fifth floor, with Jim gripping her hand as he helped her up the steep stairs. They went directly to Dr. Scott's office who opened the door and let them in silently. Dr. Rosenthal was already there. Dr. Scott suggested that Dr. Rosenthal, Debra, and Jim should begin to make a list of cultures and data they would hope to locate, which would prove to be incriminating for Steiner.

The Nashville detectives were due to arrive any minute, and while plans were being discussed, David and Andy came in the door. By now the police department had the license number and description of Steiner's gray sedan. There were several other officers in a stakeout in the parking garage and would be watching for him to leave the building. When the suspect drove out of the garage, they would let the detectives know that the coast was clear to begin the search.

At 8:45, the notification came that Steiner had driven out of the garage, and the four went silently down the stairs to the research floor. Debra could see the bulge of David's gun and holster under his heavy jacket. The hall was bathed in darkness. The maintenance department had given Dr. Scott a master key to all the rooms on the fourth floor, so the group cautiously entered room 425. Debra turned on a few of the lights and swallowed in fear while thinking how different the lab looked in the evening shadows. The familiar looked out of place, but all the equipment and reagents were just about where she had left them two days ago. Debra went to Steiner's office desk and removed the key to the private lab.

Jim began to look through the desk for research notes, while the detective went through his personal items, perhaps hoping to find an appointment book with meetings or travel plans. Dr. Rosenthal went with Debra into the smaller lab and began a search for any evidence linking Steiner to the epidemic in Greenwood.

Jim pulled several notebooks out of a drawer. He sat down on a lab stool and began to decipher the writing. Detective Cooke went through the top drawer filled with miscellaneous small pieces of papers, rubber bands, and paper clips. He immediately hit pay dirt.

"Look here what I have found!" he shouted. There were receipts for gas bought in the Greenwood area over the summer and the fall. David held them up in his hand so Jim could see the receipts. A smile spread across his face. "Two days ago, that bastard told me he did not know anything about Greenwood or care what happened to it. I knew he was lying but couldn't prove it then. Now it looks like Dr. Strangelove was using some of his free time to visit his hometown. He can't be that smart to keep damaging receipts like these."

By now everyone was crowding around the desk and looking at the first bit of evidence. Detective Cooke reminded them that just being in the town did not prove anything but to redouble their search efforts. A half an hour passed.

Then Debra in the private lab exclaimed, "I think I've found something. In one of his notebooks dated September the twentieth, he has written, 'Added 5000ml of xxy to CL, expect results in thirty days.'" Jim and Dr. Rosenthal were puzzled by the note, thinking CL referred to the symbol for Chlorine from the atomic table. But Debra remembered the lake was called Crystal Lake by the natives before it became a reservoir for Greenwood.

"Stupid moron," mumbled Dr. Rosenthal. "Why would anyone so brilliant leave such an obvious trail?" All were shocked for it now seemed that Steiner had actually documented adding something to the town's water supply.

David thought for a brief time and said, "Well folks maybe he wanted to be caught. This could be another factor pointing to mental illness. And again, it is well-known in criminology that certain types of criminals might leave obvious clues around, hoping to get caught. So maybe Steiner was doing something like that." He hypothesized.

Diligently the investigation team collected several racks of bacteria and more notebooks, which would be studied later in greater detail. They silently locked the small lab and then the main lab doors. This time they took the elevator and moved the operation to the fifth floor and Dr. Scott's office.

Dr. Scott and Detective Andy McClure were nervous waiting for their return. After seeing the receipts for the gas purchase in Greenwood and the notebook stating a chemical had been added to "CL" in September, Dr. Scott called the attorneys, who were with Dr. Katter. After a brief discussion, it was decided there was enough evidence that the police should arrest Steiner as soon as possible. Considering the enormity of this assumed crime, they were all praying the bail set by the district judge would be huge.

As Dr. Rosenthal remarked, there was no telling what other nasty tricks he might be up to or what other water systems he was planning to poison. The others looked up in concern at this unpleasant thought. Dr. Scott reminded everyone to stay calm and only wished the police could find him quickly and make the arrest.

David called the DA, who said he would have the warrant ready by the time they drove to his office. After they picked it up, the detectives planned to drive to his home and make the arrest. The human resource department at the medical center had given them the address earlier in the afternoon. Detective McClure had driven by the home later in the day to check it out. He reported it was a run-down bungalow located on the northwest side of Nashville.

As they got ready to leave, Jim wondered aloud if he would be caught asleep at this late hour or would be prowling the streets looking for more trouble. Naturally, there were still officers guarding the parking garage, who would notify them if he tried to reenter the medical center.

Debra pulled Jim aside and told him she felt they should follow the police when they went to arrest Steiner. Her rationale for this idea was the police might have trouble shifting through the contents of his house, just like they had his lab, and they could at least help them. Dr. Scott looked up from some of Steiner's notes he was trying to decipher and nodded in agreement that this was a good idea. So reluctantly the detectives agreed to let Jim and Debra follow them in Jim's car, but first they had to swing by the DA's office and pick up the arrest warrant. David told them that once they got to Steiner's house, under no circumstances could they get out of their car unless they were told to do so by him. They should sit tight until Steiner was safely locked up in a squad car.

CHAPTER TWENTY-EIGHT

With Jim and Debra following at a safe distance, the detectives drove slowly through a working-class neighborhood on the west side of Nashville. They passed a branch of the public library situated in the middle of a city park. Close by was a Dairy Queen, still open with a few customers standing in line for ice cream in spite of the chilly evening. Across the street was a small Hispanic church. Next to it was a large graveyard which covered the rest of the block. A chainlinked fence draped in garlands of brilliant gold marigolds surrounded the cemetery. Giant trees inside the grave yard were decorated with paper skeletons that hung from their branches and danced in the wind like evil spirits drunk with power.

"Look, Jim," exclaimed Debra, shaking his shoulder. "It must be the Day of the Dead since it's the first of November. You can see, the graves are decorated with flowers and gifts in remembrance for their loved ones who have died. They must have celebrated earlier today and left the decorations up."

Though Jim could see how the graves were decorated with flowers, family pictures, and gifts for the dead, he had to ask what the Day of the Dead even was. Jim was amazed to see the decorations, since he rode his bike in the area on weekends and had never seen anything like it before. Apparently, this was the first time the small church had celebrated the holiday because neither he nor Debra could remember seeing any activity in past years.

"Jim, I was on a vacation in Mexico five years ago and learned about the celebration there. The Mexican people believe the barrier between heaven and earth dissolve that day, and spirits of loved ones float down to visit their graves and greet those still alive. Unlike most of us Americans, the Mexicans embrace death. They honor their deceased relatives and celebrate the memories of their lives. The holiday is a big event there, almost like Christmas in America."

Jim, who had been raised in a religious family and made it to church when he visited his widowed mother in Kentucky, remarked in disgust how ironic it was that Steiner was going to be arrested on this Day of the Dead. He added that he believed the dead from Greenwood were now in heaven and hoped Steiner, who had killed many by a sinister and cowardly method would get the maximum punishment.

They turned right on a dark side street, following the detectives' car, and by now a second squad car filled with four officers had joined them. The cars approached Steiner's house. His gray sedan was parked on the street in front of the house. The police pulled up behind his car and silently walked to the front door, their pistols drawn, and their breath in short gasps. David knocked loudly on the door. At last a light was turned on inside. Dr. Steiner, in a rumpled shirt and jeans, answered the door. Cold, unblinking eyes stared at them. A slight beard covered his face, and his thin lips were pinched together.

David Cooke spoke quickly. "Dr. Steiner, I have in my possession a warrant for your arrest in connection with the poisoning of the water supply in Greenwood, Tennessee." And he started to read the Miranda rights to him, but before he could utter ten words, Dr. Steiner slammed the door in their faces and turned the dead bolt.

They were startled for they had not expected such a quick response from the scientist and stared dumbfounded for a second at the locked door. Luckily two of the officers who had accompanied them sprung quickly into action. They broke down the door by ramming it violently with a log that they found discarded in the yard. A frantic search of the house began.

Going in the kitchen, David saw the back door standing ajar. They rushed to the door but were too late because they could hear the sound of a motorcycle starting up behind a toolshed at the end of the yard. Unfortunately, it took off at a high rate of speed down an alley that ran behind the backyards.

"Damn, who would have thought he would have had a motorcycle hidden behind the shed!" exclaimed Andy McClure as he ran to the front of the street with his service revolver drawn and fired shots at the escaping man. He shouted for Debra and Jim to stay put, then he and David jumped in their car in hot pursuit of Steiner.

The rest of the police detail, realizing they too had been fooled, ran to their squad car and followed the detectives. The cruisers covered the neighborhood streets with their sirens blaring, moving in a frantic zigzag fashion like a Pac Man game. Unfortunately, Steiner had gotten a head start and was nowhere to be found. An all-point bulletin went out over the airways with his description and a warning that he should be considered extremely dangerous.

David and Andy pulled up in front of the house, finally admitting they had probably lost him, but in desperation, the detectives told the rest of the officers to continue their search of the Nashville streets. David got out of his cruiser and slammed his fist down on the hood in frustration. He walked over to Jim and Debra, patiently waiting in Jim's beat-up old car.

"Folks, I'm afraid I'm embarrassed to admit he got away. He's one slippery dude. Come on in and help us go through the house's contents. Maybe we'll find more evidence to send his sorry ass to death row."

By now the lights were coming on many of the houses along the block. Neighbors were standing on their porches or in their yards, trying to figure out what was going on at the Professor's home.

Jim and Debra hastily got out of the car and followed the detectives into the house. They began to methodically go over each room inch by inch, looking for anything related to the investigation. The house, being a small bungalow, was easy to search.

In addition to a living room and kitchen, there were two bedrooms and a bath. The second bedroom, at first glance, appeared to be used as an office, but what looked like to be a small office was, in reality, a makeshift lab. In addition to a very messy desk piled high with books and medical journals, there was a refrigerator, a small incubator, and sitting on a beat-up table by the window was a microscope. Just like the lab at the hospital, there were stacks of used bacteriology plates and open notebooks scattered around the room. The detectives looked over the room in disgust.

"What in the devil," David said, surprised at seeing a microscope and the other contents of the room. "Why does he need another lab here? Andy, we'd better not touch anything." And they backed carefully out of the room.

Debra peered into the room and said weakly, "I never even knew where he lived, and now I find he has another hidden lab close to the hospital, producing who knows what."

Jim and Debra put on gloves, masks, and gowns before they entered the room. They also warned David and Andy not to go in the room again. "You don't have to worry folks. That's the last place I want to spend any time in," and Andy shuddered.

Immediately, David went back to the squad car and called Dr. Scott to tell him of the new and upsetting developments who then in turn called Mark Rosenthal. After Dr. Scott relayed the news, he asked Rosenthal if he could go to Steiner's home to help Jim and Debra identify what Steiner had there.

Debra and Jim began to go through the plates lying around the small lab counter then pulled out plates and test tubes from the incubator. Jim found several large screw-top flasks filled with a cloudy liquid in the refrigerator. He was afraid they might contain more cultures of the typhoid mutant or, worse, some new bacteria Steiner had designed.

Debra was holding them up to the lamplight when Dr. Rosenthal arrived out of breath. In his haste to get there, he wore no coat in spite of temperatures in the forties and was dressed only in jeans with a pajama top hanging over the jeans. After putting on the usual protective clothing, he began to help the other two carefully make an inventory of the room's contents.

Since David and Andy had been told not to go in the office or lab, whatever it was called, they began to examine the contents of Steiner's bedroom. The covers of the bed had been thrown back, and a stack of books had been knocked off a chest of drawers in Steiner's haste to escape. It looked as though he had a minimum amount of clothes in the closet, and a few pairs of shoes were under the bed. Curiously, a large black-and-white map of the city of Nashville, unframed, hung on a wall over the chest.

At first the detectives dismissed it completely. David remarked he thought that it was a little strange to have a map on the wall rather than a print or some sort of painting. Andy jokingly suggested that maybe he used it to find his way around Nashville. David though didn't laugh at the joke but commented in a rather thoughtful manner that Steiner had lived in Nashville for several years and by now should not need a map for help finding his way around the city.

He walked over to the map and upon closer inspection could see one small area circled in red ink. This included the intersection of Eighth Avenue and Nolensville Road in downtown Nashville. They both realized simultaneously the city's reservoir was also located in the area that was highlighted.

"Holy cow!" exclaimed David. "Is Nashville next? Is he planning to poison our water too?"

David grabbed the phone and called his supervisor who in turn notified the director of the water company about possible trouble brewing. The water company people reassured them that, unlike Greenville, Nashville's water supply was heavily protected with a twenty-foot barbwire fence around the perimeter and gates manned twenty-four hours a day by an armed guard. Even still, the possibility of poisoning Nashville's water alarmed both the police and the water company executives. The mayor was notified, and he instructed the police to double the number of officers searching for Steiner, then they would sit tight and hope for the best.

The all-points bulletin on Steiner now carried more urgency. It was more obvious than ever, even to the earlier doubters, that they were dealing with a madman and, under certain definitions, a serial killer.

Two of the police back at the medical center were still in their stakeout, patiently watching the parking garage. Since the operation had now shifted into high gear, they were told to continue guarding the entrances and should be aware that Steiner was on the loose and very dangerous. It was a possibility that he might try to sneak back in his lab.

Dr. Rosenthal asked Jim to call Dr. Scott and tell him that he might want to notify his contacts in Greenwood so they could be brought up-to-date on the latest developments. David agreed, so Jim picked up the phone and began to dial Scott's number.

"Surely you don' think he would be planning to go back to Greenville, do you?" asked Debra. "After all he has done enough damage to the town to last a lifetime. The hospital is overrun with patients, the schools and businesses are closed, and the people still alive are terrified."

"Who knows," answered David in an angry tone. "We are dealing with a dangerous, unhinged person. I can say from experience that when you have someone so emotionally disturbed, anything is possible. It appears he had some longstanding grudge against a lot of people in that town, so maybe he might want to return there, check over the damage already done, or even inflict more."

They all shuddered at that thought, as Jim got Dr. Scott on the phone to tell him about the map in Steiner's bedroom showing Nashville's reservoir and the possibility that Steiner was planning to hit Nashville's water too. Jim, however ended the conversation by reassuring him that the authorities told them that Nashville's water supply was well guarded, unlike Greenwood's, and no one should worry about the safety of Nashville water.

By now it was one o'clock. The group decided they had enough evidence from Steiner's makeshift lab, so they packed up the contents, which Dr. Rosenthal placed in his car and headed over to his lab on the main campus. Before he left, Dr. Rosenthal told Jim and Debra he planned to have his lab run analysis on the plates and cultures to see if they were just more of the typhoid bacteria or some new concoction. He would still have to help his assistants prepare the new samples for analysis before he could go home to bed, he added with a yawn.

Back at Steiner's home, the detectives secured the house by putting heavy padlocks on the doors and ran yellow tape around the property denoting a crime scene. A lone policeman was assigned to stay in an unmarked car half a block down the street and guard against the possibility Steiner would try to return. Then David and Andy left for a few hours of sleep before reporting for duty at police headquarters.

CHAPTER TWENTY-NINE

EARLY THE NEXT morning Jim received a call from the police saying that they had not been able to find Steiner in spite of extensive search efforts. They warned that he and Debra should be careful if they went out. After giving Debra this bad news, Jim looked at the clock and decided to go back to work anyway. He wouldn't take the day off, as Dr. Scott had suggested, but planned to go about his job as usual, pretending nothing had happened. How much his fellow residents knew about the shenanigans that went on yesterday in the research wing was unknown to him. He told Debra he would take Annie out for a brief walk for her since she was not dressed. When they returned, Debra was watching the morning news on his small television. She told him there was no mention about Steiner or the medical center on TV in spite of the intense search that had gone on last night.

"Deb, you better sit tight again in the apartment today. While I think you're a hundred percent safe here, I still don't want you to take any chances. Steiner probably doesn't know about our relationship and that you went to Greenwood with me. Even if he does know we are friends, he sure as hell doesn't know where I live or that you are staying here, honey."

"Jim, you don't have to worry. I agree he would never think to look for me here. In the past, he wasn't interested in anything I did, only that I helped him with those damn experiments. He certainly didn't care about details of my private life or whom I was dating."

"Well, yeah, I guess you're right, anyway. I've got to leave for the hospital now. I'll call you later this morning after I talk to Scott and the detectives to give you the latest update on

Steiner. Just be careful if you take Annie out for a walk, stay on the side streets and off West End Avenue. He could be driving by and see you."

As Jim was walking to his car, he decided he was being overprotective, telling her to be careful. She, after all, was an intelligent person. However, he believed in the past she had given Steiner too much benefit of the doubt. Maybe she had been so impressed with Steiner's reputation and list of publications that she overlooked the deadness which he had seen in his eyes.

When Jim got to the hospital, the first thing he did was go to Dr. Scott's office. Dr. Scott looked exhausted from the late evening but was relieved to see him and patted him on the back before they sat down and rehashed last night's frantic events.

"Jim, I didn't know what in the devil we were getting into when I sent you to Greenwood to collect that research data." Just then, the phone rang. It was Mark Rosenthal confirming that the culture they had found in Steiner's house was the same typhoid bacteria they obtained from Greenville and Steiner's lab at the medical center. Also, it was the only bacteria found, and no new organisms were at the house.

After that conversation ended, Dr. Scott called Sam James in Greenwood to tell him even though the warrant for Steiner's arrest was issued, he had slipped through the authorities' hands. So far, the police didn't have any clues where he was but were hopeful he would be apprehended soon. After hanging up, he said to Jim, "No use telling them about the map showing Nashville's reservoir. I don't think that's something they need to know about. Dr. James said the admissions rate at the hospital has slowed down a little more, and they hope the worse is over, thank God."

Back at Jim's apartment, Debra sat by the radiator, trying to warm up. She ate a bowl of the stale cereal she found in a kitchen cabinet with some milk in the refrigerator which still had a good expiration date on it. The sun by now had come out, and it looked like it would be a warm fall day, a good day to take Annie on a walk. She already had on a nondescript jogging suit and her long hair tied back in a ponytail. She put on one of Jim's baseball caps and left the apartment to stand in front of the building, surveying the traffic. Across the street and further down the road, Centennial Park could be seen glistening like a tempting beacon of emerald green, while an unrelenting stream of traffic passed in front of her.

In the center of the park stood the white marble Parthenon, a replica of the one in Athens, she had been told. Even though Jim's warnings about staying on side streets were ringing in her ears, she and the dog ran across the busy street, dodging cars, and entered the park. It was so beautiful and peaceful there. The grass had been freshly mowed, and the leaves raked into neat piles ready to be picked up by the park's maintenance men. A small lake in the front of the Parthenon added to the serenity of the scene. A few maple leaves floated gently on the water.

The only ripples on its surface were made by ducks swimming in slow circles around the center of the lake. They were clustered together and appeared to be biding their time, looking for bread crumbs from park visitors. She started to walk around the shoreline with Annie who disturbed the silence by barking ferociously at the ducks.

On the other side of the lake, a few moms had just arrived and were sitting on the benches, while their children prepared to throw pieces of bread out to the ducks who at that moment were swimming with great urgency toward them. Debra looked at the mothers and children with envy. Would she ever be in a similar position? After the last few days, she was just thankful to be alive. As she approached the children, a child with long blond hair ran over and petted Annie, who wagged her tail in appreciation.

She continued, walking for a while more, then at last sank down on a bench directly behind the Parthenon. Over her head was a large maple tree. It was still glorious with colors of red and gold, and enough leaves left to provide shade for anyone sitting on the bench. Debra took a deep breath, shut her eyes, and simply enjoyed the silence around her. Then she heard the motorcycle before she saw it. A black motorcycle pulled up across the park road, and the owner, dressed in jeans and a dark leather jacket, sat astride it, watching her. Dread filled her body.

He walked toward her, pulling off dark glasses. Black stubble of beard covered his face. "Well, Ms. Chandler, I see you have recovered enough to take your dog for a walk and don't seem to be worried about your job with me at the medical center."

"Dr. S-Steiner, I didn't expect to see you here. I didn't even know you had a motorcycle." She searched for something more to say than those silly words while easing her body off the bench. She held Annie's leash tightly and added, "Actually, I'm planning to resign and mail the resignation letter to you later today. My parents want me to return to Clarksville because of my mother's poor health, and mine's is not so good either."

Of course, these were all white lies, but she was frantic to tell him anything and escape. Annie by now was growling softly at her feet as though she sensed danger, and it involved this man.

"Yes, I see," answered Dr. Steiner, looking her up and down. "Actually, since I tried to check on your supposed illness the other day, my situation has changed, and I may not need a lab assistant any longer. It is just as well you are planning to resign. It seems the authorities here suspect me of having something to do with the typhoid epidemic in the small Tennessee town east of Nashville, Greenwood, is its name, I believe. How ridiculous for them to think that. I have been wondering why they would suspect me. Then your name crossed my mind, you who know more about my lab than anyone else. Should I blame you for the police's interest in me? How fortunate for me I saw you in the park and can ask you that." And he took a step closer to her.

"Please, Dr. Steiner, don't blame me for anything like that. I really don't know very much about your other research. After all, you told me on several occasions not to go in that lab. I am truly sorry you're having so much trouble." Debra answered this way, trying to show sympathy for him, as she slowly backed away.

"But I'll tell you this much, I had already heard you were being investigated in connection with the illness in Greenwood. I also heard the medical center found out that you grew up there, so don't pretend you have never heard of the town. Perhaps that's why the police are making some connection with you and the epidemic. You don't have to blame me for any of this," she added as she backed farther away from him.

"The hell you say, I don't know how they discovered that little fact, but I might as well admit it. I did grow up there. My life was miserable, miserable there as a child. I hate the sound of Greenwood on my lips. The teachers didn't know how to handle me. I had such a high IQ it didn't register on their pathetic scale. Most of those idiots living there were only interested in the football team or hunting deer. I didn't care to waste my time with their stupid pursuits. I must say I was picked on for no good reason other than I was so much smarter than the rest. But enough of that sad story. I was grateful to escape by going to college, far from Greenwood, and hoped to never see the town again when I left."

This emotional outburst, from a person whom she thought had no emotions, stunned Debra. She could almost conjure up sympathy for the child who had become the man except when she remembered the pain she witnessed at the hospital or recalled the list of the dead which she read in the paper.

"Again Dr. Steiner, I'm sorry for all your problems, and apologize for not have gotten hold of you sooner to tell you about my decision to quit. I should have called again and left another message," Debra wondered, as she looked around, where she could run to, or if anyone would hear her calls for help.

He studied her intently for a few minutes as if trying to decide what to do next. He reached out, touching her face, and simply said, "Well, yes, Ms. Chandler, you can say you have resigned. I would prefer to think I've fired you. Whatever, you can go to the lab tomorrow and clear the things out of your desk. Providing the authorities will let you. Do not consider the possibility that I would give you any kind of recommendation for another job. Perhaps you should just marry that doctor you lent some of my reagents to. He looks like he would be a good romp in the hay, you know what I mean," he said with a sneer.

She stepped back and looked at him, her eyes blazing. "Goodbye, Dr. Steiner." And she couldn't help but add, "I want you to know while you're a brilliant man, you're a difficult and weird person, especially to work with, and for my part, I'm glad I'm never going to see you again." Wishing to add, but of course she didn't, she also thought he was guilty of a hideous crime and hoped the police would catch him soon.

She turned quickly and ran with Annie to the other side of the park, where she hoped he couldn't see her. She crossed the street and dashed into the hotel that sat at the corner of West End Avenue and Natchez Trace, and planned to stay there until she was sure he had not followed her.

"Oh, miss, you can't bring that dog in here!" yelled the gray-haired clerk standing at the front desk. He looked in a disapproving way at Annie, who was sniffing along the floor of the hotel's spotless lobby.

"Oh," said Debra. "I didn't realize dogs weren't allowed here. I'm sorry, but I'm desperate to go in your restroom. Could I just use it, and then I promise we'll leave. Surely you must recognize me. I've had drinks in your lounge and eaten here many times when I was in the University's grad school. My parents are from Clarksville and have stayed here often. My name is Debra Chandler."

"Oh, yes, I do recognize you now, Ms. Chandler. Your parents are lovely people and good customers. I suppose I could bend the rules a little for you. Please leave quickly after you finish in the restroom. We don't want to get in trouble with The Nashville Health Department."

"Thanks so much, I won't forget this," Debra said, out of breath, as she and Annie disappeared in the ladies' restroom. *The health department,* she thought. *If you only knew about the monster I just escaped from and what he could do to the health of a whole city, you would let me stay all day.*

After waiting as long as possible in the restroom, she came back through the lobby and left by a rear door. Immediately, she noticed the hotel's pool was still filled with water and comfortable chairs still surrounded its deck. She sat down by the side of the pool, pulling Annie close to her. Conveniently, there was a high fence around the pool so no one could see them from the street. Looking over the fence, she could see the football stadium in the distance and began to feel safer in this familiar neighborhood, hidden from view of passersby.

A pay phone was hanging on the wall. She searched in the change purse she had in her pocket for a quarter. Finding one, she went and called the police. The call was put through at once to Detective Cooke. He couldn't believe she had walked to the park or that Steiner was brazen enough to be still riding around

Nashville and had recognized her there. He promised to send patrol cars immediately to search for him around the park and warned her to stay inside the fenced pool area until she heard from him. In a few minutes, she could hear the sirens in the distance getting closer and closer. After a while, they died down, and she assumed they had no luck in finding him. She knew how slippery Dr. Steiner was and realized it could be a long time until he was apprehended.

There was a Coke machine next to the phone, so she walked back and bought one. Then she found a paper cup lying on the ground next to the phone, which she filled with water for Annie. She waited about an hour on the chaise lounge, and then just as she had given up and started to walk back to Jim's apartment, David's squad car pulled up beside her. He jumped out and first scolded her for not waiting until he gave the all-clear sign. Disappointed, he reported they had not found Steiner in spite of searching the whole area several times. He offered to give her a ride home, but she refused and said she would rather walk.

She could see the squad car following her at distance as she and Annie made their way back to Jim's apartment, this time using the side streets. *I guess they are watching to see if he will materialize again and grab me*, she thought.

When she reached Jim's apartment, David got out of his squad car and walked with her to the door. She told the detective she had no idea how Steiner could have found her in a city as large as Nashville. Probably it was a coincidence he saw her in the park.

"Well, perhaps that could have been the case, a coincidence, but, young lady, you took a terrible chance today. I guess you know that. He could have pulled a gun or knife on you and ended your life. You would be just as dead as those in Greenwood."

"I'm sorry, Officer. That was stupid of me. I should have followed Jim and your orders and stayed away from open areas and busy streets."

"That's all right. I guess the apartment got feeling small and cramped after much time there. Let's change the subject. Tell me, do you have any idea if he could be a homosexual?"

That question really floored her. It was something from time to time she had wondered about him since she had been hired a year and a half ago. "Why do you ask? Have you heard anything like that about him?"

"Well, I don't know if you know this or not, but one area around the Parthenon is well-known as a meeting place for gays. When I heard he had confronted you there, that was the first thing that popped in my mind. It's possible he had gone there to meet someone and just happened to see you there."

No, she told the detective there was no one else around when he stopped as she remembered. He simply parked his motorcycle and walked over to interrogate her, which was when her terror began, not sure what he would do to her.

Then she added after thinking some more, "I have never seen him with another man or a woman, for that matter, except in a situation related to University business, Detective Cooke. He didn't seem to be interested in people in general, sexually or otherwise. He only cared about his research. He never talked about having any friends to me, as I have told you before. He certainly never seemed to pay any attention to me or relate to me like a normal person might, never much of a smile or compliment. I don't know what he meant by touching my face or the crude remarks about my boyfriend. That seemed out of character for him."

"I don't know what he meant either. Maybe he was jealous of Dr. Tarkington in spite of you telling me he had no interest in you. But okay, everyone seems to say the same about him not being interested in friends of either sex or anything else except his work. Why I'm asking these questions is that I'm still trying to figure out what makes this guy tick. Just let me know if you think of anything else, and remember to keep out of that park." David tipped his hat to her and left.

Debra let herself in and fell down on the beat-up couch in Jim's apartment. She took several deep breaths. Shaking off nervousness, she went to the phone and called Jim at the medical center to tell him about the latest developments. A nurse took the call for him and said she would have him return the call when he got out of a meeting.

CHAPTER THIRTY

At two, Jim called back. She described the events of the morning and included the visit to the park. At first, he seemed upset and irritated with her since she had crossed West End Avenue against his advice. After hearing the tension in his voice, she decided not to mention Steiner's crude comments.

He was also shocked that Steiner had found her so easily in the park. "I don't think he was following you, and I doubt he knows where I live or that you are staying with me. He could have just been riding by and saw you crossing the street with Annie, but you were like a sitting duck in that park, Debra." He almost yelled these last words to her over the phone.

Finally, he cooled down and said he was relieved nothing had happened to her and that she was back safe in his apartment after encountering Steiner. And yes, he had heard that Centennial Park was a hangout for gays in Nashville but didn't think that was anything Steiner would be involved in. Jim too thought Steiner was the type of person who was aloof to everyone regardless of their gender and was distrustful of any type of intimacy. Then he reminded her about what her cousin had said about his childhood growing up as a loner in Greenwood.

"Jim, I agree with everything you have said, but what I can't believe is he's still hanging around Nashville. I thought he would have left the country by now. And where do you think he has been hiding? His house and his lab are locked up. Where could he get any more clothes or money for food or gas for his motorcycle, for that matter?"

"Probably he's staying in a motel where no one would recognize him, or maybe he has a second residence. I had an idea he had several bank accounts. David Cooke and I had this discussion yesterday. The police today got permission from this bank to check on his accounts, and surprise, all the accounts were closed this morning after the raid last night on his house, and the money was withdrawn. I was told the balances totaled over $800,000. I knew he was well paid but not that well paid."

"What, I can't believe he had that much money. I saw one of his paystubs on his desk, and there was no way he could have saved that much on the medical center's salary. What did he do with the money he withdrew, did the police tell you?"

"Some was taken in cash, but most of it was wired to a bank in Mexico, the Grand Caymans, probably. I think he had prepared for the possibility of being caught and set up the foreign bank account. He bought the motorcycle sometime ago. Now who can guess what other plans he has."

"At this point, Jim, I can't worry about his future plans. I only wish I knew when he is going to be captured. I don't like the thought he is roaming around out here, ready to kill me. I'll always have to be looking over my shoulder, searching for him. He had some idea that I was the one who alerted the police about the poisoning of Greenwood's water, but I certainly denied it vehemently to him. I hope he didn't realize I was quaking with fear when we were standing in the park. I tried to reassure him I hadn't talked to the police and pray he'll leave me alone."

"Debra, if you want me to guess when Steiner will be caught, I have no idea. Perhaps they'll catch him soon but then maybe not. It seems like to me they would have found him by now if they were going to. Steiner must be the master of escape, and maybe he is a master of disguise too. Those are good traits to have if you are on the run."

Debra took a deep breath and looked out the window of his apartment. "I'm exhausted and frightened about all that has happened, Jim. I no longer feel very brave. I'm afraid he will hunt me down and try to kill me. I think I should leave Nashville until he is caught. I can go to Clarksville and stay with my parents through Thanksgiving and then go visit Elizabeth. I hope you'll understand. It doesn't mean I don't want to be with you."

"Debra, baby, I'll miss you a lot, but I don't blame you for wanting to leave for a while until they catch this guy. Maybe you would be safer if you go to your parents' home, in case he's stalking you. I understand completely. Just don't forget to come back and make it sooner than later. You must know how I feel about you. Needless to say, you can stay with me as long as you like when you return. Just as I told you before, I still think you will be safe at my apartment because I don't think he knows where I live."

Abruptly, Jim changed the subject because he had some good news to share with her for a change. "They are going to let me off early tonight, probably Dr. Scott's doings. I want to take you out for dinner, nothing fancy, to make up for the one we missed last Saturday night. I know about an Italian restaurant where the parking lot is right in front of the restaurant. We can drive up practically to the door, go right in, and get a table in the back of the room. Steiner couldn't see us eating in there from the road. I think we need to spend some quiet time together, relax, and forget about all this drama for at least an evening."

"A dinner date, that sounds like a good idea. I would like to forget about this nightmare too for a few hours, and we need some time together, a dinner date, great. I love the sound of it. I agree one hundred percent."

She then took a deep breath and asked, "Please, you must know that I care a lot about you, Jim, even though we haven't known each other for such a long time. And I hesitate to bring this up, but I probably would like to know where our relationship is headed."

Jim thought to himself, *Where is this conversation headed?* He told her they should save that topic to be answered at another time and promised he would get off early and pick her up at the apartment. Then he hung up the phone and returned to the ward.

True to his word, they went out for a needed break. The evening proved relaxing for both of them, much to Debra's surprised since she had been worried they would have to be on the lookout for Steiner, not only that night, but for a long time to come. She laughed at Jim's silly jokes and put thoughts of her former boss behind her for the evening.

The lasagna could have been made in Italy and the cheap red wine went down easily. When they finished the bottle, they toasted each other. Jim leaned over and pulled her head close to his, and gave her a lingering kiss. Several other diners looked at the attractive couple in the corner and smiled. No one would have any idea what they had been through the last few days or guess they had helped solve the water-poisoning incident in Greenwood to which the media had given round the clock coverage.

After dinner, they drove to her vacant town house, and she picked up clothes for her trip. Jim sat in the car and watched for Steiner while she was in the house. The street was deserted. There was no sign of him or his motorcycle. As they were pulling out of the complex's circular drive, a squad car cruised by. They concluded that in addition to keeping a watch over them, the police were periodically driving by her house, probably checking it out in case Steiner tried to break in.

The next day at the apartment before she could leave, she got a call from David Cooke saying that the police needed more help. He asked her to come in and go through Dr. Steiner's personal things in his office desk even though they had searched there several times previously. He also had more questions that he thought she could help answer. She drove to the hospital to meet with him, nervous to be around the lab and the medical center again.

In Steiner's office were dusty piles of old journals, minutes from meetings he had attended on undergraduate education across campus, and correspondence with scientists from other parts of the country. It all looked innocent enough. None of the material she looked through seemed to link him to the water poisoning or was damaging in any way. There was nothing suggesting anything out of the ordinary, unlike what they had found in the locked lab or his house. She couldn't shed any light on his things, and disappointed, the detective started to leave.

Just then, Debra found his Day Timer, which had been hidden under a pile of journals on DNA research. She handed David Cooke the pocket-sized calendar. Together they looked at his day-by-day schedule for the last five months. David turned to the weekend they were most interested in, September 20 to September 22, but there was nothing there except a note as a reminder to get wood for the fireplace.

David commented, "That's sure strange. As I recall, the bungalow had no fireplace, but I better check that out again. I'm not giving up on Steiner as the prime suspect, Debra. After all, it's too much of a coincidence for someone to have developed new bacteria, have the same cultures in his lab at work and home, and also the same bacteria was found in Greenwood patients and their water supply. I don't think it was a strange coincidence that all this has happened. Just because his lab notes said something was added to CL might not mean Crystal Lake, but in my mind it did, it was the reservoir."

The detective was disappointed since, essentially, no new information had been found in his office. Everyone was hoping the case would be tied up nice and tidy, and the suspect arrested. He told Debra he would continue to look for any new information and would let her know later how the investigation stood. Then he gave her a weak smile and left the lab.

Debra ate lunch in the cafeteria with her friends one last time after telling them she could not talk about Dr. Steiner's lab being closed and planned to visit her parents for several weeks. Then she went back to room 425 and cleaned out her own desk. She packed up her notebooks, reference books, and an assortment of pens and folders in several boxes. There was a picture of Annie playing with a ball, which she wrapped carefully in paper and put in her purse.

Human resources had already offered her a new position in another section of the medical center's complex. But she decided to decline the offer at least for a while. She felt the uncontrollable urge to get away from the medical center and all the bad memories she associated with it.

She planned to stay with her parents in Clarksville at least through Thanksgiving. There she would feel safe and not be always looking over her shoulder for Steiner. In spite of trying to get a good night's sleep last night, she had tossed and turned, being still emotionally and mentally exhausted by the week's events. She hoped she could recover her sense of equilibrium in her parents' quiet home. Even running into her ex on the street or in a store didn't seem so bad now.

After spending Thanksgiving with them, she might decide to go on to Greenwood to visit Elizabeth and could return to Nashville by the first of December, providing Steiner was caught. When she explained to Jim what her final plans were, he was very understanding. She had already invited him to spend Christmas at her parents' home and told him that she knew they would like him as much as she.

Yesterday, she called them to say she was coming home and would stay until after Thanksgiving. They were shocked. Her mother seemed especially worried and thought it spelled trouble with her new boyfriend. Her father suspected it had to do with her job and right away asked how she could take off so much time from work. When she answered, it was a complicated story, but in essence, she had quit, there was silence on the other end of the line.

Her mother asked one question after another in such rapid fashion she had to say, "Stop, Mom, I'll tell you the whole story when I get home tomorrow." By now she could see they were probably thinking their talented daughter whom they used to be so proud of seemed to be in a mess again, first the divorce and now no job after spending two years getting a master's degree.

She looked in her rearview mirror at the medical center as she drove away. What a great feeling to leave that large complex of buildings behind and the problems brewing there. The decision not to take another job for at least a while was certainly the right choice for her.

Now that she had decided to leave and there was no turning back, Debra could hardly wait to get out of the city. She drove straight to Jim's apartment to pick up Annie and her suitcase. She said goodbye to the building's janitor, who shook his head over all the comings and goings of Dr. Tarkington and his woman. He hoped they weren't in any trouble because the police had been there yesterday asking about them again.

As she headed toward Clarksville, she felt she might be able relax and smile in the comfort of her parents' home. A wonderful sense of relief washed over her body the farther she got from Nashville. She would have to handle carefully any questions from her parents and only give them a brief overview of the situation at the medical center. She hoped she could explain the situation leaving out many details so not to alarm them too much. Of course, she wouldn't mention to her father, yet, she had been staying at Jim's apartment, leaving the town house empty and unguarded. Actually, the police went by at times, checking to see if Steiner was around, so she wasn't worried about it, but all that worrisome information would be better held back for another day.

CHAPTER THIRTY-ONE

For the next few weeks, Jim himself could barely keep up with the department's admissions as early cases of flu hit the Nashville area. He fell badly behind with his research at the medical center and was so busy during the long work days he hardly knew Debra had left, not that he would tell her that. She called several times to ask how he was doing; usually late in the evening when she knew he would be at home. He could picture her wearing white pajamas and lying in her Clarksville bed, dark hair spread out over the pillows while she talked to him. Then as exhausted as he was, he later had trouble falling asleep, missing her kisses and warm body in the frigid temperature of the University apartment.

Jim didn't tell Debra over the phone, but he knew from the first time he spoke to her that, he could easily fall in love. Secretly, he was planning to visit a jeweler another resident had recommended when he found time. He knew the purchase had to be before the visit to Clarksville to meet her parents since he wanted to surprise her with a ring at Christmas. When the actual wedding date could be, he was not sure perhaps, late spring.

Naturally the ring's cost was a problem since his bank account was low with no hope of increasing until he went out in practice. He knew Debra was used to very nice things though she never talked much about her material possessions. But after all, her dad, probably had tons of money since he was a bank president in Clarksville, and her ex's family even owned a furniture store.

The days relentlessly rolled on, and he spent every spare minute working on the paper about a modern-day typhoid epidemic to be published in Dr. Scott's journal. The major part of the paper would be the identification and description of the bacteria mutant and its development by Steiner.

The CDC had sent pages of data, which would have to be deciphered. Their information was in a more sophisticated form than that of Mark Rosenthal's from the campus labs. Because of the huge amount of complex data, Dr. Scott had even half-jokingly said he would have to come down to Jim's lab and help.

He wanted Jim to prepare some graphs and charts comparing the two sets of data, which would help them get a handle on how to write the paper. It was exciting stuff, as Dr. Scott mentioned several times, and he was anxious for Jim to finish the paper. Just to think, a town's water supply had been poisoned by an artificially developed mutant. This was an electrifying subject, and no one in their right mind would have thought it possible in the past.

The cat was still not out of the bag about Steiner's exact role in poisoning the water in Greenwood. Rumors and more rumors swirled around the medical center, which had not allowed Dr. Scott, Mark Rosenthal, or Jim to give out any additional information other than what was already known. Regardless, local and national news organizations were clamoring for interviews. The attorneys were still worried about the University's reputation if word got out that Steiner had actually produced the mutation on the medical center's property. They hoped to downplay its involvement in the trouble at Greenwood.

The police and district attorney would only say that a person of interest who had worked at the medical center was being sought in the Nashville area, and it was hoped he might know something about the water problems in Greenwood.

Greenwood itself was slowly recovering from the devastating events of a few weeks ago, but progress was difficult to measure. Those patients who were infected and didn't die immediately suffered from the lingering symptoms of the infection, which would probably plague them for many months to come. No one in the city seemed to be in a good mood even if they had not been sick. Those people were still nervous about catching the disease or worried about the return of the illness in other family members and friends.

No one trusted the water supply, Harry, or his staff anymore. People only felt safe if either their water came from a well or if they lived in the area around the hospital whose water was on a separate system. To the relief of those working at the hospital, the patients with the severest form of the disease finally responded to advanced types of experimental antibiotics developed by the CDC. After the first two weeks, no more deaths occurred, and most of the survivors were on a slow but difficult road for recovery.

The city fathers tried to reassure their citizens that the water was now safe to use, safe to drink, and they could use it without fearing the illness. The city had received a federal grant to try to help life return to normal, but so far, it was a slow process. As the mayor liked to say, next spring they would worry about the return of the tourists and their economy, but for now, they were taking one day at a time.

In Atlanta, the CDC was attempting to further decipher the DNA strands of the mutant. It was hard to understand how it was able to slip through the filtration and chemical procedures of the water company. Dr. Marcum made several trips back to Greenwood and met with Harry at the water company and the people at the clinical lab. So far, much of the action of the bacteria remained a mystery to everyone.

As it had been said many times, the bacteria seemed to look like a simple *E. coli*, but in fact, under its membrane was hidden a DNA sequence more deadly than that found in nature. Many of the microbiologists had questioned the role that the colonies' faint pink color played in the life cycle of the mutant. The CDC could only answer that when Steiner developed the mutant, he had either on purpose or accidently added a genetic tag whose DNA produced the pigment. While it seemed to have no role in the metabolism of the bacteria, the color was certainly useful in the isolation of its colonies as the researchers noted.

Misery and gloom was the atmosphere in the town when Debra arrived at Elizabeth's home the Friday after Thanksgiving for a visit. She had spent most of November with her parents and celebrated a peaceful Thanksgiving there. Her parents fortunately didn't ask too any questions, so Debra felt rested and refreshed when she left and enjoyed the beautiful drive to Greenwood while she listened to music on WSM.

Elizabeth met her at the kitchen door of her home with a hug and kiss on her cheek. "You don't know how I've missed you!" she exclaimed with tears in her eyes. Even though Debra and she had talked several times on the phone, there was still a lot of catching up to do. Elizabeth had made a pizza, and the two sat up for several hours after dinner, going over all the incredible events of the last few weeks.

Elizabeth told Debra that her boss, Taylor Whitney, was seeing forty to fifty patients a day either at the office or the hospital, as were most of the other doctors. She also added almost as a sad afterthought, he and his wife had gotten back together after they almost lost their younger child to typhoid fever. Taylor acted embarrassed, but confessed to Elizabeth about the reunion with his wife one day after the office had closed. He had given up the studio apartment he had been living in and moved back in the big house last weekend. Surely he prayed their marriage would be stronger after the near death of their son.

"As I told you, Debra, the weekend the epidemic hit, Claudia was still planning to go to Nashville again with some of her girlfriends she runs around with, you know, Greenwood's country club set. As usual, she would have left poor Taylor at home to babysit rather than catch up on his sleep. I think he had some trouble persuading her to cancel the trip even when he was overwhelmed seeing patients in the hospital and half the town was sick."

"Well, Elizabeth, how did she think he could take care of the patients and his children at the same time?"

Elizabeth shook her head in disgust. "Who knows how her mind works, I can hardly stand to be in the same room with her, Debra. After almost losing her son to typhoid, I guess Claudia finally realized their family and marriage meant more to her than she knew. Taylor said she was very shaken and asked for forgiveness for her irresponsible behavior and filing for the divorce. Do you know before he moved back in, she came every day, looking very sexy, and brought lunch to him for a week? They ate in his office with the door closed. Peggy and I could only use our imagination with what was going on inside."

Elizabeth stared out the window and added, "One day, she stopped by in the afternoon and told us she was planning to redecorate the office in the spring. She felt the decor had been neglected and needed updated. According to her, new furniture will make the patients relax and forget the horrors of the epidemic. That's just what Peggy and I need, Claudia and her decorator moving furniture around and measuring for drapes while we have an office full of patients."

And then she explained to Debra while wiping away tears, "He's a wonderful man, the kindest man in the world. I only hope Claudia can appreciate him. I personally can't forgive her for trying to turn the children against their father. Then speak of poetic justice, their son was stricken with typhoid, and this kind husband whom she wanted to divorce was responsible for saving the child's life and others in the hospital too. I would say she always has had misplaced priorities, shopping and running around with the party set. At one time, I heard she was having an affair with the thirty-year-old tennis pro at the club, but I don't know if that was true or not." She then went back to the kitchen to return with the bottle of Chardonnay to refill their glasses.

Even though she had never told Debra her true feelings for Taylor Whitney, obviously Debra knew but wisely said nothing and only patted Elizabeth on the back. Elizabeth collapsed on the sofa with more tears.

After calming down and getting her emotions in check, Elizabeth said she wanted to hear more details about the events in Nashville. She never really understood how Debra's boss was implicated in the typhoid epidemic. First, Debra said that Elizabeth would have to promise everything she heard would be held in confidence. Elizabeth naturally agreed. Debra then told her in greater detail than she had over the phone how she and Jim had stolen the cultures from Steiner's lab, then explained how the campus microbiology department had identified it, and shown it was a new form of the typhoid bacteria. When the lab proved it was the same terrible bacteria that had been found in Greenwood, the University authorities and the police decided to arrest Steiner.

"You see Elizabeth, I had seen pink tinted colonies in his locked lab a year and a half before the mutant showed up in the reservoir so he must had been experimenting with it for months."

Debra continued, "Guess what, Elizabeth, the day before they planned to arrest him, I called in sick I was so terrified of him by then, and the next morning he came by my house and banged on the door, I suppose to see if I was really ill. When I didn't answer, he left a note that said he needed me to help run an important experiment and wanted to discuss the future of my job with him. After that visit, I was even more scared than ever. Now he knew where I lived. Jim urged me to move in with him, which I did. We didn't think Steiner would know where to search for me in a large apartment building."

"I guess that was nice for both of you at that point," Elizabeth added with a smile and wink.

"It was, except when I was worrying about being killed, really, Elizabeth! Well, anyway, when the police tried to arrest him on the night of November the first, he escaped and continued to elude the dragnet the police set out for him. Now this was not the smartest thing I've ever done, but a day or two later, I got bored sitting in Jim's apartment and decided to take Annie for a walk in Centennial Park. You may not believe this, but somehow Steiner found me there and threatened me in no uncertain terms. I thought he was going to kill me at that point, but for some reason, he allowed me to escape. I ran to the hotel across the street and called the police and stayed there until a Nashville detective found me."

"Gosh, Debra, I can see how you were scared he would kill you when he found you in the park. I know you think you're lucky to be alive, but I don't think he would have tried to kill you in the open like that with cars and people around. He does sound like the creepiest of creeps in my book. Thank heavens you had Jim and the Nashville police looking out for you."

"Well, I should have been carrying a can of mace in my pocket, but I didn't have one. Maybe Annie would have attacked him if he tried to hurt me, who knows. In the past, I felt very confident that I could take care of myself in most situations, until all these awful events occurred. But now I don't know how brave I am. I was afraid much of the time when I was in Nashville in spite of Jim being there. To tell you the truth, Elizabeth, we are all vulnerable when we are confronted by a mentally ill person like Dr. Steiner. Regardless, in the park he let me go, but if I ever meet him again, I may not be so lucky."

"Mentally ill or is he just evil, Debra? It seems to me he is some of both. Don't ever feel sorry for him. There must have been something more analytical going in his mind than just acting like a textbook case from psychology 101. He planned to kill so many innocent people and did kill some of them. Was it some ego trip to see how much damage he could do? It's almost as though he created a Frankenstein-like bacteria instead of a monster like in Shelley's tale."

Debra thought and answered carefully, "Some would say it was the pain inflicted on him as a child that caused him to act the way he did. Because of this, he wasn't completely responsible for his actions. But others might argue his soul was consumed with evil, and he didn't care about the consequences of his actions, even enjoyed knowing about the pain he caused others to suffer. A Catholic priest I knew in graduate school might have taken this side of the argument and said evil walks the earth as do good angels."

"Well, evil or mentally ill, who knows what he is. The only thing I know is killing is a sin, and that is what he did even if by an unusual method. Do you remember that guy who shot the people from the bell tower at the University of Texas? I have been thinking about him and how angry he apparently was, taking it out on complete strangers walking across campus. Steiner's actions could be similar, but he used poison in our water instead of bullets. I guess he hoped to get some of those who teased him when he lived here, but he killed innocent strangers too."

Then Elizabeth put the dirty plates and wine glasses in the dishwasher and continued, "I think maybe we should go talk with someone who knew him when he lived in Greenwood as a kid. If we find out anything worthwhile, you could pass the information along to the Nashville police."

Elizabeth suggested. "Maybe what we learn might help them to track him down. They could use any information we come up with to try to figure out his motives or even where he could be hiding."

So with this scheme in mind, Elizabeth arranged for them to meet the retired head of the high school chemistry department. According to the school personnel office, Steiner had been his star pupil. They hoped to find out what he remembered about a younger Steiner when they met with him tomorrow.

CHAPTER THIRTY-TWO

ON THE THIRD day of Debra's visit, they drove to a small frame house in an older part of town and were invited in by Mitchell Ball, a short bald man in his mid-seventies. After seating the women in his pleasant living room, he brought out a tray of tea and cookies for them to share. Mr. Ball told them immediately how lucky he was to have escaped the illness and still be alive. They were the first guests he had had in weeks, and he was pleased to have them pay him a visit now that the worse danger was over.

"Once I read about the citywide illness in the paper, because of my age, I didn't think I should go out. I just stayed in the house, afraid to leave. Now I still think I should keep away from crowds as much as possible and not take any chances. So I have gone out only to buy groceries and have skipped church and the Kiwanis meetings I usually attended each week. I've heard all the reports about the water's safety but don't believe their accuracy. I'm still using bottled water. Not only do I drink it, but I use boiled water to brush my teeth and take a bath. It's a pain to heat that much water on the stove, I must admit."

Elizabeth agreed with him that all the residents living in Greenwood couldn't afford to be careless. She was doing much of the same as he at her office where they were still using bottled water to drink or water that had been boiled for other uses.

"Fortunately, I live in the county and can use my well water which is safe to drink. Now I'm going to change the subject and want to inquire what you remember about a student you had had a long time ago, a Joe Steiner," she carefully asked.

"Yes, of course, I remember him well, ladies," Mr. Ball said as he slowly sipped the tea. "He was probably the most brilliant student I ever taught. He never forgot a fact and could reason his way through any problem I might present to him. If mine were not tough enough, he would find one in a book which would be more challenging. His parents were certainly proud of his success. When he won the scholarship to the big eastern University, they were ecstatic. Of course, that is the bright side of the story. He had a dark side to his personality as well."

Debra leaned closer to his chair and asked him to explain what he meant by that comment, but actually, she already felt she knew what he was going to say. She hoped he would fill them in on more particulars of his high school years and homelife.

"Well, Steiner never smiled much or seemed to enjoy a joke, anyone would tell you that, but the problems with his personality went much deeper. In fact, it seemed he could not understand the most basic human manners or kindness. For instance, he never thanked me for the extra time I spent with him or for the glowing recommendations that I wrote to various colleges for his admittance. After he won the scholarship and left for the school up east, I never heard from him again. I have no idea where he is now, nor do I much care. He had no friends at school, and I always understood why."

Elizabeth told him about the incident on the school bus that she had witnessed and how sorry she felt for the then boy.

"Well, I guess things like that made him resentful of the other kids with good reason. I know he spent a lot of time in his family's cabin deep in the woods doing God knows what. I saw that cabin a few years ago, still standing, but barely, while I was hiking. I believe his parents, whom he treated with great indifference are both dead now, passed away quite a few years ago, but why did you want to know about Steiner?"

Debra spoke up and asked Mr. Ball to hold what she was about to tell him in great confidentiality and slowly explained that he might not be able to believe the information she was going to give him today. First Joseph Steiner had become a world authority on recumbent DNA research, and she had worked for him in Nashville. Then as carefully as possible, she described the trouble his former student was in. Even though he had reached the pinnacle of success in DNA research, he was now wanted by the police in several states in connection with the possible poisoning of Greenwood's water.

At first, Mitchell Ball could hardly believe a person who was so well-known and accomplished in science could have done such a thing. He was dumbfounded and also surprised to learn he had been living in Nashville for some time because he remembered him saying he hated the South. But then he began to recall the weird peculiarities and arrogance a younger Steiner had exhibited. After thinking some more, he conceded that perhaps he was capable of such deliberate actions. He told them he would be glad to talk to the police to shed any light on Steiner's school history or motives from his earlier life. He had no idea where he could be now since he had lost all contact with him after graduation. He only prayed the police would apprehend him soon. As the meeting ended and they were leaving, he thanked them profusely for coming, adding he hoped they would keep him posted on Steiner's whereabouts.

As they drove away, Debra glanced around the neighborhoods they were passing through and remarked how disturbing it was to see the turmoil that still existed in Greenwood. Unlike the pristine city that she would have enjoyed visiting four weeks ago, it appeared almost like a war zone in a foreign country and certainly not in the United States.

"Look, Elizabeth, at this trash and garbage still piled up on all the streets, what a disgusting mess!" exclaimed Debra.

"Well, the sanitation people have experienced as much illness as any other department in the city government and are just now catching up on the pickups. Nothing is working now in Greenwood."

While they were driving, Elizabeth told Debra even educated people like Mr. Ball were nervous about drinking the water, so they also were using bottled water for drinking and washing their teeth. A few like him would not even use the water for bathing unless they first boiled it.

Morale was low in Greenwood, and nothing the authorities could say seemed to improve the people's mood. Many of the city services, like the sanitation department, were not running at full steam. For instance, the parks and recreation department had not even bothered to put up any Christmas lights, and the annual Christmas parade had been canceled. Schools were back in session, but not all the students had returned. Several of her teacher friends reported their classes were behind several weeks with lesson plans.

Usually the trendy shops at this time of year were decorated to the hilt for the holidays, but now the merchants had only made half-hearted attempts to get the shoppers in the Christmas spirit with a few trees and anemic strings of lights. Sales were down, and no wonder, with many of the residents either recovering from the illness or helping other family members get back on their feet.

Both the water company and the health department had issued reports saying the tests had confirmed the water was safe now to drink, but most people didn't believe them. The new ozone treatment, extra filtration, and chemical treatments had apparently removed all traces of the bacteria, according to Harry. These reports came out at the end of November and were followed by the CDC bulletins saying essentially the same. Still people ignored the reports, and no one could blame them. At least there was no news of other water systems being poisoned, and state officials were almost ready to breathe a sigh of relief, according to the news media and Elizabeth.

After leaving Mr. Ball's home, Elizabeth suggested they should take a detour and visit Aunt Susan at the nursing home, which was in another part of the county. Susan had been asking about Debra, and she agreed they should stop by for a short visit.

When they pulled on the driveway of Sunshine Retirement Home, Debra could see a low-lying ranch structure arranged in the shape of a U. Elizabeth told her the home had been built by a local doctor twenty years ago and was so popular with the county's older folk there was a long waiting list to get in. Debra had not seen Susan for several years and was a little shocked to see how she had aged when she met them in the entrance hall. The three of them had a pleasant time sitting on the home's sun porch talking about relatives they all remembered from family reunions at the state park. As they were leaving, several of the residents told Elizabeth, whom they knew worked for a local doctor, how lucky they felt to have well water to drink at the home and not have to use city water. Debra wondered out loud if the water company would ever get its good reputation back.

Debra offered to take Elizabeth out to dinner after they left the nursing home since it was after five, but Elizabeth chose to go back to the house and cook. While she was frying pork chops, she admitted she was a little like Mr. Ball because she wasn't sure about the city's water and preferred to drink the well water, which she knew was safe.

A few nights before Debra left, Elizabeth's friend Roger came over after work for dinner. He brought her a dozen long-stemmed roses in a cut glass vase and told Debra he was very grateful to Elizabeth for helping him when he was ill. He chatted easily with them, bringing both up-to-date on how the store's employees were doing. About half had been hospitalized, while others were still out sick, recovering at home.

He found that actually, the store could operate just fine with a few less clerks and was in an upbeat mood being particularly pleased at the sales increase the store had had since the epidemic hit. Bottled water sales, especially, were off the charts, and his suppliers could hardly keep up with the demand.

When they were cleaning up the kitchen after he left, Debra told Elizabeth he seemed very kind and sincere. Probably, she should give him a second look. Debra thought to herself that Elizabeth needed to settle down with a stable man like Roger and not be pining over what was already taken. But she didn't repeat thoughts like these to Elizabeth and only added she liked Roger and found him attractive.

CHAPTER THIRTY-THREE

Debra stayed three more days at Elizabeth's and talked to Jim late every night after he got off work. Finally, they decided there was too much heartache not to be together, so the next morning, she put Annie and her suitcase in the car, said goodbye to Elizabeth, and drove back to Nashville. As she told Jim, she was sick and tired of wondering if Steiner would reappear in their lives. They should refuse to be a victim in his plans and pretend the past month had been a bad dream. Everything that happened with Steiner should be forgotten, and they should get on with their lives.

She carried her suitcase into Jim's apartment, using the key he had given her. This felt like it was her home now too. She had no thoughts of even considering going back to the town house. During the many conversations Jim and she had had over the phone, they had come to some type of understanding about their relationship though it would be hard for her to put the commitment in so many words. She knew they agreed they would be together no matter what happened, but exactly what together meant hadn't been spelled out.

Jim flatly told her he was too busy until Christmas to figure out how a formal commitment and future plans would work. After all, in July, he would have to decided on a place to practice, and Debra might not want to live where he had offers to go. Debra didn't tell him, but she knew she wouldn't be picky where they were going to live as long as he would be there too. Wisely, she was willing to let him take his time deciding about their permanent relationship.

Debra knew her parents were anxious to meet Jim. Her mother was especially worried about Debra's future and hoped

Jim would make her happier than the first husband whom she had approved of at first, heavens knows why. Debra had told them in general details about the trouble she had had with Steiner, leaving out the more troublesome details. After hearing only the censored version of Steiner' misdeeds, they were still horrified and relieved that she was living with Jim and not by herself. Of course, they might say publicly they believed in marriage and not cohabitation, but Nashville was far enough away that their church friends wouldn't know about Debra's living arrangement.

What to do with the town house was a problem. Debra wasn't sure how to solve that. Jim still thought it was too risky to live there since Steiner knew where it was, and no one knew where Steiner was. She had told her parents she would rather stay in the house staff apartment building, as decrepit and crowded as it was, rather than move back to the town house. She suggested her parents could possibly rent it or even put it on the market now. They talked it over and told her to wait and see what would happen in the next few months before any hasty decisions were made. She didn't tell them, but she felt she would be moving wherever Jim chose to go in practice in July when his training came to an end. Then they would have an empty town house on their hands.

Debra hung her clothes in the small closet and had been in the apartment waiting for several hours when she finally heard the key in the lock. She threw herself in his arms and broke down in tears of joy to be with him again. Jim wiped his own eyes as they sank into the old couch.

After several hours of joyful lovemaking and they were sitting across from each other, half dressed, at the tiny kitchen table, Jim went over what had transpired in the Steiner investigation, which was essentially nothing.

"Deb, I hate to tell you this, but the police seem still stymied, no leads or any sign of him. If they know anything, they aren't sharing it with Dr. Scott or me. I heard that most of the patients in Greenwood are getting better, so at least that's positive. We all learned much more than we wished to about a disease which was eradicated fifty years ago in most of the world."

Debra was happy to be back in Nashville and, on the first three days, caught up on the mail that she had told the post office to hold while she was out of town. Jim was working day and night and hardly had time to talk to her after the passionate reunion the first night. Finally, needing something to do, she looked around the sparse apartment and tried to rearrange the furniture in the tiny space. That proved to be impossible, considering what she had to work with. Then she gave the place a much-needed cleaning, even scrubbing the tile on the kitchen and bathroom floors.

At the end of her first week in Jim's apartment, Detective Cooke called to talk to Debra to arrange a meeting, hoping she had thought of some leads for him to follow. As he told Debra, they had reached a cold trail, seemingly with no possibilities of finding Steiner. The police guessed by now he was living in another country under an alias. The following morning, David met her for coffee in the same hotel to which she had escaped after being accosted by Steiner in the park.

He told her she looked much better than the last time he saw her, scared and exhausted, as he ordered coffee and doughnuts for them both. She took a sip of the hot beverage and at first said she had nothing new to add to the information she had originally given him. Then suddenly she remembered a part of the conversation she and Elizabeth had with Professor Ball.

"David, I remember he said Dr. Steiner spent a lot of time as a youth playing in the woods since his parents had a cabin about five miles from town. He didn't know if it was still standing now, but a few years ago, he was hiking and saw it from the trail. It was covered with vegetation and difficult to see from the road."

David Cooke wrinkled his nose and thought for a minute. Then thought some more and said, "Well, maybe that is something I should look into. It's possible he could be hiding out in the cabin, and after all, there was that strange note in Steiner's Day Timer about remembering to buy firewood though his house in Nashville had no fireplace." The more he thought, the more excited he got and abruptly left, with Debra still sitting at the table with a cold cup of coffee and a half-eaten doughnut.

Since that meeting with David, she heard nothing from the Nashville police. After another week of sitting around the apartment with only a few books to read and Annie for company, she got really, really bored. The park was off-limits to walk to, not that she would care to repeat that dreadful morning when Dr. Steiner had confronted her there, so she walked Annie each day on the few side streets close to the apartment.

She had been in contact with Michelle and Linda after she got back, so she decided to go to the hospital and have lunch with them one day. They were waiting for her at the entrance of the cafeteria and each friend gave her a hug and kiss when she came through the door. They insisted on buying her lunch and then after going through the food line found their old table and sat down to eat.

Of course, from the newspaper and TV reports, everyone at the hospital knew about Steiner's run-in with the police, being fired by the administration, and the closure of his research facilities. Because of this information and gossip floating around, her friends knew Debra no longer had a job but were careful not to mention this fact, not wanting to embarrass her. They also knew she was staying in Jim's apartment and were happy for her but were not sure why she no longer lived in her comfortable townhouse or for that matter why the both of them didn't live there instead of the awful staff apartment building. So they avoided that topic too.

Just as they were starting on their sandwiches, Carolyn Moss breezed through the cafeteria doors and joined them for lunch. She told Debra she was glad to find her in the cafeteria since she didn't have her current phone number and knew Debra no longer worked at the medical center. Her department was in a pickle because one of the girls in microbiology was going on maternity leave next week. The C-section was scheduled for the following Friday. She wondered if Debra would like to substitute for about eight weeks there. It would really help her department, and she hoped Debra could work until the other girl returned.

"Gosh, Carolyn, you're asking me at just the right time. You don't know how bored I am after a week just sitting in Jim's apartment. The temporary job sounds like something I'd like to do. I'll say yes, but before I do, I need to ask you if I can have a few days off at Christmas. I've already promised my parents I would come home, and I've invited Jim to come along too."

Linda punched Michelle under the table, thinking there might be a spring wedding for them to attend after all.

"Of course, you can have Christmas off, darling. I'm just relieved you can take the job." Carolyn was thrilled she had solved a problem for the lab director because it wasn't easy to get someone to help for such a relatively short time. After finishing lunch, the women walked out of the cafeteria together. Carolyn suggested she and Debra should go up to the clinical lab so Debra could sign some paperwork before she started to work the next week.

"Just remember, Carolyn, I don't know a lot about the clinical side of lab work, but I feel confident you'll be a great teacher," Debra warned before she picked up the pen. Then she thought that history is repeating itself since she had told the med tech in Greenwood about her lack of training in clinical labs too.

After Debra showed up for work in the clinical lab on the following Monday, Carolyn monitored her every move, but after a few days, Carolyn could see Debra knew what she was doing, so she turned her loose, identifying in coming samples and talking to doctors about their patients' lab results. Carolyn was grateful she had someone she could trust working in the lab, thinking our lab's gain was the research department's loss.

CHAPTER THIRTY-FOUR

TWO WEEKS AFTER Debra left Greenwood, Elizabeth finished work on Friday afternoon. She decided to stop by a small grocery on her way home. A cold wind was blowing in from the north, and snow flurries were predicted for later that night. She knew that the large chain grocery where she usually shopped would be packed this time of day with everyone buying supplies for the weekend since snow was in the forecast. The small grocery, little more than a 7-Eleven, was on the edge of town and was uncharacteristically crowded that afternoon. It seemed many people had the same idea as she had. Elizabeth was in the cereal aisle, trying to decide between a box of Special K, which she knew was healthy because she had just finished diligently reading the label, on a box of Frosted Flakes, which she had loved since a child. She was wrestling with her conscience, when one of the girls from the hospital's clinical lab approached her, pushing a small cart piled high with groceries.

"Hi, Elizabeth, I guess you're loading up too, in case we get more snow than they're predicting. I'm so glad I've run into you because I wanted to ask, how's your cousin doing? You may not remember, but she really helped us for a few hours when we were overwhelmed with specimens that first weekend of the epidemic. When typhoid fever hit our town, no one knew what it was or what to do, so doctors were ordering every test in the book. We were knee-deep in requests, and she helped us plate out the swabs. Debra seemed so talented and picked up our procedures very easily. We loved having someone with her training in our lab. We really didn't have to show her anything. I understand she works in some high-powered research lab in Nashville."

"I guess I did know she helped you but had forgotten. That weekend seems so long ago now," Elizabeth replied in a tired voice, thinking how she would like to forget all memories about the epidemic.

"I was told she was here with a friend, a boyfriend and a doctor too, I suppose. He was cute. Actually, I saw him in the cafeteria talking with some local doctors. She told us he was collecting data about the epidemic for his research in Nashville. Whatever became of that report? Did he ever write it, or do you know?"

Elizabeth lowered her voice so everyone around them would not overhear their conversation and answered, "I believe he is probably working on the paper as we speak. The subject matter is complicated and not something he can finish in a short time. I would guess it won't be published until next year. Oh yes, you asked about Debra too. Well, she was just here two weeks ago. She spent Thanksgiving with her parents before coming here for a visit to see me. Then she went back to Nashville, where her boyfriend lives. And about her job, actually she no longer has that job in Nashville."

Judith Anne, the girl talking to Elizabeth, obviously had a strong curiosity streak but not much tact and asked, "She lost her job, do you mean she got fired? She told me her boss in Nashville was really difficult to work for, and I'm not surprised to hear she no longer works for him. I would have lasted about one month with a dude like that."

"Well, yes and no, she really didn't get fired technically," Elizabeth hedged. "I guess I could tell you the real story of why she lost her job if you promise not to tell anyone. I don't think it had anything to do with her abilities, Judith Ann. She would say that she was planning to quit when her boss fired her for causing trouble for him with the medical center and the police."

"Wow, can you fill in with a little more detail? Why did she report him to the police? This sounds like something on a weekday soap opera," exclaimed Judith Ann, whose eyes sparkled with more curiosity.

Elizabeth lowered her voice more and continued with the story, "The authorities in Nashville know all about this that I'm going to tell you. Probably the hospital administration and the doctors here know the details too. You may have read in the papers that the Nashville police are searching for a person of interest, and that person was a scientist at the medical center. The article said he may have been connected in some way with the poisoning of our water or have some knowledge about it."

"Well, sure, I read all the articles about Greenwood either in our paper or the Nashville one. All of us in the lab have been speculating, whatever could a Nashville person know about the epidemic here?"

"Well, I can tell you, that person they are searching for is who Debra used to work with in Nashville, that is, until a few weeks ago. Debra knew some things about his research that did not seem right and tipped off the authorities he could have had something to do with the Greenwood's water problems. After a lot of medical detective work, an arrest warrant was issued, but he managed to escape."

Shocked, Judith Ann leaned closer to hear Elizabeth as she continued, "Her boss put two and two together and accused her of talking to the police. By then she was planning to quit anyway, he frightened her that much. Before she could send him a written notice, the medical center fired him and closed down his lab, so technically at that point she didn't have a job anyway. Debra was too frightened to stay in Nashville until he was caught and left to go to her parents' home and then visit me. She finally decided after staying with me herefor a few days to go back to Nashville because that's where her boyfriend lives. I told her she was lucky to get away from her boss and not get killed by him. He may be some type of scary sociopath. So far the police have no leads where he might be."

Judith Ann could hardly believe her ears and asked angrily, "If the authorities could prove this scientist had caused the epidemic, would he be tried for murder, Elizabeth? Gosh, some of my friends and neighbors died, and many more are still sick, our town may never be the same. I wonder how much evidence the police have against him. There could be a long court battle in Greenwood with hospital employees like myself called to testify."

"Oh, I don't know anything about more evidence other than what Debra told me and perhaps I've said too much. Judith Ann, we had better finish the grocery shopping and leave before the roads get slick. I'll just say this before I go. I think everyone has heard rumors, and as far as I know, nothing has been proven yet. The most frightening thing is if he did do this, no one knows where he might be, or if he is planning anything else."

A man dressed in hunting clothes had been looking at a magazine around the corner from the two women. A heavy beard covered his face, and a brown hat was pulled down over his forehead, hiding his features. At first, he appeared not to be paying attention to their conversation. Then overhearing something one of them said, he suddenly looked up and began to edge closer to them, listening intently. After hearing the discussion about the link between the water disaster in Greenwood and the scientist who Debra worked for in Nashville, he pitched the magazine on a pile of others and ran from the building, almost colliding with a shopping cart pushed by an elderly woman. A beat-up pickup truck was parked on the front row of the grocery's parking lot. The man jumped in and left in a swirl of dirt and gravel.

"Wow, did you see that guy run out of here?" a clerk asked the other one who was standing at the end of the checkout lane, waiting to bag groceries for customers.

"He must have heard we are getting more snow than he had planned on," the other said with a laugh. "Seriously, have you ever seen that dude before? He looks like a stranger to me and not a hunter type either."

"Well, I sold him some groceries, a big order, about a week ago, but I never had seen him before that. He had a funny accent, maybe a guy from the West Coast, maybe from the East Coast. I lived in San Diego for a while but never picked up the way they talk, but I know how they sound. I could have sworn though he was riding a motorcycle when he came in last week."

Elizabeth appeared at the checkout lane, and the two clerks stopped their conversation to wait on her. Elizabeth left carrying two bags of groceries, followed closely by Judith Ann, who waved goodbye with a promise to call soon. A few snowflakes fell on both of them as they walked to their cars.

Elizabeth pulled cautiously out of the parking lot. While she drove slowly down the narrow country road now covered with patches of snow, Elizabeth wondered what Taylor was doing now. It seemed he and Claudia were still trying to make a go at their marriage, and she supposed she wished them well. After all, they had two children to raise. Of the children whom she had seen as patients in the office, those with only one parent usually had a harder time growing up. In her opinion, Claudia would not win any awards for motherhood, but usually two parents were better than one.

Roger had invited her to go out for dinner tomorrow night, and she probably would unless they had too much snow. Right before she left, Debra made her promise to see more of Roger, whom she thought was attractive and had a promising future in store management. *And maybe I will, if I think about this a little more,* she said to herself.

As Elizabeth turned down the driveway to her aunt's house, the Christmas lights came on around the door and windows.

It was perfect timing with the delayed switch that Roger had installed last weekend. He had hung strand after strand of the white lights, working in the cold for several hours. The whole house looked grand, she had to admit, as she pulled in the garage, looking forward to a cozy evening in front of the fire. She planned to bring her aunt and a few of her friends from the nursing home over on Sunday afternoon so they could admire the holiday decorations and have punch and cookies.

From the road, a beat-up truck slowed down, and the driver noted the name on the mailbox and drove on. The snow was falling faster now, and the truck's tracks were covered in a few minutes.

CHAPTER THIRTY-FIVE

MITCHELL BALL WAS reading a favorite book of poetry on Saturday morning when his bell rang. Two large men were at his door and showed him their badges.

"Mr. Ball, I'm Detective David Cooke with the Nashville police, and this is my assistant, Andy McClure. Could we come in for a few minutes and get out of the cold? We would like to ask you some questions about a former student of yours, Joseph Steiner."

Gee, Mitchell thought as he let the policemen in, *first the two lovely girls and now the Nashville police, all wanting to know something about Steiner.* His quiet retirement was getting more interesting and lively for sure.

After sitting down, David started the interview by saying, "I believe Debra Chandler told you about our futile hunt for Dr. Steiner and all the trouble he is in, sir."

"Yes, she certainly did. I knew he had some personality quirks and was even strange as a youth and certainly not very popular with others, but in my wildest dreams, I never could have imagined all this."

"I understand how you must feel, Mr. Ball. In meeting with Ms. Chandler a few days ago she mentioned that you told her his parents owned a cabin in the woods where he spent a lot of time, growing up here as a boy. It occurred to me that he could be hiding out there, so we need your help in locating this cabin."

"Well, yes, that's good thinking. I remember the general area, and as I told Debra, I guess it's still standing since I saw it three years ago on a hiking trip. I could draw you a map, it's off Highway 57, but the cabin can't be seen from the road.

However, it's close to a trail which is popular with hikers because it leads to one of our area's waterfalls. I can add some detail to the map which will help you find the cabin." He pulled out a pen and a piece of paper and drew a map which would be easy for the detectives to follow.

Four hours later, David and Andy accompanied by three heavily armed Greenwood policemen maneuvered through the snow and approached a deserted and half-collapsed cabin, surrounded by tall pine trees. They slowly pushed open the unlocked door.

And just like his home in Nashville, the cabin contained books, a microscope, and small incubator. A pile of dirty clothes were tossed in the corner of the cold room and in the fireplace were the remnants of a fire, but there was nothing else to suggest the cabin was still occupied. Dr. Steiner had again escaped the clutches of the law.

At the water company, Harry was working in his office Saturday morning, reading some reports about the epidemic. There was also an intimidating stack of scientific journals covering topics from monitoring water systems to new methods in DNA research on his desk. He was getting a headache from reading the pages and pages of lab data.

At least the situation at the water company was going better for him personally. The board no longer held him responsible for the infected water and wasn't planning to fire him as he feared earlier. People were still drinking bottled water though since many in the town didn't believe him or the CDC's announcements that the water was safe. He supposed that it would take time for the trust to return.

He had eaten lunch at the drugstore a few days ago, and everyone had greeted him in a friendly fashion. That was good since it would have not been the case the first weekend after the epidemic hit. None of the docs who usually ate lunch at Hopkin's Drug Store were there due to the large number of patients they were still seeing. The chief of police was sitting, however, at the lunch counter and told the group that the Nashville police had paid him a visit. They were trying to figure out if a former resident of Greenwood might have returned to the area and, if so, where he might be. Of course, that raised everyone's curiosity, but the chief wouldn't say anything more. Harry wondered if the person the Nashville police were searching for could be Joe Steiner who he understood was a suspect in the poisoning of their water.

At one o'clock, Harry decided he needed a breather and food after spending four hours poring over the reports stacked on his desk. He left the office and drove to the lodge to say hello to some of his buddies and watch a few minutes of the season final between Tennessee and Georgia. Several of the guys had been deathly sick and were still recovering. Others hadn't been stricken, and he was glad to see their cars when he pulled in the parking lot.

It was strange; he couldn't hear any noise when he pushed open the door, nor did he see anyone around the TV or standing at the snack bar. He walked into the large rec room and stepped in front of the couch. There, three of his classmates were lying on the floor, looking shockingly very dead. He had known them well for over thirty years because they had been on the football team together. An open box from the local pizza shop was on the coffee table, and in it was a partly eaten pizza. Harry ran to the first man and felt for a pulse—there was none. He quickly moved to the other two but couldn't find any signs of life in either of the two men. Blood had drained from their mouths and pooled under each body.

Shaken and nauseated, he went to the kitchen phone and called the police, reporting what he found when he entered the lodge. In minutes, several officers arrived, then the coroner and detectives. After the detectives interrogated him, and asked numerous questions, they got the men's addresses and the names of next of kin. Then the bodies were removed. The officer in charge told Harry the men could have been poisoned for there was no evidence of gunshot wounds or struggles. The truth could be established only after autopsies were done. He asked Harry if he wanted to notify their families, but Harry declined. The medical technicians carefully wrapped up the pizza box and the partly eaten pizza and said they planned to send it to the state lab for analysis.

Harry collapsed in an armchair, not believing he was seeing more deaths and these of friends who had escaped the epidemic. He called Joyce to tell her what had happened and that he was coming home. He couldn't work anymore today. A migraine headache had taken hold of his body. Sharp pains stabbed his forehead and behind his eyes. He finally pulled himself together enough to call the president of the lodge to give him the bad news. Then he went out the door, and sadly locked it. Already around the porch and steps of the old building, yellow police tape was draped. Several people stopped to stare and ask Harry what had happened. He ignored their questions and got in his car and drove away slowly, his hands gripping the wheel.

Sunday Harry had spent a miserable day answering phone calls, but that evening he and Joyce were trying to watch *Sixty Minutes* when the phone rang again. The police wanted him to know that the initial autopsies showed all three men had died of some unknown poison. Interesting, the local pizza store said that while they had sold a good number of pizzas before noon that day, only three had the same ingredients of Canadian bacon and onions as those found at the lodge. Of the three pizzas, two went to a local barbershop because the girl at the counter knew the barber who picked them up. The other one was ordered over the phone, and a man, rough looking and unknown to her or others in the shop picked it up at 11:30.

CHAPTER THIRTY-SIX

DEBRA HAD LEARNED most of the common procedures in the microbiology department after a few days under Carolyn's careful instructions. She had been there about two weeks, relieved to have a job and something to do during the day while Jim worked such long hours. The worry and fear about Dr. Steiner had faded in the back of her consciousness. She enjoyed being back at the hospital and able to see her old friends again.

After getting off work at 4:30 one day, she found herself riding the elevator to the fourth floor and turning down the research wing to see if Jim was working in his lab though she thought it was too early for him to be there. She walked down the familiar corridor, and looked at familiar doors. Suddenly, she knew she had come too far, because she was standing in front of room 425. Posted on the door was an old announcement from the administration which said that the suite of rooms was closed by order of the Nashville Police Department. No one was to enter the area.

Debra, for no reason at all, reached out and tried the doorknob. Much to her surprise, the knob turned, and the door swung open. Just like housekeeping to mess up the police orders, she thought. She hesitated a second and walked into the lab then quickly shut the door behind her. Amazingly, the lab looked much the same as it did on that day in November when she met with the police before she had picked up her belongings and left for Clarksville. Many of the chemicals and solutions whose names had been meticulously labeled by Debra herself were still on the shelves above the lab counters. She was looking over some of the bottles of reagents when she heard the door open behind her. She turned to see an ill-kept man in army fatigues silently enter the lab. A cap was pulled down over his forehead, and his face was covered with a heavy beard.

"Ms. Chandler what are you doing here in my old lab?" he asked in an accusing manner as he pulled off the sunglasses, and she found herself staring into the cold, empty eyes of Joseph Steiner.

He continued, "Perhaps, I should call you Debra now that you no longer work for me, and our paths seem destined to cross. Listen you bitch, I know now you implicated me with the typhoid bacteria they found in Greenwood's water supply. You and your doctor boyfriend stole my laboratory cultures. After much hocus-pocus with Dr. Scott and the campus microbiology department, who are a bunch of fools by the way, they decided to call the police and attempt to arrest me." And he stared at her with disgust.

Slowly he pulled a long hunting knife from his pocket. "I should have killed you when I saw you that day in the park. Then I wasn't sure of your guilt, but now I am. The people in Greenwood which you felt so sorry for didn't deserve to live. Most of the people in the town are no-good, stupid fools."

"How can you say that about innocent people, Dr. Steiner?" Debra stammered. "You truly are a monster." Debra began to back slowly toward the floor-length window at the back of the lab.

"I admired you when I first started working for you. I was in awe of your genius. I thought that you were interested in helping mankind with the DNA discoveries you made, surely not to kill innocent people and destroy towns. What kind of person are you really? How can you sleep at night?"

He gave a short laugh and said, "Most of mankind has not progressed since they got out of the trees and learned to stand up right, Debra. The majority isn't worth much and doesn't need to use up precious resources on our planet that could benefit the truly talented. Three of those fat fools from the Greenwood football team are perfect examples of using resources and not doing one ounce of good for the planet. Somehow, they escaped the effects of Greenwood water, but now another discovery has corrected that situation."

Debra almost gagged, "I read about the mysterious poisoning of some lodge members in Greenwood with a pizza. Don't tell me you were connected with that too, Dr. Steiner?"

"That's for me to know and you to find out, Debra." Then he gave a short laugh. "I was in a grocery in Greenwood recently and overheard your cousin telling another hospital person how you and your boyfriend stole my bacteria and gave it to the medical center people who called the police. I suspected as much, and now I know it's true. I plan to deal with your boyfriend and your cousin after I finish with you. I remember she was such a brat when growing up there. I never liked her. She needs killing too," and he grinned hideously.

"Dr. Steiner, are you insane? Come to your senses. The authorities can help you, turn yourself in!" Debra stammered.

"It's too late for that, Debra. Because of you, my life is in turmoil. I no longer have a place to work and continue my research. I have only a little makeshift lab where I'm living now, but it's not well equipped nor suitable for more concentrated efforts. Luckily, a foreign power know about my research and will make a final offer soon. I'll help their government in exchange for funds to build a truly great facility for myself. Also, I'll be given a large sum of money so I will never have to think where my next meal is coming from. Unfortunately, I may have to live on foreign soil to accomplish this, but so be it."

Debra's mouth hung open on hearing this latest information. All the meetings on undergraduate education he was always attending may not have been on campus after all but had a darker, more sinister purpose.

"But enough of this boring talk, my dear, I followed you up here to see what kind of mischief you were going to get into before I end your life. You could be a great danger to my future plans. Rest assured Debra you will die quickly and feel little pain with one swipe of my knife." And he fingered the hunting knife again, feeling the sharp edge of the blade.

Debra reached behind her back and, through a sideways glance, knew her hand was on a bottle of sulfuric acid. Swiftly, she swung the bottle around breaking it open on the countertop and flinging its corrosive contents in Steiner's face.

He screamed in agony as he lunged toward her with his knife, stabbing blindly in the air. At the same time, the lab door was flung open, and Detective Cooke yelled, "Dr. Steiner, drop that knife! Down on the floor or I will shoot!"

Steiner spun around, acid dripping off his face and threw the knife at the sound of Detective Cooke's voice as several shots rang out. Then as if in slow motion, the knife buried itself in the wall behind Cooke's head, and Dr. Steiner collapsed in a pool of blood at Debra's feet.

Debra too collapsed, sobbing on the floor. David helped her up after checking to see if Steiner was dead. Mercifully he was and David's eyes had shut momentarily with relief.

Still supporting her by her elbows, David said, "Debra, that tip you gave me a week ago proved right on and probably saved your life today. Mr. Ball gave us directions for finding the cabin. We went up there and found signs someone had been living there. And sure enough, the next day Steiner appeared in hunting clothes, no less, and when he saw us, he jumped over a wood pile, raced to his truck, and escaped again. None of us would have even recognized him in that disguise if we had not been tipped off by you. We lost his trail several times but picked it up again today. I saw him in the hospital parking lot a few minutes ago and followed him up here. I believe he saw you earlier in the cafeteria and waited for the opportunity to find you alone in order to kill you."

At that moment, Jim arrived completely out of breath. He stared at the scene in disbelief. Debra had almost lost her life again to the madman. He pulled her close and held her in a tight embrace.

Once more room 425 was corded off with yellow police tape after Dr. Steiner's body was removed. Several of the people who had known him gathered in the hallway to watch the gurney, carrying his body, being rolled toward the elevator. Dr. Scott leaned against the wall, thanking God that the end to this saga had finally come, and they were all safe.

EPILOGUE

THE WEDDING WAS small. A private affair held in the chapel of a Presbyterian Church on West End Avenue. Debra wanted it to take place as close as possible to Valentine's Day. Since the church was available on the twelfth, that day was chosen. In spite of ice and two inches of snow that fell the day before, Jim's mother and Debra's family gathered at four for a quiet ceremony. She wore a beige silk suit and carried a small bouquet of red roses. It was so unlike her first wedding with six bridesmaids and, as it seemed to her, half the town of Clarksville in attendance.

The reception followed and was held at the same hotel that was across the street from Centennial Park, the scene of Debra's first encounter with Dr. Steiner. Her mother couldn't understand why she would choose that particular hotel, but Debra had always liked it in the past, even before the park incident. She felt hiding there had saved her life from Dr. Steiner. In fact, every time she drove past now, she was reminded that she had won the battle with the sociopath scientist and in doing so perhaps saved other towns from the fate of Greenwood.

The hotel's staff had outdone themselves with Valentine decorations and a holiday menu for the reception. Several round buffet tables were set up and loaded with everything from shrimp and oysters on the half shell to rounds of beef and country ham with homemade biscuits. After Debra and Jim cut a cake decorated with red roses, they mingled with the crowd, overcome with happiness.

Many of their friends from the medical center came to the reception, some straight from work still in their uniforms. They stayed and stayed drinking the French wine or aged

Tennessee whiskey Debra's father had ordered. In spite of the snow, Elizabeth made the treacherous drive from Greenwood and brought along her Aunt Susan and Roger and his mother.

David Cooke and his partner, Andy, had even been invited. They told Jim they were not used to receiving invitations unless it was a summons for a court appearance. As Andy was standing at the bar trying to order a second whisky and soda, David bumped into Dr. Scott. He was munching on a plate of ham and biscuits while discussing the department's patients with two interns still in hospital whites. David pulled Dr. Scott over to a corner of the room and brought him up-to-date on how the investigation had ended, and finally, how all the loose ends were tied up.

"Dr. Scott, we found more incriminating evidence in his cabin hidden in the woods outside of Greenwood. He had plans to mass-produce the bacteria and spread it all over the country. It was a good thing that Nashville's water supply was so heavily guarded. I can also tell you that he really was planning to get a foreign power to finance his research as he had hinted to Debra before he was killed. There was several months of correspondence on his desk in the cabin from them, and you know, that money in his accounts, that was from them too. If they had been able to finalize the deal with him, he would have used his discoveries to spread the evil poison around the world. I don't have the liberty to tell you which country it was but can only say the state department is looking at the situation very carefully."

"Good lord, he was even worse than I imagined. Well, what about the members of the lodge who were found dead in Greenwood, Dave, did Steiner have anything to do with that?" Dr. Scott asked.

"Well, as far as what caused those deaths at the lodge, the state proved they had been poisoned with an unknown substance sprinkled on the pizza, probably another one of his discoveries. It appeared to be colorless and difficult to trace with the typical autopsy, a perfect poison.

As a sidenote, we always wondered about his personality, his lack of human contact, and I wondered how he really felt about Debra. Believe it or not, he had several pictures of her pasted to his bedroom wall in the cabin. They were taken from his office with a long-range lens while she was working at her lab desk. To this day, I don't know if he had her targeted for revenge or was in some strange way infatuated with her."

"Well, we will never know because, thank heavens, he's dead and can no longer hurt anyone, especially Debra. Look at her, David. She and Jim are so happy now with their whole lives in front of them. If it hadn't been for their detective work in connecting the Greenwood bacteria to that in Steiner's lab, he would still be loose, causing more deaths, more destruction. I believe this nightmare is finally over. My thanks to you and your partner, Andy, for tracking him down and letting all of us get back to the business of teaching students and healing patients."

And he smiled and patted David on the shoulder before returning to his conversation with the interns.

ABOUT THE AUTHOR

MELISSA DAVIS BAIZE is a retired financial service representative and insurance broker, She lives with her husband in Central Kentucky and has two children, a stepchild and four grandchildren. In addition to working as a volunteer at several non- profit groups, she enjoys gardening and traveling in her spare time. In her first novel, she has drawn from experiences in the seventies which were a time when women were just emerging from the dominance of a male workplace, especially in the health care system. It is in that era in which the book is set. Melissa holds an undergraduate and a master's degree in microbiology from the University of Kentucky and earlier worked in research labs in Nashville, Tennessee, and Lexington, Kentucky.